AF431113

THE Ultimate
SAVE
BROOKLYN BLADES 2
FELICE STEVENS

BROOKLYN
BLADES

Published by Good Man Press

Edited by Keren Reed
Copyediting by Flat Earth Editing
Proofreading by Virginia Tesi Carey
Additional Proofreading by Lyrical Lines

Cover Art by Reese Dante
Cover Photography by: RafaCatalana

ISBN Digital: 979-8-88949-104-0
ISBN Print: 979-8-88949-105-7
ISBN Alternate Print: 979-8-88949-106-4

DEDICATION

To my family, my ultimate loves.

ACKNOWLEDGMENTS

Thanks as always to my editor, Keren Reed. To Hope from Flat Earth Editing, you are the ultimate. To Dianne, from Lyrical Lines, I couldn't do it without you. Thank you to Virginia-Tesi Carey for your last looks. To Reese, thank you for everything and more.
And to the readers, you are the reason and make it all worthwhile.

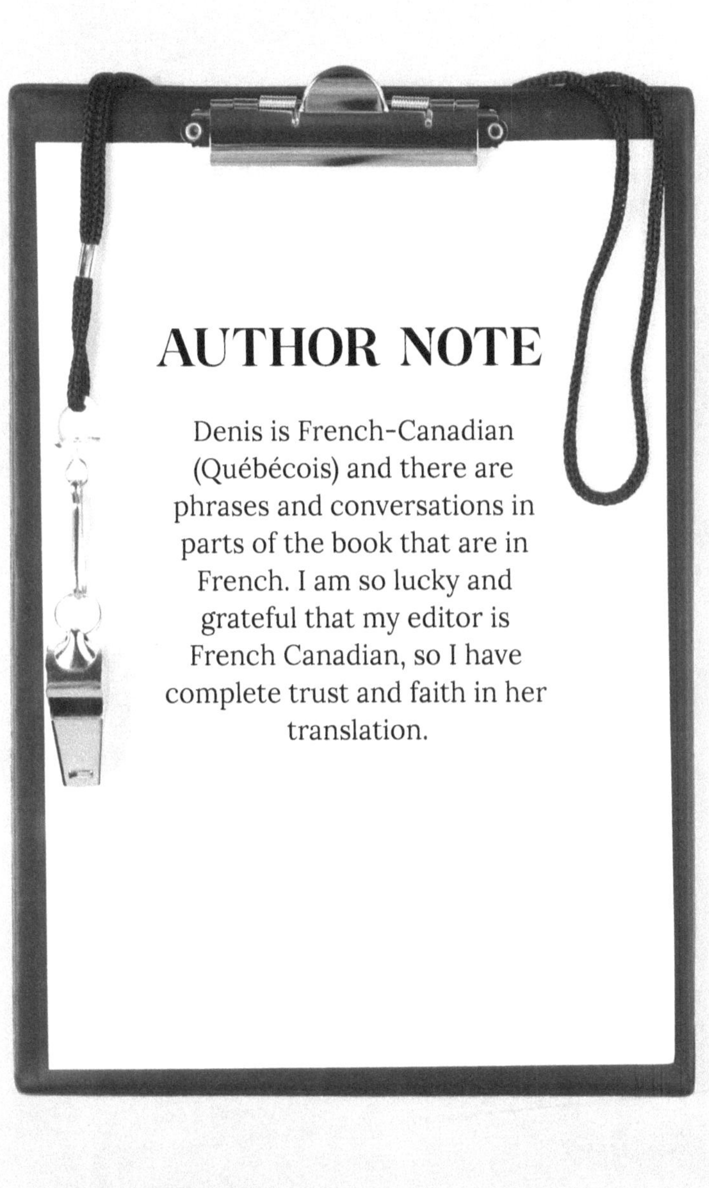

AUTHOR NOTE

Denis is French-Canadian (Québécois) and there are phrases and conversations in parts of the book that are in French. I am so lucky and grateful that my editor is French Canadian, so I have complete trust and faith in her translation.

CHAPTER ONE
Denis

All my life I'd wanted to be a hockey player. I was Canadian; ice ran side by side with blood in our veins. We learned to skate as soon as we could walk–sometimes before.

The Stanley Cup. I'd dreamed about it, never believing it might happen. Wished so hard that it had consumed my every living, breathing moment.

Hockey. It was everything.

Every boy in Canada grew up wanting to be a professional hockey player. I'd achieved my dream. Now I had two Stanley Cups in a row, a beautiful apartment in Brooklyn overlooking the river, and I'd made millions of dollars. I'd been awarded numerous MVP titles and Vezina trophies.

So why was I so damned miserable?

The celebration around me grew wilder, and I smiled and drank champagne. Pretending all was right in my world. And it should be. I could have anything I wanted.

Except the one man I'd let get away.

Vous voyez, je suis bien niaiseux. I'm such a fool.

"Don't lie to yourself. You didn't let him get away." I guzzled the remainder of the champagne bottle and grabbed another one. "You ruined it. As usual." My head spun, and I knew I'd have a wicked hangover in the morning, but I didn't care. I had no one to get up for. The talk shows would have to put up with me as I was. As they expected. *Denis Bouvier, bad boy of hockey.*

I grimaced and narrowed my eyes. "What's he doing here?" A tall man in a perfectly tailored suit stood at the entrance to Slapshots, looking uncomfortable and out of place. Sterling Forest, nighttime anchor of Channel 8 News. He scanned the room and homed in on Rip and Adrian. "Of course. He's looking for his protégé. Pompous dick."

Forest worked his way through the crowd and, when he reached Adrian, began to talk. Adrian nodded, and Rip set his champagne bottle on the table and moved away slightly. From his tight shoulders and frown, I sensed he was annoyed. My temper shot to the surface.

"It's his fucking night," I swore and got to my feet. I didn't stop to wonder if I was welcome in their space. Still holding my bottle, I strode past my teammates and others to talk to Rip.

"Why's he here?"

A bit hazy-eyed, Rip shrugged. "Who knows? Something about a news story."

I snorted. "*Mais bien sûr.* It always is with him. But can't he leave you alone for just one night?"

Rip grinned. "Aww, you're feeling bad for me? That's kinda sweet and a little ironic coming from you, don't you think?"

"Maybe, but you said that guy is always on Adrian about work. Let him celebrate with you."

Rip's gaze settled on Adrian and Forest, still deep in conversation. "Yeah, well, Adrian's in awe of him, and Sterling's a big deal in the news business, so he wants to make a good impression. And since Sterling's taken a liking to him, Adrian is going to do what he wants. Within reason, of course."

"He looks like he's got a stick up his ass. So uptight."

"He is." Rip chuckled. "I don't think I've ever seen him smile. But from the times I met him, he seems like an okay guy." An amused expression on his face, Rip took my bottle, drank from it, then wiped his mouth. "Don't tell me you're still upset because of what he said about hockey players? He apologized to me and said it was a mean-spirited thing to say."

When it was announced on air that the Blades had won the Cup, and the rest of the news team had celebrated, Sterling was the only one who'd remained unaffected. He'd been caught on a hot mic with his unsolicited opinion.

"I'm glad the season's finished. I never understood the allure of grown men beating each other senseless over a puck on the ice. I'm surprised more people don't wind up with permanent brain injuries. Or maybe they have, considering the way some behave. Like thugs and hulks."

I sniffed. "I guess growing up in Beverly Hills and that fancy college education makes him think he's better than the rest of us. But I never gave it a second thought." Except he'd made an enemy of me.

A raucous burst of laughter caught my attention from the other side of the bar, and I spotted Rudy. My heart squeezed tight. For the better part of the past six months, he and I had been together. The sex was good, and we'd had fun together. I'd thought maybe he was the one.

Until he'd blindsided me and said he was leaving. That I wasn't giving him what he needed, whatever the fuck that meant. We'd gone out to the clubs, had dinners at great restaurants every night. He worked for the Blades training staff, and I knew he didn't make much money, so I'd paid for most things—clothes, all the designer crap he liked, VIP at the clubs and dinners. What more could he want? I watched him slip his arm around some big guy, and they began to kiss. I turned my back. My mood grew dark, and I guzzled more champagne.

Rip put a hand on my arm. "Hey. What's wrong?"

"Nothing. We just won the Cup. Everything is right." I brandished my bottle. "Another round of champagne."

"That's bullshit. You don't look happy. I'm sorry about you and Rudy."

I was glad Rip thought he knew me. Maybe he could tell me who I was, besides Denis Bouvier, star goalie and master of failed relationships. I cracked a brittle smile. "Don't be. It was just a fling. There's always someone new waiting to warm my bed. No shortage of willing participants." At that precise moment, Adrian passed by me with a frowning Sterling Forest at his side. I swore I could smell the man's disdain oozing from every expensive, spa-loving pore.

"Hi," Adrian said. "Sterling wanted to fill me in on something that came in late to the newsroom."

"Must be earth-shattering to track you down at your fiancé's celebration," I sneered. "I hope it was worth it."

"It's not for public consumption until verified," Forest stated, and I rolled my eyes. He was an automaton wrapped in a beautiful package.

"*Mon dieu.* Such secrets."

"It might be. I'm sorry to intrude on your night," he told Rip, sounding contrite, but the side-eye he gave me dripped with ego.

"It's not a problem. I know how hard Adrian's been working lately. If you need to go to the newsroom, it's okay." Rip kissed Adrian. "I'll hang out here for a while, then go home. We should start thinking about the weekend plans. I'll call Neil and Lisa and tell them."

"I can't believe it," Adrian exclaimed and leaned into Rip.

"Believe what?" I asked. "Is something special happening?"

Bright-eyed, Rip slung an arm around Adrian's neck. "We're getting married. This weekend at my brother's summer house upstate. We'd love it if you could come, Denis. I know it might seem strange since we were once together, but that was a lifetime ago, wasn't it?"

My smile was thin. "*Mmm. Vraiment.*" I'd thrown it all away. But then, you never knew what you had until you lost it.

"Absolutely, Denis," Adrian added. "I mean, I know Rip would love it if you came."

But not you.

"*Mais oui*, how could I turn down such a heartfelt invitation?" Tempering my sarcasm, I extended my hand. "Truly, I'm honored. Thank you. I'd be happy to come and share your special day."

Adrian beamed and turned to Forest. "Sterling, it would mean the world to me if you could come as well."

"I-I'm not sure. But thank you for inviting me." Of course the stiff-necked suit couldn't give a straight answer.

"I'm sure Adrian is going to invite Rob DeVine," Rip added. "We'd love to have you as well. Adrian thinks so highly of you and tells me how much he's learned working under you."

"Rob's on vacation this week," Adrian offered. "Or of course I'd invite him. I hope you can make it, Sterling. It's not going to be super formal or gigantic." He gave his sweet smile to Forest, and I could see why Rip loved him. The man was pure goodness wrapped in a very pretty package.

I smirked. "I'm sure he'll want to come to the most important event of your life."

Forest directed a withering look my way. "I hardly need anyone, especially you, to answer for me."

"Especially me?" I arched a brow and took a long pull from my champagne bottle. "What does that mean?"

He didn't answer, checking his phone instead. "Hunt, we need to go. My source isn't going to wait forever."

Adrian kissed Rip's cheek, and he and Sterling hurried off.

Rip and I stood side by side. "So, married, eh? I'm very happy for you."

"Thanks." He drank some more champagne and laughed as Chitty climbed on the bar, beat his chest, and chugged down almost a full pitcher of beer. "Kid's gonna be sick before the night is over."

Seb approached us, carrying a bottle. "Hey, guys, why so serious? We should be dancing. Two in two years, baby."

"Not sad at all," Rip said. "Matter of fact, I was just coming to get you. This weekend at Neil and Lisa's place upstate. Adrian and I are getting married."

"Yeeeeessssss." Seb let out an ear-piercing scream and flung himself into Rip's arms. The entire bar turned silent and craned their necks to look.

"Just two men hugging it out, *mes amies*. Nothing to see. Go back to celebrating. Go, Blades!" I yelled, held up my bottle, and finished it in one long guzzle. I'd had enough playing nice and mingling for the evening. I needed to get filthy, stinking drunk. Get laid. Maybe both.

I set out to accomplish that by pushing my six-foot-four bulk to the end of the bar and waving to the cute bartender with the curly hair, wearing a Blades cap and a jersey. My jersey. He blushed when I grinned at him.

"Hello, there. You're new, aren't you?" I purred.

"Uh, yeah. Just started last week. I'm a huge hockey fan, so this is kinda like my dream job."

"What's your name?"

"Marshall."

"Well, Marshall…" I swiped my tongue across my lower lip, and he ducked his head. "I see you're wearing my jersey. Am I your favorite player?"

His face was bright red now, and I could see the rapid rise and fall of his chest. "Yeah. I think you're the best goalie in the league, Mr. Bouvier. I've followed you from the beginning of your career with the LA Seals, then the Icers." He grew talkative, and I was entranced by his mouth. I wanted to bite it. Taste it. "I was so excited when you came to the Blades."

"I'm very excited to be here too. Especially tonight. Call me Denis, please. Mr. Bouvier is so formal. And I'd like us to become friends. Would you like that?"

Marshall's big blue eyes grew wide. "Oh, my God. Yes. That would be so cool."

"How about another bottle of champagne? Your best."

Marshall's jaw dropped. "That's the Dom. I'd have to go to the back refrigerator for it. We don't keep it out here."

"I'll wait."

He hurried away, giving me a perfect view of his lovely ass. I sighed. For all the jibes at Rip about how much younger Adrian was than him, Marshall was no different. He couldn't be more than thirty, if that.

Marshall returned, holding the bottle. "There's only one chilled. There isn't enough to share with all your teammates."

"Let them drink Moët. You and I are sharing this."

Marshall's mouth made an O. "Mr. Bou—I mean Denis. They charge a hundred dollars a glass for it here. I can't—"

I reached out and put a hand over his. "But I can. It goes on my tab. Now, let's share."

He popped the cork, and with a slightly shaky hand, poured two flutes. I lifted mine. "To you, Marshall, and to me. Our new friendship."

We clinked, and I watched him taste the drink. "Oh, wow. This is so good. Totally different from the stuff we drink on New Year's or when we make mimosas."

"*Mais oui*. It's the best. Have some more."

He hesitated. "I really shouldn't. It's not fair to let the other guys work while I'm talking to you."

"You're very sweet. And thoughtful. I like that. We can continue the conversation later if you'd like." I drank some more. "In my apartment."

His Adam's apple bobbed. "Uh…yeah…uh…that would be…yeah." He bit his lip. "I get off at midnight."

"I can wait." I pushed off the bar and grabbed the bottle. "Don't worry. There's plenty more of this at my place. See you later, Marshall."

My evening plans arranged, I could enjoy the rest of the partying. I made sure to find the buffet and grabbed plenty to eat to coat my stomach for all the alcohol I'd imbibed. With a plateful of food, I leaned against a table and listened to the chatter of my teammates.

"This is the best night ever," Chitty exclaimed, and I couldn't help smiling at his enthusiasm. "I'm the luckiest guy in the world."

Varhov had his arm around his pretty woman, loving her up. "Ready to go soon, babe? I love these guys, but I wanna be alone with you."

On my other side, I heard, "When do you think Rip is gonna retire? I thought last season he'd go after his knee injury and the win, but now? I'm not so sure," Lindy was grousing to Lemoine, and I perked up to listen.

"Why should he? Rip's the captain—the best in the league. If you wanna go, talk to your agent about a trade. Shit. Two Cups already, and I've only been in the league five years? Fuck it. No way am I going anywhere unless they trade me."

I'd need to remind myself to tell Rip to watch out for Lindstrom. Guy was good but had the bad luck of being on a team with the best center in the league. Like our second goalie, Ellis. I had no intention of retiring anytime soon, and I'd made that perfectly clear.

I finished my bottle, used the restroom, and as I walked down the hallway to the bar, I saw Marshall, my new friend and hopefully bed partner later in the night. He faced the wall and was on his phone. Yeah, it was wrong to eavesdrop, but sue me. Marshall was very into his conversation and didn't hear me when I stopped less than four feet from him.

"Yeah, I know, babe, but it's Denis Bouvier. I figured I'd get him drunk, grab some stuff, and leave without having to do anything. He's pretty trashed right now, so it won't be too hard."

The fuck I was. Hearing how the sweet-faced Marshall was about to play me...*steal* from me, sobered my ass up pretty damn quick. I strained to listen. I couldn't hear what was being said, but Marshall disagreed with vehemence.

"No way. I'd never fuck him. You wouldn't mind if I kissed him, though? That's not cheating, and I don't wanna seem like a cock tease."

The voice on the other end rose, loud enough that even I could hear it. "*Why the fuck would you wanna kiss him?*"

Marshall huffed. "Joey, I don't want to. Trust me, the thought makes me wanna puke. But I wanna get him to sign my jersey and get some pics. Maybe he'll give me a puck or something. Plus, he's got a ton of cash in his wallet. He'll never miss a few hundred. You know I'd never cheat on you."

My anger grew with each breath I took. My control snapped, and I stormed over to Marshall and took the phone from his hand. "Joey? It's Denis Bouvier. Your loving boyfriend was ready to get on his knees and suck my dick in front of everyone in the bar, he was so into me. He's a lying little turd." I put the phone back into a shocked Marshall's hand. "And you'd better be ready to pay for that bottle of Dom yourself."

Leaving him standing, I walked out of the bar and into the cool spring evening. The glow from the Blades Arena lit up the street in the team colors of blue and gold. *Your Stanley Cup Champions Brooklyn Blades* played across the illuminated screen. A promo picture of Rip, Seb, and me flashed up first, then other ones with the rest of the team. I glanced behind me, watching them all continuing to celebrate, most likely not even realizing I'd left. And yet they were still closer to me than my actual family.

I wiped the wetness off my face and began to walk home. Alone.

CHAPTER TWO
Sterling

I woke to the alarm, an anomaly, since I was usually up before it began its incessant beeping. Annoyance flooded me as I recalled the wasted trip Adrian and I had made. My source never showed, and the information—that the mayor didn't actually live in New York City and never had—couldn't be used without other independent verification.

I doused my face in cold water to wake up completely and tighten my pores. Once I'd hit forty, I'd become hyper-aware of how I appeared on camera. Someone like Adrian Hunt, young and startlingly handsome, would have no trouble filling my seat. A focus group had proved what I knew: viewers wanted their news read by youthful anchors.

The age of the wise and trusted gray-haired reporter had vanished, maybe forever.

It was almost the weekend, and as I ate my breakfast, I regretted telling Adrian I'd go to his wedding. Long ago I'd learned not to socialize with people I worked with. That would only lead to questions I had no intention of answering. Channel 8 was a close-knit group, which made me wary of spending time with any of them out of the newsroom, but showing up to Adrian's wedding would effectively kick that resolution to the curb.

"Damn the kid for being so...nice." I strode across my apartment, gazing out the windows where the sun had begun to peek over the tips of the skyscrapers, and hopped on my exercise bike. "I should've said no, but he's too earnest." Sweat dripped down my face. "Well, I can show up and then leave after they say I do. They won't even notice I'm gone."

My ten miles completed, I stripped and showered, scrubbing my scalp vigorously. I applied my hair-thickening serum and weighed myself, noting with satisfaction that I'd dropped a few pounds. I'd watched a tape of one of my broadcasts and I'd looked a little bloated, so I'd gone on a strict juice cleanse, and it seemed to have done the trick.

I flipped on the morning news, and it was all about the Blades winning the Stanley Cup. No matter what station I turned to, all I saw was Adrian's boyfriend and that big hulk who'd kept getting in my face the prior evening. Denis Bouvier. The snide bastard was sexy as hell, I'd give him that. I made a face for taking notice. Arrogant too. I'd concentrate on that fault.

"Jesus Christ, isn't there any real news? Who gives a damn about this bullshit sports crap when there's corruption and crime happening all around us?" I drank the rest of my green tea and checked my emails. "Murder, subway delays, and an impending storm. Another fun day in fun city." I might complain, yet I'd fallen in love with New York City from my first day and wouldn't want to live anywhere else.

I dressed in one of my charcoal suits, with a starched white shirt and blue silk tie that perfectly matched my eyes—or so I'd once been told—and headed out the door to the station. The air was still cool, so I opted to walk and add that to my daily exercise regime.

It was June and the weatherman promised warmth later in the day, so I turned the air conditioning in the office higher and made another green tea while I read the morning reports. Again, I had to sift through the sports to read that the city was planning on raising parking-meter rates and that the state wanted to screw new workers out of a percentage of their pension.

I had a blessed hour of peace where I took notes and sent directives to the news team. By nine, the rest of the group trickled in and filled the conference room. Adrian, first as always, sat intent, his laptop at the ready.

Of course, everyone in the room was congratulating him on the win and thanking him for the tickets he'd given them. I hadn't used mine, as I had little desire to be trapped in a closed space with thousands of screaming people for an event I knew nothing about and cared even less to watch. It had taken everything in me to go find Adrian in that crowded bar.

"Good morning, everyone. There's been a few exciting developments overnight that we can report on for the evening news."

"We know. We were there. The Blades were awesome," Lars Peterson called out. He was the Brooklyn news director and a good reporter, but this shit had to end.

"All right. Can we all congratulate Adrian for his fiancé's win and move on? There's more going on in the world than hockey."

"Come on, Sterling. This is big news. It took New York almost twenty years to get a Stanley Cup, and we've never had two wins in a row. Plus, it's Friday."

Scanning the people sitting at the table, I arched a brow. "And? Does the world stop on Friday? Are you saying there's no news? Because I read some stories I think New Yorkers will be interested in long after some silly hockey game is played." I caught Adrian's downcast eyes and instantly regretted how harsh I sounded. "But yes, congratulations to Adrian, who, more importantly than a winning hockey game, is getting married tomorrow. So lunch will be on me today for the whole news staff."

After the applause and thank-yous, we got to business. It turned out to be a busy day, and we had some breaking news of an oil-tanker fire spilling fuel across the northbound lanes of I-95—a major artery in the East Coast—as well as a shootout on the George Washington Bridge. Adrian had followed up on the pension question, and we had a good clip of the head of the largest city union trying to wiggle out from answering his question as to whether older city workers would see their pension affected by the new rate.

We closed out with, naturally, more hockey highlights and accolades, including interviews with the players. Once again, Denis Bouvier ate up all the oxygen whenever the microphone was in his face. The guy loved the spotlight, and unfortunately, it loved him back. Sure, he was big and brawny and stupidly gorgeous, but he was way too full of himself.

After that, my night was far from over. I had to remain for the ten o'clock broadcast. We'd use the earlier clips for viewers who'd missed the six p.m. news, but we had different staff do night-beat reporting, and there was always something going on in the city that never slept.

"Good show, everyone." I gave Tanya Slidell, the meteorologist, and Bryan Held, the sports reporter, a brief nod. I left the anchor desk and the studio to use the restroom, then returned to my office to check my appearance in the full-length mirror I kept behind the door. Someone knocked, and I frowned. I rarely spoke to anyone between sets, preferring to read or listen to music.

I opened the door to see Bryan Held standing in front of me. "Can I help you?"

"I was curious about something."

"Yes?" I made no move to invite him in.

"How is Adrian doing?"

The question took me by surprise. I knew the two weren't friendly. "Why are you asking?"

"I mean, let's face it. The kid's only here because of who he's sleeping with. He was a washout as Louie's fill-in." To my annoyance, he stepped inside and closed the door behind him.

I remained neutral. "And you're telling me this, why?" I folded my arms. "Did you forget I also worked here at that time?"

Ignoring my question, he smirked. "So you know." He shifted closer, and I had to take shallow breaths. His cologne threatened to suffocate me.

"Know what?" I grew impatient. "You obviously have an agenda. Spit it out."

"Why would you pick him? That one little segment he did for the arena collapse wasn't so special. He helped some people—big deal. But to give him a camera-facing spot on prime-time news as a political reporter? And he still gets his own show in sports, which really should be mine. I don't get it." Bryan shook his head.

"So you wouldn't have done squat for the kid." I attempted that old-boy attitude. "Even with Rob DeVine telling everyone Adrian had the chops, you think he doesn't deserve it."

"Rob and Louie are close, and Louie's softhearted for Adrian. Maybe he's gay too, I don't know. I mean, the guy's never been married."

"And that's an indicator that a man's gay? Because he never married?" My smile was thin. "I'm not married."

Bryan flushed. "I-I didn't mean that. If you're gay, that's cool. I don't care."

"I'm not sure what someone's sexuality has to do with their job performance, unless they're a prostitute. Then satisfaction is a necessity." My gaze turned icy. "What I don't understand is one colleague seeking me out to bash another, unless it's out of professional jealousy."

Bryan's jaw worked. "I'm not jealous. But I've got years of experience on him."

"True," I murmured. "And yet you were Louie's backup and the Saturday night sports reporter. Not the most sought-after position."

His face flamed. "I'm the full-time reporter now."

"Yes. I'm aware. But let's see." I held up a hand and counted on my fingers. "Adrian has, in the span of a little more than a year, filled in for a sports legend, Louie Rozner; pitched and gotten a very successful sports talk show; was hailed on national television for assisting in a near disaster; and gotten promoted to a coveted news position. All while being extremely well liked by all the staff. Except, it seems, you."

"I don't...you know what? Forget it. You don't understand."

"Yes, I do. You're trying to create tension in the newsroom where there is none. You're envious of Adrian's success and his abilities. He's younger than you, better-looking than you, smarter than you. Now why don't you leave? Go study some stupid statistic like shots on net or how many points Adrian's boyfriend made in his game."

Bryan snorted. "I see you know nothing about sports. You act so above it all, but people need an outlet to wind down from the day's work and connect to each other. Sports satisfies that. Watching a game brings people together. Maybe you should try it. It would loosen you up." He spun on his heel and left.

"I'm plenty loose," I muttered. "Just because I don't like watching grown men run around throwing or hitting a ball doesn't make me a bad person."

I closed the door to my office and turned on the television. Nothing new to report for the ten o'clock spot, so I flipped the channels, stopping on a replay of the hockey game. Maybe if I forced myself to watch, I'd understand what the hell the fuss was.

"Okay, well, yeah, that was pretty awesome," I said, watching Rip skate backward while passing a puck. The speed the players maintained, all the while keeping their feet under them and watching the puck, was impressive. I sat forward as the opposing team's player raced toward the Blades' net. Recalling that the obnoxious Denis was the goalie, I homed in on him. There was a scuffle in front of the net, and I couldn't see how Denis prevented the puck from going in, but he did. "All right. That was good."

I ended up watching the entire game. It was fast-paced, heart-pounding, and I hated to admit, damned awesome. And yes, Denis Bouvier was an incredible machine, slapping away shots left and right. I understood why Rip was named the Most Valuable Player, but in my mind, Denis had earned it. Not that I'd ever mention it to that pompous jerk.

I checked my phone, shocked to see I only had about half an hour to review the script and see what we were going live with. "Dammit. I never should've watched that stupid game."

I turned on the lighted mirror on my desk and checked my face. "Pretty good, considering you've been up since six." I brushed my hair and checked my shirt and tie. The television show had moved on from the hockey game to "Superstars Then and Now" in hockey, and I was treated to Denis's publicity picture. Snapping dark eyes, a wicked grin, and slightly longer hair gave him a rakish appeal, almost like a pirate. I couldn't look away as they showed him and Rip hugging after their first Stanley Cup win the previous year.

What would it be like...?

Horrified at my thought, I hurried out of the office to the newsroom.

The drive to Adrian's brother's house upstate took close to two hours. I could've taken the train, but that would put me at the mercy of someone else's schedule, and I liked to be in control of my time. Especially when it came to leaving.

The house was a beautiful Tudor on several acres of land surrounded by towering trees. Birds chirped overhead. I'd worried about parking, but a valet had been arranged, and all I'd needed was to hand my keys to a kid in a white jacket.

A woman with a clipboard in hand met me on the path leading to the house, and behind her, a server waited with a tray of champagne flutes, the golden bubbles sparkling in the sunlight. I rarely drank, but my one weakness was champagne.

"Hello. May I have your name?" Her eyes widened. "Oh, how silly of me. You're Sterling Forest, the newscaster. Adrian told me to be on the lookout for you. Just go right up the path. Please have some champagne and enjoy yourself, Mr. Forest."

"Thank you."

I took a flute and meandered around the house, enjoying the sunlight and birdsong. I entered the back-yard—a huge expanse where a billowy white tent had been set up. An arched canopy filled with flowers stood at the end of a runner, and white chairs were set in rows. A violinist and flutist played softly, but I saw a DJ booth under the tent and knew I'd be long gone before that part of the evening started. As expected, I didn't recognize anyone—almost all the men were large and obviously athletes. Some were with women, others with men or single. I spotted Adrian with Rip at his side, talking to the only other person I recognized, Adrian's brother, and walked over to greet them.

"You made it," Adrian exclaimed. "I'm so glad. Thank you so much for coming. It means a lot to me."

"Thank you for having me, and congratulations." I raised my glass in a toast and took a sip. The bubbles danced on my tongue. He really was a sweet guy, and it was clear that he adored Rip. And from the possessive heat in Rip's eyes, the feeling was mutual. I wondered what it would be like, giving myself up so completely to someone.

I drank more champagne.

"You've met my brother, but not Lisa, his wife." Adrian introduced us, and I smiled.

"Hello. You have a beautiful home. Thank you for having me."

"Thanks, but that's only because I had a cleaning crew in." Her good-natured laughter rose in the air. "With two kids, three dogs, a cat, and a rabbit, it's impossible otherwise.

We come up here for the summer and long weekends, and it's amazing what can accumulate."

"Don't listen to her," Neil said with affection and kissed her cheek. "She's the glue. All that plus a full-time job. I couldn't do it."

"Of course not, darling." She patted his shoulder. "It's so nice to finally meet you, Sterling. Adrian talks about you all the time, and of course we watch your newscast. You've elevated Channel 8 the past few years."

I didn't normally allow compliments to go to my head, but I couldn't help the rush of pleasure. "Thank you. I'm trying to make this local station be more investigative and not into the fluff. More like the national news." I tipped my head to Adrian. "And I was lucky to have Adrian join me. I think he's got a terrific future in newscasting."

Adrian blushed. "Thank you. That means the world to me."

We stood for a minute or two, idly chatting. I finished my champagne and handed the flute to a passing server.

"We really should mingle," Rip pointed out to Adrian. "I see some of the guys, and Dev and Brody just showed up. Plus a few board members from GAINS."

"GAINS?" My brow furrowed. "What's that?"

"Gay Athletes in Sports," Adrian explained. "Rip, along with Devlin Summers and Brody Martin from the Brooklyn Kings, are the co-founders. Other gay athletes have joined as well. I'd better go say hello." Adrian gave us a quick smile before hurrying off with Rip.

"Would you excuse me for a moment too, please?" Lisa asked. "I need to check with the caterer."

"Of course." I was left with Neil Hunt, whom I knew to be in charge of a vast sports media conglomerate. "I'm not much of a sports person, I'm afraid. Neither of those names mean much to me other than they're on a New York team. I'm sure I won't know any of the people here."

"*Au contraire, monsieur journaliste de télévision*," a husky voice purred in my ear. "You know me."

I turned, and despite my dislike of the man, I almost swallowed my tongue. Denis Bouvier stood before me in a navy-blue suit and white shirt open at the neck. Golden stubble shadowed his jaw while his hard eyes clashed with mine.

A grin—evil or devilish, I couldn't decide which—kicked up his lips. "We meet again."

CHAPTER THREE
Denis

After his rude behavior toward me, I wanted to say something cutting to Sterling but couldn't. Call me shallow, but he was melt-my-bones-like-butter hot. Blue eyes as clear as an endless summer sky, glossy dark hair, and a jawline that could cut diamonds.

Sterling Forest was perfection.

Until he opened his mouth.

"I hardly think a few words exchanged in a bar qualifies us as friends."

I pretended to think hard. "Did I say that? I wasn't aware."

Neil grimaced. "Denis."

I tipped my head, attempting to be gracious. "It's good to see you again, Neil. Where is your beautiful wife?"

Rip and I might've made up and put our past behind us, but Neil and I hadn't. "She's here somewhere." He spoke directly to Sterling. "Would you excuse me, please?"

He hurried off, and Sterling's lips quirked. "What did you do to piss him off? Or was it simply you being you?"

"What is your problem?" I took a glass of champagne from the tray of a passing server and handed it to Sterling, then took one for myself.

"I don't recall saying I wanted a drink," Sterling grumbled.

"I don't drink alone. That would be pathetic."

He raised a brow but took a sip. And another.

We watched the crowd filter in.

"I thought this would be small. Adrian used the word *intimate*." Sterling glanced around. "There are over fifty people here."

"At least. But Rip has the team, his friends from GAINS, and other people he's close with. He's not the type to leave someone out."

"And you'd know his type, how? Because you've played on the same team for a few years? You're his best friend?"

I studied his face to see if he was joking, but he remained unreadable. Did the man not know our history?

"We play hockey together, plus at one time...we played in the sheets." At his stare, I laughed out loud. "As a newsman, you didn't know? Rip and I were lovers." I drained my glass.

For the first time I saw this uptight man at a loss for words. "Yet you're here? And Adrian invited you. I was there." He dropped his voice to a growl. "Don't tell me he doesn't know, and you're lying to him."

Hmm, he was even hotter when he turned growly. My dick twitched. *Merde. I must be hard up if this jerk is getting to me.* I needed to get laid.

"I see you too have fallen under the spell of our Adrian. No, no. Not at all. Adrian knows everything. But Rip and I...it was a long time ago. We're adults, and we've put the past behind us." Surprisingly, that shut him up, and I couldn't help poking the bear. "That's the mature way to handle it, don't you think?"

"The smartest thing would have been to never sleep with someone you work with in the first place." He finished his glass.

In the distance, I watched Rip and Adrian laughing with Seb, Varhov, and some of the others. Once I'd split with Rip, I'd been frozen out of their little friendship club. I pretended not to care. I pretended a great many things.

"*L'amour*, Sterling. Sometimes the passion is too great. Too strong." I met his eyes and took a step closer. His breath hitched. "You get caught up and can't help yourself."

His gaze clashed with mine. "Boundaries need to be set and respected."

My lip curled. "Some people can't live within boundaries and fences. They need to be free. Free to be who they are without fear of repercussions or that they won't be liked."

"Is that what happened to you? Someone tried to cage your untamed spirit and you broke free?"

You have no idea, and you never will.

"Didn't anyone ever tell you sarcasm is an ugly habit?" Without breaking eye contact, I beckoned a server carrying champagne. I gave him our empty glasses and took two more. I handed Sterling one. "Here."

He took it, our fingers brushing, and every hair on my body rose. I covered by gulping more champagne. Sterling held his glass but didn't drink.

"What's wrong?" he asked.

I couldn't answer as I still struggled to bring myself under control. What the hell? Maybe I should slow the drinking. It was beginning to affect my judgment.

"Nothing. Let's get back to you. Are you saying you've never been attracted to someone you've worked with? Not our beautiful Adrian because he is madly in love with Rip. They are the perfect couple."

Did I sound bitter? I didn't believe so, but I must've failed miserably because something that looked like pity filled his eyes.

"I'm sorry. Were you and Rip together long?"

"Two years. But it was my fault. I was stupid."

"You cheated." His voice turned flat.

I lifted a shoulder. "I said I was stupid. There's no need to get into anything else. Rip and I are friends now, and that's all that matters."

"For him, maybe. It proves he's a nice guy. But you?" Forest shrugged.

"I guess you've never made a mistake?"

"If I believed in relationships, I would never cheat."

"A cynic. How sad."

His mouth tightened, and some demented part of me wanted to kiss the scowl right off his face. I'd probably get punched in the nose, but it might be worth it. Maybe under that buttoned-up exterior lay a tiger waiting to be unleashed.

Rawr.

He grimaced. "I'm not a cynic. I'm a realist. Statistics prove most marriages end in divorce. In the research I once did for a news story, a scientist came up with a theory that mating for life in humans wasn't natural. From the fifty percent divorce rate and all the commitment phobes, I'm betting he's right."

I made a face. "A *clinical* cynic. The worst kind. Bah."

Now he smiled, and his eyes sparkled in the sunlight. "You don't believe in science? In facts?" He sipped his drink.

"Where's the room for passion? For being swept off one's feet?"

"You're kidding." He chuckled, and I stared—I'd never seen him with anything but a scowl. But I wasn't laughing, and the smile faded from his face.

"No, of course I'm not. Sometimes you see a person and it clicks. You can't stop yourself. You want to know what they sound like. Feel like." I brought the glass to my mouth and drained it. "Taste like." I swiped my tongue over my bottom lip. "You get caught up in the moment, helpless to stop it."

Our eyes locked, and I watched the pulse beat at the base of his throat. His chest rose and fell, and my heart pounded. I enjoyed the sparring, but he didn't act as though he were ready to get naked. He gave off more of a don't-touch-me vibe. Which, curiously, only made me want him more.

"Denis, the ceremony is starting." Seb clapped a hand on my shoulder. "Take your seat."

"Okay, best man."

Seb winked. "Finally he acknowledges the truth." He strode away, pointing the others to the filling seats.

I snickered and shook my head. "Don't push your luck, wingman," I called after him and walked along the lawn, noticing after a few steps that Sterling wasn't following. I stopped and turned around. He stood awkwardly, out of place. "Are you coming?"

He frowned and straightened his shoulders. "I have to sit in the last row. I'm leaving right after the ceremony."

My turn to frown. "Why would you do that?"

"I only came to show support for Adrian."

"Which you do by staying for the dinner. There will be music...dancing..."

His lips thinned. "I don't dance."

"*Quelle surprise*," I murmured but continued. "A delicious dinner." I sat in one of the gilt chairs.

"I'm on a strict diet."

"God, you're *such* an uptight hard-ass."

"And you're a hedonist," he sniped right back.

My brows shot up, and I grinned. "Thank you. Maybe I'll tell my agent to put it in my bio."

He snorted. "You would." Ignoring the empty chair next to me, he deliberately chose a seat several rows behind.

The ceremony was brief but meaningful. Rip had always spoken about wanting a family of his own, and Adrian was his perfect match. Adrian's parents beamed, Rip's father wore an ear-to-ear smile. Neil and Seb stood up for them. It was a picture-perfect wedding. Everyone was filled with joy and happiness.

So why did I feel like a black cloud hung over me? It wasn't that I'd lost out on a forever with Rip. I hadn't lost it; I'd thrown it away. And to be honest, we'd never had what he and Adrian did. They truly loved each other in a way that went beyond the physical.

Maybe I didn't believe I'd ever find that all-encompassing love. I huffed and made my way to the bar. Why was I stressing? I didn't need love or even a boyfriend. All any relationship had shown me was that I was bad at them. But sex? *That* I excelled in. So I might as well give up trying for something I kept failing at and couldn't possibly find, and instead keep on doing what I did best: having fabulous sex. Spread the wealth, so to speak.

Rip and Adrian had created a signature drink—a champagne cocktail—and I sipped it, watching them take pictures with their families and close friends.

"They're going to be deliriously happy, aren't they?" Seb stopped by on his way to the shoot. His hands were jammed into the pockets of his pants, and that earlier friendly face? A distant memory.

"I think they are."

"Just stay away from them. I know we've all made up and play nice now, but if you pull any shit, I swear—"

"Fuck off, Seb. Go find your beautiful wife and leave me the hell alone."

He glared at me but left, and I watched him take Jolie's hand and join Adrian and Rip. Perhaps I'd deserved the warning. In the beginning, I *had* tried to get between the two of them, but it had been more because I was unhappy in another failed relationship at that time than wanting Rip back. Plus, I didn't go after married men.

As I drank a glass of water, my gaze lit on Sterling sitting at the end of the bar, his eyes pinned on Adrian and Rip. I crooked my finger at the bartender.

"Send a double of the special cocktail to that gentleman." I pointed toward Sterling, then pulled a hundred out of my wallet and handed it to him.

"Sure thing, Mr. Bouvier." He mixed it up and brought it over to Sterling, who turned around. I grinned and wiggled my fingers. Of course that earned me a frown and a shake of his head. I picked up my glass and joined him. I was already a little buzzed and had a feeling I'd be calling a car to take me home or finding a hotel room for the night.

"You can't say no. I had him make it special for you."

Sterling snorted. "Sure you did. But I've had enough. More than enough, for that matter. I don't usually drink so much." A slight smile lifted his lips. "Unfortunately, I have a weakness for champagne."

"As do I. I keep a fabulous collection in my apartment." I leaned in close and felt him stiffen with shock. It gave me the opportunity to breathe deep of his scent. Hot and sweet. Like honey. "Maybe you'll come see it sometime."

"Is that the new *come see my etchings*? An excuse to get me alone?" he rasped.

Well, well. The iceman's blood runs warm.

"Do I need one?"

"I watched your game," he murmured.

Now I was actually shocked. I pulled away and stared him in the face. "You what?"

He took a drink of the cocktail. A long one, I noticed. "I wanted to see what the hype was all about."

Amused, I leaned on the bar. "And?"

"You—I mean the Blades—are good."

"So we live up to the accolades."

His cheeks flushed pink. "I guess. I mean, it was a winning game, so yeah. It was good."

The music stopped, and Neil took the mic. "Dinnertime, everyone. Take your seats."

People filed off the dance floor to the tables placed around the perimeter, but Sterling and I remained at the bar, him sitting and me standing by his side.

"I'm not really that hungry," I told him. "Are you?"

A tiny shake of his head.

"So." I shifted closer. "You thought we were only good. How many games have you watched?"

His lashes fanned down. "It was my first."

"*Incroyable,*" I muttered. "You only think we were good. In the final game of a seven-game championship series with a 1-0 score."

"Yeah. Okay. It was very good."

I loomed over him, and his blue eyes blew open wide. "So this is how it's going to work. You are going to come to preseason opening day and watch us play. Then you're going to come opening night at Blades Arena and watch the game."

He had the nerve to glare at me. "No."

"No? Why the hell not?"

"Because, if you thought about it for a moment, you'd realize I have a job that requires me to be at the station for a six p.m. and a ten p.m. show. I can't just take off to watch you play your games."

Dammit. I hated that he was right. But…he didn't say he wouldn't come. Merely that the time wasn't right.

"That's fine. You can come on the weekends. We play afternoon games sometimes."

"I never said I wanted to." His brows knitted, and I grinned.

"You haven't said no."

"Since when do I owe you explanations for what I do? Listen, you've attached yourself to me this whole afternoon. Why don't you go play with your other little hockey friends and leave me alone?"

"Attached? Play with my little friends?" I sputtered. "Did you seriously say that to me?"

He pushed off the chair and knocked against me as he walked away. "Deal with it."

"Obnoxious prick."

I decided to stop drinking completely before I made a fool of myself, and I asked for water. I refused to allow Seb, Neil, or anyone to think that seeing Rip find love and getting married in such a warm and accepting environment hurt like a kidney punch.

"Stupid fool," I muttered, seeing Neil stop Sterling, put an arm around his waist, and lead him into the house.

Was I talking about him or me?

CHAPTER FOUR
Sterling

Coming from Beverly Hills, this wasn't the first celebrity wedding I'd attended. My own mother had three failed ones.

Dahlia Dumont was one of the most recognizable movie actresses in the world, famed for her beauty and sweetness. Talent too, of course. She'd won numerous awards—Oscars, Film Critic Awards, Golden Globe—and there was a dedicated room for them all in her Bel-Air mansion.

But for someone who spent her life in the public eye and made her fortune from embracing the media, Dahlia had a dirty little secret.

Me.

Her son.

The child she'd had at fifteen before running away from home and heading to Hollywood.

I was probably lucky she hadn't left me behind or given me away. Her backstory read like a novel: At sixteen she'd been discovered at the mall by an agent and signed to a movie deal to play a virginal ingenue. At seventeen her first movie had become an unexpected blockbuster, and the money had poured in as she'd risen to fame playing that same part—the young, sweet girl falling in love with the bad boy and redeeming him. She'd bought a big house and hired staff. I'd grown up thinking I was Marisel the housekeeper's child.

Until one night when I was sixteen, I'd heard them fighting. I'd stood frozen outside Dahlia's bedroom door, but their raised voices had been as clear as if they were standing in front of me.

"Listen, Dahlia. I never asked to pretend to be Sterling's mother. You paid me, and I did it. But now, if you want me to keep your secret, it's gonna cost you more."

"You've had a very nice life from what I see," Dahlia drawled. "I'm rarely here, and you have the run of the place. I even have a housekeeper for you...my housekeeper. I give you my clothes and bags, plus I pay you damn well."

"And I want more," Marisel said. "If you don't, I'll go to the gossip magazines and tell them how you don't give a damn about your bastard son and hid him away because you were embarrassed of him."

"You bitch."

"I know you can afford it. I saw your bank statements."

My heart pounded, and spots floated before my eyes. Dahlia Dumont, one of the most famous movie stars in the world, was my mother.

But she was ashamed of me. Didn't want me.

"Fine. How much?"

"Five million."

A shriek of laughter. "You've got to be kidding me."

"You made over fifty million on your last movie alone. I read the papers. I know."

"No one would believe you."

"That's fine. You wanna take that chance? I have Elsa Halpern's cell number from Entertainment Weekly. She's always after me to give her some dirt, but I ignore her calls. Next time I won't. You know what they say. Where there's smoke, there's fire. You want them to start digging? You never told me nothing about his father. What's he, a criminal? You on the run or something?"

I crept closer.

"Don't be ridiculous," Dahlia hissed. "But only this once. Sterling will be eighteen in two years, and then he'll be out of the house and our lives."

My stomach cramped. Out at eighteen for good? My chest hurt. Where would I go? I almost got sick on the pristine floor. My whole life was a lie. I was going to be homeless and alone in two years.

"Doesn't matter to me. I want that money in my account."

At the sound of heels clicking on the polished floors, I scurried away and around the corner. I waited until I saw Marisel—formerly Mom—skip down the stairs.

Now it all made sense—why Marisel was always distant, why she never showed up to my school plays or parents' nights at school. She was basically an actor. Dahlia was my mother but, she didn't give a damn. My life story was only worth five million dollars to Marisel.

My jaw hardened. If that was the way the world worked, I fully intended to get my share.

I retraced my steps and walked into Dahlia's room.

"Sterling? Why are you here? Why didn't you knock?"

I smiled. "Hello, Mom." She turned white.

I had been paid well to keep her secret. I'd left home at eighteen, and had never needed to worry about college or graduate-school tuition or my living expenses. When I'd wanted my own condo, I'd had the money to buy it, anywhere I wanted, mortgage-free. Plus, I'd gotten the Malibu house. I needed a private hideaway.

From the time I'd confronted Dahlia Dumont, she'd given me whatever I asked for, except a mother's love. But as I'd never known what that meant, I'd learned to live without it and had turned out pretty damned well. I'd graduated with honors and received a master's in journalism. I'd worked my way up in the newsroom in the LA market on my own. Her actions—unintentionally—had imparted to me one of life's greatest lessons: *Everything you show to people is a mask. Just make sure what they see, what you choose to show them, is perfect. That you're perfect. Appearances are all that matters to get ahead in the world.*

At the moment, I was feeling far from perfect. Before I made a fool of myself and got sick all over the lush green grass, I needed to leave. I'd never had so much to drink. Ever. *Damn Bouvier.*

"It's all his fault," I mumbled. "Jerk kept giving me drinks." The fact that I'd sucked them down fast was irrelevant.

I walked across the lawn—slowly, carefully—but dammit all to hell, Adrian's brother blocked my escape route. Good manners dictated I couldn't sneak away without speaking to him.

"You're not leaving, are you? Dinner's about to be served."

My smile was quick and my answer ready. "Yeah, sorry. It was a wonderful ceremony. They look very happy."

"They are." Neil peered at me. "Are you okay to drive?"

I blinked and drew in a deep breath. My lips felt a little fuzzy, but I had water in the car. I'd drink the bottle and leave. "*Mm*, yeah, of course." A rumble of thunder sounded in the distance. "I'd better get going. It's a long drive to the city, and I don't want to get stuck in a storm. Thanks for everything."

God, why won't he leave me alone?

"You were drinking a lot at the bar. With Denis." His gaze sharpened. "He didn't say anything to make you leave, did he?" A look of distaste clouded his normally pleasant expression. "He can be an obnoxious son of a bitch if he wants to."

Laughter ripped from my chest. "He must want to all the time, then."

"Trust me, I'd love an excuse to kick him out. I know Adrian and Rip have made their peace with him, but that doesn't mean squat to me."

I fished the car keys out of my pocket but dropped them. "Shit. Crap." I fumbled for a bit before I picked them up, but to my shock, Neil swiped them from my fingers, and I jerked my head up to meet his concerned face.

"Sterling, I'm sorry, but I'm not letting you drive in this condition."

I scowled. "Condition? What the hell are you talking about?" *Ugh*, my stomach felt as if I were on a roller coaster hurtling at breakneck speed. I swallowed. "Could you tell me where your bathroom is?"

Neil put his arm around my waist, propping me up. "Come with me. I'll show you."

I grimaced, but with my belly doing a tap dance, I couldn't object. We walked inside, and he led me to a spacious bathroom.

"Thanks. And again, it was a beautiful wedding." I closed the door in his face and promptly got sick in the toilet. After making sure I left the room as pristine as I found it, I rinsed my mouth. One look in the mirror, and I almost died. I looked...well, I looked as drunk as I felt. My face was pale and sweaty, my eyes red and glassy.

"God." I hung my head and closed my hand in a fist. "How could you be so stupid?" It was all that idiot hockey player's fault, but in my heart I couldn't rest the blame on him completely. I searched for and found some extra-strength aspirin in the medicine cabinet and popped three, cupped water in my hands, and drank it. And drank some more. I patted my cheeks with a towel, did some deep breathing. This was as good as I was going to get, so I opened the door…and found Neil waiting.

"Feeling better?" He was nothing but sympathetic, and this time my nausea was from humiliation rather than overindulgence.

"Not now. I should leave." I attempted to push past him, but he gripped my arm.

"No damn way am I letting you out of here. Come with me."

"Neil—"

"You might be able to intimidate my brother, but it doesn't work with me."

Horribly embarrassed, I followed him through the house to a bedroom. He stepped aside. "Please. Take a nap. I'll tell my wife so you won't be disturbed. If you need to spend the night, no worries. We have others who'll be staying over, and you won't be the only guest for breakfast in the morning. So do yourself a favor. Stretch out and sleep it off. Don't be embarrassed. It happens to all of us." He closed the door, then reopened it. "Oh. And just in case you try and leave, I'll be keeping your car keys." This time the door stayed shut.

I sank on the bed and kicked off my shoes. I refused to go to bed dressed and end up looking a wrinkled mess, so I slipped my clothes off and laid them on the bed, not bothering to even hang them up. So unlike me, but I hadn't gotten drunk in ages.

I was so tired, and the room was spinning a bit. There was a bottle of water by the bedside, and I finished it. I lay down, rested my head on the pillow, and closed my eyes.

Warm. I was so warm. And comfortable. I opened my eyes, and it took me a minute to remember where I was. Neil's house. I stretched, enjoying the feel of the cool sheets on my naked body. I had no idea what time it was—later that night? Dawn? Next afternoon? God, what a disaster. Too much to drink with that big lug of a hockey player. Asshole thought I was interested in him? He was strictly where he belonged—buried in my fantasy sex life.

I heard a sound from behind me. Water was running in the en suite. A shower. Someone was in the shower. I closed my eyes, and flashes of memory rolled through my brain.

Firm, warm lips skimmed mine.

Big, rough hands held me close.

A stubbled cheek rasped against my jaw.

Long hair tickled my face.

"No," I whispered. "No, no, no." Behind the door, the water stopped. Frantic now, I searched the room for my clothes and found them draped on the club chair in the corner. I had one leg in my briefs and was about to slip the other one through the opening, when the bathroom door opened and Denis appeared, water dripping from his hair to his shoulders and chest.

His very broad, sculpted chest.

All the air in the room vanished. I couldn't stop staring. I'd never seen abs so beautiful. Like rows and rows of bricks built on top of each other to form a solid wall. Pure muscular perfection. I wanted to look away. I needed to but couldn't break my focus on that swirl of golden hair leading down...down...

"Ah...*bonsoir.*"

That husky voice with an undertone of laughter sent a frisson of unwanted desire through my bloodstream. Glancing up to see his amused face, I panicked and backed away. To my mortification, my feet tangled in the underwear at my ankles, and with my dick hanging in the breeze, I fell on the bed.

Humiliated didn't begin to describe how I felt. And I had no time to move, as Denis approached. "I'm sorry. Did I scare you?"

Burning up from embarrassment, I pulled up my briefs to cover myself and waited a second before I glared at him. "What the hell are you doing here? And what time is it?"

"It's nine p.m. You've been asleep for about five hours."

I ran a hand through my hair. "Oh. I thought it was Sunday." My eyes narrowed. "And why did you take a shower?"

"After dinner, a bunch of us decided to change and go to the local rink to play a game. Too bad you missed it. I was fantastic. Blocked twenty shots on goal in an hour."

"Oh." I bit my lip. "I thought..." Feeling foolish at my racing thoughts, I shook my head. "Forget about it." I huffed. "Do you mind? I want to get dressed."

But Denis didn't move. "You thought what?" His dark eyes searched mine, and that wicked grin I despised—mainly because it turned me inside out—tipped up his lips. He leaned in close, and my breath caught as my heart pounded. "Maybe we kissed? Or something else?"

"No," I bit out. My composure rested on a hair trigger, and I prayed he wouldn't try to touch me because I knew there wasn't a fucking chance in hell I'd be able to resist. "Why would I think that? Or want it?"

We were so close, I could almost taste him. His mouth hovered next to mine.

"I will admit, I was tempted. But I figured when I do fuck you, we should both be clearheaded. And alone, not in someone else's house. Because it's going to be loud. Very, very loud." He chuckled and ran his knuckles along my flaming face. "You were so very enticing, I might've stolen a brief kiss, *mon cher*. But only on your cheek. Like this." Something wet licked me. His tongue. I should have been disgusted. Instead, I was turned-on. Excited.

I froze and jerked away.

"Don't ever do that again. And there will never be a first time for us. Only in your dreams. I don't want you to kiss me, never mind fuck me. I don't even like you."

If I thought my insult would upset him, I was wrong. His smile grew broader, and like a fly in a spider's trap, I found myself helpless to move in his glittering web of lust.

"You don't have to like me to want me to fuck you. You know how good it will be."

God help me, he's right. I could imagine his hot mouth on mine, those big arms holding me, those powerful thighs pinning me to the bed. I wanted him with a deep ache in my bones that sensed with some primeval instinct how incredible the sex would be. The seconds ticked away, and I panicked. Breathless and shaking, I forced the words past my trembling lips. "Get out of my way and let me get dressed. I have to leave."

"You can't. Lisa has prepared a late-night meal for those of us caught in the rain. Now that you're awake, you'll join us."

"Rain?" I glanced at the window, at the water beating against the panes. I grimaced and met his fathomless eyes. Eyes a person could get lost in if they allowed themselves to. Which I refused to do.

"Who the hell are you to tell me what to do?"

He dropped the towel, and before I turned my head, I caught a glimpse of his dick. Half-hard, it was…large. Very large. And thick. Tension wove ropes around me, and I released a sigh of relief when he strode away to his pile of clothes on the dresser.

"Let's see. You get drunk at her house, and she's kind enough to let you sleep it off, so you thank her by sneaking away without saying *au revoir*? No thank-you for her hospitality?" He tsked and finished buttoning his shirt. "Such poor manners, *mon ami*. I wouldn't have believed that for someone as proper as you." Fully dressed now, he folded his arms. "Get ready, and we'll go to the kitchen."

It was irritating that he stood there, indecently perfect with no sign he'd been drinking as much as I had. "How the hell are you so…sober?"

"I drank water after. Lots of it." His eyes danced. "And I suppose I can handle my liquor while you cannot." His smirk grew. "Plus, I'm bigger than you. Although I'd have no complaints." His gaze dropped to my half-hard crotch, and I itched to punch him in his perfect face for my body's lusty response to his words.

Annoyed that he was correct yet again, I went to the bathroom, washed my face, combed my hair with my fingers, and rinsed with mouthwash. I took some more aspirin, drank water from the tap, and thank the fucking gods, I felt mostly human after sleeping.

I returned to the room and swiftly dressed, peering at myself in the mirror. I looked…not my best, but there was nothing more I could do. I didn't subscribe to wearing the stubble so many men favored, and grimaced at the shadow darkening my jaw, but that couldn't be helped.

"I'm ready."

I followed him down the hall, wondering what fresh hell awaited me.

CHAPTER FIVE

Denis

I should've felt sorry for the man. He was completely out of his element, and I could've made it easier for him. But he'd been such a sanctimonious little shit that I let him squirm like a worm on a hook and muddle his way through his embarrassment.

"Here he is," I announced to the room of people. "All cleaned up and hopefully hangover free."

"Bastard," he hissed in my ear. Sterling cleared his throat and stepped around me. "Lisa, may I speak to you a moment?"

Always a sweetheart, Lisa excused herself from the conversation and approached us. "I'm glad you're awake.

Are you feeling better? We have some late-night snacks, and I still have food from the wedding, if you'd like."

Big blue eyes filled with venom shot to me. "Do you mind? I'd like to speak to Lisa in private."

"*Absolument.*" I strolled away and found a seat at the end of the large dining table across from Adrian and Rip. A feast had been set out—sandwiches, bagels, all kinds of spreads, and cold cuts. Cookies and pastries took up a side table, along with a large coffee urn. I counted twenty people including me.

Adrian leaned over to speak to me. "How is he?"

I could play it two ways. Tell the truth and say he was drunk as a skunk and had passed out, or be the gentleman and say he wasn't feeling well and thought it was best to rest instead of attempting the long drive home.

I took half a bagel and put it on my plate. "Better, now that he's slept. I don't think he'll have too bad of a hang-over." I couldn't help it. Sinners had much more fun.

Adrian's brows shot up. "Hangover? He always said he barely drinks. Sterling's very into his health—no coffee, only green tea, has a strict gym routine."

"I guess everyone needs to let go once in a while." I spread cream cheese on my bagel, placed capers and toma-toes on it, then piled smoked salmon on top.

"You seem to be enjoying this, Denis. You and Sterling were having a very intense conversation at the bar before dinner." Rip lazed in his chair, his fingers playing with Adrian's hair. The light picked up the gold glint of his wedding band.

"Enjoying what? A wedding? Of course." I swept my hand in front of me. "My two favorite people together at last."

Rip studied me. "How are you doing?"

I chewed and swallowed. "Me? You saw tonight. I'm great. I might be thirty-six, but I'm as quick as Ellis, even though he's more than ten years younger."

"I'm not talking about hockey, Denis. I mean you, as a person. We didn't have a chance to talk about it at Slapshots after the win, but now that the season is finished and Adrian and I are married, we should try and catch up."

My throat grew tight, but I forced a smile on my face. "About what?"

"I don't know. I feel like we never got to know each other."

"Of course we did. I'm an open book."

He laughed. "You're a great liar, but you can't fool me. Every time I asked about meeting your family, you pushed me off. I only met Gil once, and that was a brief hello at a playoff game. I know he's been a huge influence in your life. We never talked about anything of importance except hockey."

"Is anything else but hockey important?" I joked.

"Do you really believe that?" His brow puckered. "There's more to life than the game. It's our job."

"I mean, there's sex, but I doubt we need to talk about that."

"No," he responded with a scornful tilt of his lips. "Don't even go there. Dammit, I thought you'd changed."

I immediately sought to smooth things over. "No, no. I'm sorry. I'm kidding." The last thing I wanted was to upset the tenuous bonds of friendship Rip and I were weaving. "My family? There's not much to tell. I grew up in Canada, I left home to play hockey, and that's that."

"And that's that," he repeated. "You're kidding me. I know more about the guy I buy my coffee from than you've ever given me. Friends share, Denis. They open themselves up."

Rip might be speaking to me, but my concentration was on Sterling. Lisa had seated him by her and Neil, and they were attempting to draw him into conversation. Knowing the little I did of the man, it would be in vain. He was as tight-lipped as they came.

And tight lips were only good if they were sucking my dick, which wasn't about to happen with Sterling, no matter how hot it would be to see him on his knees, those angry blue eyes shooting daggers as he pleasured me. He was an arrogant, annoying bastard, but perversely, that made him eminently desirable. I suppose it was the thrill of the chase and ultimate capture.

"Denis," Rip spoke sharply, and I focused on him again.

"Open up? Trust me, *mon ami*, the last thing I want to do at your wedding is talk about my family. That chapter of my life is closed." The food rolled in my belly, and I needed air. "Excuse me."

I rose from my seat and exited through the kitchen, where I remembered from the times Rip had brought me here, a door led out to a deck and the spacious grounds.

The rain had ceased, and the air was fresh and clean up here. It reminded me of my home, an hour north of Montreal. The cold weather began in August, and snow was common in October. We were playing hockey by mid-month.

I was the biggest kid in my Timbits—U-7 league—and like my father and grandfather, chosen to play goalie. "*The Bouvier legacy*," *Papa* had proclaimed to our family, all puffed up with pride, and every minute out of school, after I'd finished my homework, he and *Oncle* Marc would work with me. We'd practice on the frozen lake behind our homes in the winters and in the town's indoor rink in summertime. My little cousin Davide had been born with some ailment and couldn't play sports, so my uncle Marc had poured everything into me.

Life had been perfect.

Until I turned fifteen and realized I hadn't been interested in kissing Thérèse, my next-door neighbor, who'd walked to school with me every day, but instead, my dreams had revolved around her older brother, Georges. A tall, tawny-haired god with long-lashed brown eyes and a chipped front tooth from a wayward puck that had made his smile even more adorable. I'd tried to fight the urges, forced myself to go out with girls, kiss them even, though it had always turned out to be a disappointing mess.

"Open up, he says," I muttered now, taking the stairs to the backyard and walking on the wet grass. The house sat on several acres, and I made my way across the lawn, my shoes squelching in the puddles. They'd be ruined by night's end, but I didn't care. I reached the swing set and leaned on the redwood post. Gazing at the moonlit sky, at stars spread out overhead, I thought about Georges for the first time in years.

"You're going to do great in the NHL," I told him in English, practicing to get more confident speaking it, then froze at his presence behind me. Hot breath hit my neck.

"You think so?" A shiver ran through me feeling his lips touch my ear. "I'm a little nervous about leaving. I'll miss you, Denis." Georges was eighteen, two years older than me, and leaving for hockey training camp, having been drafted out of high school.

"Y-you will? But you'll meet lots of new people."

His hands splayed across my stomach, making fire explode in my belly. My vision blurred, my words ending on a hiss of pleasure when he cupped my crotch.

"I knew it," he whispered in my ear as he slipped a hand inside my sweats, pushing them and my briefs halfway down my thighs. "You want me, don't you?"

I couldn't speak, couldn't do anything except fight for my next breath as he touched me. I was harder than I'd ever been. At some point his pants had come off too, and he was naked against me. His teeth buried themselves in my shoulder as I fell apart, and he groaned.

"You're so fucking hot, and I've wanted this all year."

"I...I've never. I mean. I haven't..."

"I figured. It's hard to know who to trust in a small town. Especially for me." He turned me around, and his eyes were earnest and soft. "But you won't say anything to anyone." He put a hand on my shoulder. "Will you?"

Before I could answer, his lips settled over mine, and I almost swooned. Those few sloppy kisses I'd shared with girls were nothing like this all-consuming heat.

Georges slid his fingers through my hair and took control. His tongue pushed to meet mine, and they teased and played together. I clutched his shoulders as he owned my mouth, and I was hard. Aching. And I could see he was stiff as well.

"Georges," I moaned. "Please."

Georges nipped and bit my lips. "Please what?"

"I-I don't know. Just touch me again." In the hockey rink I was so self-assured. I knew what I was supposed to do and how to do it. Here, I was lost.

Instead, Georges took my hand and put it on his dick. I'd never touched another man, and I held it awkwardly.

"On your knees. I'll tell you what to do. Teach you. You do me first, and after I'll do you."

I sank to the floor and opened my mouth. The door to his bedroom opened.

"Georges!" his mother screamed.

He pushed me to the floor, and I scrambled for my clothes to cover myself as he cursed me and told his mother how he'd been doing me a favor, showing me hockey moves, and I'd forced myself on him while he was changing. He joined his mother in screaming at me to get away from him, and I pulled my clothes on, ran down the stairs and out of the house.

Georges's father was walking up the path. "Bonsoir, Denis."

"Révérend." Without making eye contact, I crossed the lawns between our two houses.

I sat on the swing. It was small for my height, but I let it sway me back and forth. I remembered hearing that

Georges had been transferred to the Miami Manatees after he'd failed to impress during his rookie year, and that he'd died in a boating accident off the Florida Keys.

Maybe it was the cool wind that brought tears to my eyes. It had picked up a bit since I walked outside, but I welcomed the chill. Rip insisting I should talk about my family had resulted in this, and I resented him for it. Not everyone needed to spill their guts, especially when it led to pain.

Just then I heard, "Time for me to leave this lovefest," and saw a solitary figure walking toward me. Sterling. I quickly wiped my face of all traces of wetness, but he turned sharply to the right and took out his phone, clearly oblivious that he had company.

My interest was piqued. Who was he calling? He had his car, so it wasn't a ride. With zero remorse, I crept up behind him to listen.

"You did? Listen, I'm not in the city, but I can be there in two hours. Where are you?"

A male voice on the other end rumbled loud enough for me to overhear, "There's a diner on the corner of Columbia Street and Congress in Brooklyn. Meet you there."

The conversation finished, Forest slipped the phone into his pocket.

"A news story?" I asked, watching him jump at the sound of my voice.

"Are you spying on me?" he sputtered, eyes blazing blue fire. "Who the fuck do you think you are?"

"I was out here first. And it's a free country. Or yard. You don't own the air space." It was fun to make him mad. See him lose that icy front.

Without another word, he turned and walked away. I trailed after him up the stairs and into the kitchen. He found Lisa and apologized again.

"I do have to leave. I'm sorry. Thank you very much for putting up with my appalling behavior."

"What? No, Sterling. There's nothing to apologize for. Are you sure you're all right to drive?"

His smile was thin. "Yes. Totally. I drank tons of water, took aspirin, and had something to eat. The sleep did me good and—"

"And nothing," I interjected. "There's no way your blood alcohol is normal. If you get stopped by the police, you'll get a DUI, and that wouldn't look good for your sterling reputation." I smirked. "Pun intended."

His jaw hard, he pinned me with that defiant gaze. "You're involving yourself in a conversation that has nothing to do with you." But his expression turned doubtful, and he chewed his lip. I could see my words had hit home.

Lisa's worried eyes met mine. "Do you think so? You did have a lot to drink, Sterling. I'm afraid for you. The troopers up here are no joke."

"I only had three, and that was hours ago. Can I please have my keys? Neil took them earlier."

"It was more like four. Maybe even five. I'll drive you," I offered and said to Lisa, "I'm fine, and even if the police stop us, I'm a hockey player with a bad reputation. One more strike won't matter."

She shook her head. "No, Denis, that's not a good solution either."

"But it's the best one. Can you ask Neil for the keys?"

"What's wrong?" Adrian approached us. Lisa explained the situation, and Adrian looked agonized. "I should go with you. If you're after a news story, I should be there."

"It's not a news story. And it's your honeymoon," Sterling insisted. "There's no way I'd allow you to leave. You're not coming with me." Frustrated, he pulled out his phone. "You know what? Forget it. I'll call a car service and have them take me." He tapped the screen. "They'll be here in eight minutes. Lisa, thank you for everything." He held out a hand to Lisa, then Adrian. "Thank you so much for the beautiful wedding and the aftercare. I appreciate it, and I'm horribly embarrassed. I'll have someone pick up the car later in the week, if that's okay. Are Rip and Neil inside? I need to say good-bye to them."

She nodded. "Of course it is. Everyone's just having cake and coffee now."

I followed them all, and from the doorway, watched him make the rounds, so proper, as if he were at a formal dinner.

"You like him, don't you?"

I gazed down at Adrian at my shoulder and laughed. "Beauty, brains, *and* a fabulous sense of humor. Rip was smart as hell to scoop you up."

An annoyed expression marred his normally smooth brow, and he pursed his lips as if he'd bitten a lemon. "No one scooped me up. See? That's what I think your problem is."

I allowed a smile because he was a newlywed and cute, so I'd humor him. "Tell me, Dr. Hunt. Analyze me." Better men than him had tried and failed. Mostly because I had zero desire to talk about a past that held little beside ugly memories.

"You think love is a game to be played and won. But it's not."

I snorted. Cute only went so far. "Love? You're wrong, *mon ami*. Your boss is annoying as hell, uptight, and obsessed with rules and appearances. He's fun to play with to see his reactions. Like a cat with a mouse."

"You've been obsessed with him since that comment he made about hockey players. And tonight you were with him every moment from the ceremony onward. Why? From what I know of you, which, granted, isn't much, Sterling's not your type."

Adrian knew nothing about me, but it was obvious he still held a grudge over my threesome suggestion to Rip. That had to be the reason for this overprotective behavior toward his boss.

"Obsessed?" This was growing tiresome. "I hate to tell you, but I don't get obsessed with anyone. It's usually the opposite. People are obsessed with me. Matter of fact, both you and your husband seem to be more interested in me and my personal life than your own." I bared my teeth in a semblance of a smile. "Now, I'm going to collect my clothes, make my rounds, and leave you to your family celebration. I think I've overstayed my welcome."

I left him standing there and made a beeline for Rip. "Thank you for inviting me. It was a wonderful time."

"Are you sure you don't want to stay?"

While he was most likely sincere, the last thing Rip needed was his old lover hanging around on his wedding night. I knew I certainly could find something better to do.

"I'm positive. *Félicitations pour ton marriage, mon ami.* I am very, very happy for you. I am truly glad we've become real friends this time."

"I am too."

We shared a smile and clasped hands.

I waved farewell to the rest of the guests and went to collect my things. I noticed a car had pulled up front, and through the large bay window I observed Sterling sliding inside. The car pulled away, and I took out my phone.

My car showed up in less than ten minutes, and I sank into the back seat. "Long drive, huh?" the driver commented.

"Yes." *And hopefully you won't talk the whole way*, I wanted to add but held my tongue, considering he was speeding down the Thruway at seventy miles per hour.

"Columbia Street and Congress? They got a good diner there."

"So I've heard. Wake me up when we get there, please."

I closed my eyes, wondering whom a pompous, stuffy guy like Sterling Forest was going to meet in the middle of the night.

CHAPTER SIX
Sterling

What the hell was I doing, at midnight in an area of Brooklyn I would never frequent? Actually, there was no area of Brooklyn I chose to frequent—I failed to see the hype. Manhattan had everything I needed. And if it didn't, I could order it.

Yet here I was, walking into some greasy restaurant straight out of an old Raymond Chandler novel, late on a Saturday night. Why? Not for the story about the mayor cheating on his residency and taxes. That I would relish, the prospect of which would even get me to go to Staten Island. No, this, today, was information I'd first requested years ago at my first job in the newsroom at KLOS. I'd been living on my own once I'd left for college, and it wasn't the loneliness that ate away at my soul. It was the deep-seated need to know where I came from, aside from the sleek and tanned loins of Dahlia Dumont.

There was no birth certificate with her name on it, only Marisel's, which was a fake. I'd confronted Dahlia, and she'd refused to tell me where she'd come from or who my father was. But the issue had come up again because I'd needed my Social Security number, and I'd had to threaten her with blackmail to learn more. A small town in the middle of Amish country, Pennsylvania. A home birth with a midwife. No hospital records, only the family bible. That had been all she would give me.

I pushed open the door to the diner and spotted Tanner Robbins, the investigator I'd hired when I'd come to New York—the fourth one, in fact, the previous three having failed to breach the silent wall of mistrust the Amish community had for the "English" who came and tried to poke their noses into their lives. I was frustrated at the lack of progress all these years.

From a booth in the corner, he raised a hand in acknowledgment, and I slid onto the ripped vinyl seat across from him. I tried not to touch the sticky Formica table. "Well, what did you find out?"

"Guess you don't believe in pleasantries." He chuckled, the smile fading from his lips when I remained stoic. He was a beefy blond guy who'd worked Intelligence in the Army before retiring. I found his name the time I had to research for a report on missing children. He'd had success where others failed.

"Not at midnight."

A dispirited server approached us, and I ordered tea.

"All right, then." He pulled out his notepad. "Here's what I was able to find out. Your mother, Rachel Younk, had an older English boyfriend she kept secret not only from her family, but the whole community. They would meet after school, or she'd find ways to slip out of her house after dark."

"And she got pregnant."

He blew out a sigh. "Looks that way. From what I've gathered, Rachel—Dahlia—was always a bit wild. She was beautiful, and she matured early and was interested in boys. At fifteen, she met Peter at a local grocery store where her family sent her shopping. He was a delivery man, and they started a love affair. Peter was twenty-seven."

Jesus. It was my family history but read like a bad novel.

"What happened?"

"She had to admit the affair because eventually she couldn't hide her pregnancy. Being so religious, her family called her every name in the book, as you can imagine. Wicked, whore. They treated her like a pariah."

"You're fucking kidding me."

"I wish I was. Her family was old-order Amish. The strictest and most closed off of the sect."

What little I knew of them came from books or movies. I already knew the ending of her story, but I wanted all the facts.

"Go on, please."

"They hid her on the farm until the baby was born. Her family was very influential in the church and found her a husband. A thirty-five-year-old widower with four kids."

The horror story continued to get worse. Pity for Dahlia—Rachel—wasn't something I'd expected, and I struggled against it.

"So she ran away. With me."

"Yeah."

"And you're sure of this story? How did you get all this detailed information when no one else could?"

He sipped his coffee. "Yeah, I'm sure. My wife was born into the sect but left after her Rumspringa—the time when

Amish teens are allowed out in the English community to mingle and try new things. She's from Ohio, but they have family in Pennsylvania." He laughed. "Everyone is related somehow. Anyway, Sarah—my wife—decided she didn't want to live the Amish life and left. Moved to DC, got a job as a waitress, and we met."

"I didn't ask for the story of your life, just how you got the information."

His lips pressed tight. "Right. Well, Sarah's cousin, Johanna, is married to one of Rachel's brothers. I guess he would be your uncle. Johanna and Rachel were close friends, and Rachel confided the whole story to Johanna."

A thought popped into my head. "So she was married to the older man before she left?" Was Dahlia a bigamist? Jesus, this was getting weirder and weirder.

Tanner shook his head. "No, the man wanted to wait until after the baby was born to make sure it was healthy. Supposedly, he thought God might punish her for her wanton ways by harming the baby, and in that case, he didn't want to be responsible for taking care of it."

Imagining what my life would've been like, living on an Amish farm, my sexuality denied, I suppressed a shudder. "Sounds like a charming person. Guess I got off lucky, then."

"Of course, none of this information is legally verifiable. But I do have a written statement from Johanna if that helps."

"I would like that, yes."

He pulled a sheet of paper out of his leather portfolio and handed it to me. That was it. My history, reduced to a single sheet of paper.

"Thank you." Without looking at it, I folded it in half and slipped it into the jacket pocket of my suit.

"One more thing you should know. Peter confessed that he and Rachel had sex, and he was arrested. Spent four years in jail for statutory rape."

I froze. "D-do you know where he is?"

"I do. If you want his address, let me know. He's still in the same small town, married with five children."

About to say yes, I held off. What the hell would that accomplish? Half brothers and sisters I had nothing in common with, plus I doubted my presence would be welcomed after forty years. Most importantly, what twenty-seven-year-old man sleeps with a fifteen-year-old girl? My already sour stomach turned over.

"No. I'll pass." I glanced at my untouched tea. "Anything else?" I motioned to the server. "Check, please."

The server tossed the paper onto the table. "Pay me."

I took out a twenty. "Keep the change." It was the least I could do, considering the crappy working conditions and lousy hours she had to work.

Her eyes widened. "Thanks."

Tanner and I got to our feet and shook hands. "If you need any other information, I'm always available."

For the money I paid him, both for the information and his silence, I bet he was. I gave a curt nod and watched him walk out. Always cautious about who was watching, I waited several minutes, then left the diner. The night air wasn't as cool as it had been upstate, but for some reason, I couldn't stop shivering. I reached into my pocket to get my phone to call a car.

"Cold, *mon ami*?"

Stunned, I spun to face a smirking Denis Bouvier. He raised a brow at my silence.

"*Oui. C'est moi.* In the flesh."

"Were you...did you *follow* me?" I gritted out. "What the hell are you doing here?"

"Funny enough, the world does not revolve around you. I happen to live not far."

"Really?" I snorted. "You live near here."

"Close enough."

"And you just happened to be walking on this block. Where I am."

That infuriating grin grew wider. "You know what they say. New York is just a small town."

"No," I snapped. "I've never heard that. And I don't believe anything you say."

He loomed over me, his handsome face dark. "Are you calling me a liar?"

"I'm not calling you anything at all. I'm going home." I took out my phone to get a car. To my horror, he plucked it from my fingers.

"No. I think you're going to come with me."

"Give me my phone." I tried to grab the phone, but he held it out of reach.

"You'll get it when you come to my apartment and see I'm not lying."

"Fine, I believe you. Please. Just leave me alone already." At this point I'd say anything to get rid of him. I was too emotional and worn out from the earlier news to fight.

The teasing light vanished from his eyes, and he peered closely into my face. "Something's wrong. What is it?"

The chance of me telling Denis Bouvier what I'd discussed was about as likely as me fucking him on a public street. "Nothing. I'm tired. It's been a hell of a day. I need to go home and be alone."

"You're lying. Something happened between you and that man who left right before you."

I had little strength left to fight, much less speak. "Please stop," I murmured.

"Come with me. You can't go home like this by yourself. You're ready to fall apart."

I allowed him to take my arm, and we walked to a giant building overlooking the river. We entered the sleek, modern lobby.

"Hello, Denis."

"Frank, how goes it?"

I averted my face, turning it into Denis's biceps, hoping the concierge didn't recognize me.

"Very well, thank you," Frank replied. "Have a good night."

"You too."

Still hiding my face, now almost in Denis's armpit, I was led into an elevator and whooshed up twenty-five floors. He unlocked the door, and we walked inside. I caught a glimpse of huge windows overlooking the harbor and the Statute of Liberty. Denis led me to a chair at his gigantic island.

"I'll make coffee."

"I don't drink coffee."

He chuckled. "You can't be serious."

"Do I look like I have a sense of humor?" I left the chair and headed to the windows. My forehead pressed against the cool glass. It was all too much—the drinking today, this sad discovery, and now I was trapped with an infuriating, exasperating and—God help me—desirable man who wouldn't leave me alone. I wished I could sail away into the pitch black and disappear.

Denis stood beside me. "Not in the least. But you do look upset. And sick to your stomach. Drink this."

Without even bothering to look, I shook my head. "I said I don't drink coffee."

"I heard you. This is tea. Green tea. My nutritionist recommends it. Go on. It's burning my hand."

I took the mug, and he wasn't lying. It was green tea. Blowing on it first, I took a tentative sip. "It's good. Thanks."

"Were you afraid I'd poison you? Really, *mon cher*, that would be the height of inappropriateness."

"I suppose you think you're funny. Charming, even."

"The thought has crossed my mind. Many times, in fact."

His dark eyes sparkled. Did they always glitter like onyx, or was it the overhead lighting? It wouldn't surprise me if he had special bulbs created to accentuate his good looks. But I'd sooner cut my tongue out than ever admit to those thoughts. At the moment, the one and only thing I had to do was find a way to leave.

"Look, Denis. Thank you for the tea, but I have to get home. It's very late, and I'm exhausted. I have work to prepare for Monday. I'm not on a six-month vacation like you, free to hang out and do nothing but play around while I wait for the games to start again."

A switch in his eyes flipped, and his lips curled in a sneer. "Perhaps you should learn to count. It's now mid-June, and the preseason begins in September. As for doing nothing..." His hair hung in his face, giving him an almost ferocious appearance. For whatever reason, it turned me the fuck on, and my biggest fear was that he could hear my heart thundering. "I train every day." He ran a hand over his chest down to those rock-hard abs. "Perfection like this is only achieved through hard, physical work. Many days I exercise in the park. It's hot. Sweaty. You should come watch."

I was caught in the deep recesses of his unreadable gaze. "I-I have my own routine in the summer."

"Do you?" His teeth flashed white. "What is it?"

"I run and bike. Practice yoga."

"How flexible of you." His lips twitched, and he was unable to contain a chuckle. "I'd like to see it in action."

Dammit, my face burned. Why was it that only with this boorish idiot did I lose my cool? "I'm leaving. Good-bye." I strode away from him, returning to the kitchen, where I set the mug on the island.

I pulled open the door, but he called out to me. "I also do a lot of charity work. I wouldn't want you to think I'm just another pretty face."

I let the door slam behind me. I needed to get away.

I wanted him to come after me.

God, what the hell was wrong with me? I didn't lust after men. I barely thought about sex. My work had kept me satisfied all these years. It was what drove me every day. That and the search for information about my mother's past and anything concerning my father, hoping maybe there would be a possible connection we might grow. Now that I knew the history of my birth, I wiped all further thoughts of looking for him from my mind.

The car dropped me off, and I was finally home. I dumped my clothes on the chair to be picked up for dry cleaning, showered, and got ready for bed. I was safe here. Safe from being lied to, safe from being hurt. Spending the day surrounded by people, making conversation, being *on* all the time when I only wanted to turn off, was fucking exhausting. I had enough of that every day at work and on camera.

I was and always would be better off alone.

CHAPTER SEVEN
Denis

It was September, and I was so fucking bored. Preseason started in a few days, and I couldn't wait.

There were only so many hours in the day I could exercise, and I saw my therapist, but I remained restless. I visited Gil, but he had his own routine, and I couldn't simply hang around there all day. I had read all the books I'd wanted to and had satisfied all my promotional contracts for the month.

Television held no interest for me, and I only watched the news to see Sterling. Those big blue eyes shone from the screen. He had leading-man good looks and a soothing voice that gave off trust-me vibes. Adrian appeared as a political reporter, and I could instantly see the difference between them, though Adrian was pretty good too at asking hard questions. His sweet smile could be deceptively charming. Channel 8 might not be the top-rated news station, but they certainly had the best-looking reporters.

It was five a.m., and for the past twenty minutes I'd tossed and turned. The sun hadn't even risen, yet I knew what my day would be like: breakfast, exercise, checking with my agent about any trade rumors, then going through social media to see what was being said about me. I'd spent yesterday at a children's hospital ward, followed by a hockey summer camp at Chelsea Piers, and had a blast. I did love the kids–they were so pure and sweet. I wanted to protect them from everything ugly that waited for them out in the world. Yeah, I had a soft spot for children.

I was restless as hell, and when that happened, I did stupid things. Before I knew what I was doing, I'd gathered up my things and called for a car. Next stop, Central Park.

It was barely six, and the sun had finished rising like a glowing copper penny up from the East River to chase away the faint lavender haze of dawn. I sipped from my ice-cold water bottle, drops of condensation wetting my hand. My skin felt clammy from humidity, and I rubbed my neck, longing for fall and winter. Snow and ice. The rush of skaters barreling at me, trying to defeat me. The fans cheering. I needed hockey. It fed my empty soul.

The car dropped me off at an entrance on Central Park West. Now...if I were an obnoxious, introverted asshole, where would I go to exercise? I slid my shades over my eyes and began to walk, scanning faces as I passed. Finding a path, I began a light jog toward the Reservoir. It was relatively early still, but already people who had been away from the city all summer had come trickling home. Sweat slicked my neck, and I twisted my hair up in a bun. Every year I contemplated cutting it but never did. I liked it a little long. And guys did too. I enjoyed a little pleasure-pain when they tugged on it as we rolled around on the bed. Although now that I thought about it, I hadn't had sex in months. No wonder I was cranky.

I rounded the curve and saw him. He was stretching on the side, hadn't yet begun to run. Taut thigh muscles and a firm ass pulled tight under thin jogging shorts. The cut of his biceps gleamed with a light coating of sweat.

Mmm...

I ran up behind him. "*Bonjour. Comment ça va?*"

As I'd anticipated, Sterling jumped and gave me his outraged face. "Wh-what're you doing here?" he sputtered.

"Exercising. I need to keep up my cardio activities. Preseason begins in a few days." I jogged in place and read mistrust in those narrowed blue eyes.

"Why are you in Manhattan and in Central Park? You live in Brooklyn."

"Really, Sterling, how long have you lived here? Don't you know real New Yorkers call it the city? You're a news anchor. You need to at least act like you're of the people in the city you're reporting about."

"God, you're an ass."

My grin broadened, and I glanced behind me. "It is one of my better features. After my eyes." I batted my lashes.

"I have to go." And he took off.

I caught up to him easily, and we jogged in silence for five minutes before he spoke.

"Why are you here? You never answered me."

"I told you. I'm exercising. I got bored with my usual runs, so I decided to come here." I winked at him, knowing I'd get a reaction. "The scenery is prettier."

His neck turned red. Good to know he wasn't immune to my teasing.

"Not from my perspective. There's all this hot air around me."

Ahhh, nice to see he could give as well as take. I liked it.

"Was that an attempt at a joke?"

"I saw you smile," he responded with a slight upward tilt of his lips.

"Didn't you miss me? It's been a few months."

"Were you gone? I hadn't noticed."

We pounded the pavement, and he easily kept up with me.

"You wound me, *mon ami*. Here I thought we were friends."

"You're ridiculous. We barely know each other." That scowl I'd come to expect thinned his lips. Why did I enjoy pushing his buttons so much? I had my pick of men—all I had to do was go out to a club, and I was bombarded with hands, mouths, and tongues. No shortage of guys wanting to fuck a champion.

Instead, I focused on this hard-ass, somewhat rude, straitlaced man who sent out mixed signals. He might be the same in bed—stiff and unyielding. Afraid to let go. But I'd lay bets that if he was freed, he'd be a wild man. The most uptight men usually were after shedding their skin. I wanted to be the one to unlock his chains.

"Hey, you're Denis Bouvier from the Blades. Can't wait for the season to start." Fist-pumping, a couple of men ran past us.

"Me too. Make sure you come by to support us." I eyed Sterling. "Don't forget."

He rolled his eyes and jogged away. We did the loop, then began another circuit. By this time, the sun had decided to fully grace us with its presence, and both our shirts and shorts were soaked through with sweat, but I wouldn't stop before Sterling. He darted a look over at me as we continued to run, his jaw hard, face tight. I knew he wouldn't give up, and I wanted to see how long he could last.

At the last check of my watch, we'd been running for an hour and ten minutes. I had to admire his stamina.

Though our training conditioned us for endurance, I wasn't sure many of my teammates could keep this level of activity up, especially in the heat.

Panting heavily, he finally slowed, and I shortened my stride, coming to a stop the same time he did. He walked off the path and put his head between his legs, bracing his hands on his thighs, giving me a perfect view of his beautiful ass. I might have been winded, but I wasn't dead. Even smelly and dripping with sweat, he was fucking gorgeous. Of course, I'd never tell him that.

He glanced over his shoulder and caught me looking. I grinned and received a world-class glare in return.

"How are you not breathing hard?"

"Training. Lots and lots of training. I've told you, this kind of perfection takes hard work to maintain." I smirked, and he rolled his eyes and shook his head.

"Do you ever stop?"

"Stop what?" I checked my watch. "Should we get breakfast? All this running made me hungry."

Sterling pushed a sweaty hank of hair out of his face. "I have breakfast at home before I go to the office. I can't go to a restaurant like this. I need to shower." With those words, he walked away toward the park exit, and I followed. When we were walking up Central Park West, he stopped. "Why are you following me?"

"I'm not. You asked me to come to breakfast at your apartment."

His dark brows flew up. "I did not."

"You did. I said we should get something to eat, and you distinctly told me, 'I have breakfast at home.'"

"For me, you idiot. Not you."

I pouted. "That's not very nice." I nudged his shoulder. "It's only breakfast. Come on. A bagel. A little schmear."

His lips twitched, reluctantly, it seemed. "Schmear? Where'd you pick that up?"

I snickered. "My agent. He's teaching me all kinds of fun words."

"I don't have bagels. They're pure carbohydrates and not healthy for you."

At least he hadn't said no outright. "So what do you eat in the morning?"

"Homemade granola, plain yogurt, chia seeds, wheat germ, and cold-pressed juice."

I repressed a shudder of disgust. "Sounds...good to me. I'm in."

Sterling continued to walk with me on his heels. "You're not going to leave me alone, are you?" I fluttered my eyelashes, and he huffed with annoyance. "God, you're a pain in the ass." My smile broadened. "Fine. Come in. Whatever."

We stopped in front of one of those imposing buildings on the park always featured on television. A doorman opened the entrance, and the concierge greeted Sterling.

"Mr. Forest, hot day out there."

"It is, Leon."

"*Bonjour*," I said, and Leon's eyes grew wide. "Wait. Whoa. You're...Denis Bouvier. The hockey player."

"*C'est moi*," I responded with a flourish, noticing Sterling's wince.

"Looking forward to the season starting."

"As am I." Sterling had left me and waited by the elevators. "I'd best be leaving." We went up, and it wasn't until we entered the apartment that he spoke to me.

"Don't you ever get tired of people recognizing you and talking about hockey all the time?"

Astonished, I cocked my head. "Why would I? It's my job, and I'm a sports figure in New York City. The biggest media market in the world. Of course people will recognize me. I don't mind. In fact, if they didn't, I'd be worried." I plucked the sticky shirt from my chest. "Do you mind if I take that shower? I don't want to sit on your furniture smelling like this."

For the first time that morning, a genuine smile lit his face, and I let its warmth soak into me. It had been a long time since I'd seen it, and I'd almost forgotten how it transformed him from good-looking to stunning.

"That would be a disaster. But I'm not sure I have any clothing big enough for you."

"Don't you have a washer and dryer? Just throw them in while we eat breakfast."

"Fine. I'll get you a towel."

"Make sure it's big enough." I winked. "I usually use the extra-large size."

"Obviously. You need it for your swollen ego." He opened a door in the hallway, took out a large white towel, and tossed it to me.

"Thanks." I pulled the shirt over my head and bent to peel the socks off my feet. Sterling retreated to the kitchen, giving me his back while I stepped out of my shorts.

"You know, you could go to the bathroom to undress instead of giving my neighbors a free show."

"You have peeping Toms in this fancy building? Besides, I'm used to it. In the locker room we're naked all the time." I wrapped the towel around my waist. "It's safe to look now." He turned, and I picked up my clothes from the floor. With a snicker, I let the towel slip a little, flashing my naked butt.

"Denis," he growled.

"What? I can't help it. My hands are full. The towel can only hide so much."

"Bathroom is that way. Give me your things, and I'll put them in the wash."

He took them from me, keeping them at arm's length.

"How many bedrooms?"

"Two, and two bathrooms. Now if you'll excuse me, I need to shower as well."

He shut the door to his bedroom in my face, and I went to get cleaned up. When I came out, I heard the water running, so I decided to do a little snooping and entered his bedroom. As expected, his bedroom was as organized and sterile as a hospital room and just as inviting. White sheets, plain gray comforter. No pictures on the nightstands or on the walls. Just a large television.

A file sat on top of his bureau, and I knew I should have walked away and not looked, but I never did the things I should.

Dahlia Dumont.

My brow furrowed. Why was Sterling investigating the movie star Dahlia Dumont?

The water stopped. I should've left and waited for him in the living room, but I didn't move.

Completely naked, he stepped into the bedroom and froze. "What the hell are you doing in my bedroom?" he spat at me and ran back into the bathroom, grabbed a towel, and covered himself. "You have no right to be in here."

"Maybe I wanted to see where the magic happens."

"Go away."

"I'm hungry. You promised me breakfast, and you know that's the most important meal of the day." As I spoke, I moved across the room to stand in front of him. Blue eyes wide, chest heaving, cheeks burning red. "Although there are other things I like in my mouth first thing in the morning." He blinked but didn't move. My fingers slid across the edge of the towel, dipping beneath, reaching to touch him. "Should I show you?" His breath caught, and I gave a tug—and found myself shoved so hard, I tripped backward on the bed.

"I said go away. Get out of my bedroom."

Unwilling to be at a disadvantage, I scrambled to my feet and met him nose-to-nose. "You're a tease. You can't make up your mind whether you want to kiss me or punch me."

Heat blazed from his eyes, but I had no idea if it was anger or lust. "Trust me, I have no desire to kiss you."

"You invited me here."

A harsh bark of laughter escaped him. "*Invited* is a warped way of looking at it. You bullied your way into having breakfast with me, and now you're stalking me in my bedroom. Are you that hard up for sex? They have people you can pay to take care of your problem. I'm sure you know all about that."

"Sex isn't a problem. And for your information, I've never had to pay for sex. Usually it's the opposite for me. So many men, so little time."

"Pardon me while I get ill." He tightened his grip on the towel. "Do you mind leaving so I can get dressed? I found some clothes that should fit you." He grabbed them from the chair in the corner and tossed them to me. "Here. You can use the bathroom to change."

"No need for that." I deliberately let my towel drop and put the shirt on first, giving him an eyeful of my naked body, including my dick, which had grown hard during our argument. I always did like a little push and pull. It got my juices flowing.

But when I yanked the shirt down over my head, I found myself alone.

"Spoilsport. Just when it was getting fun."

I finished dressing and gave one last glance to that file on the bureau. What connection did Sterling Forest the news anchor have with Dahlia Dumont, one of the most famous movie actresses in Hollywood? And how the hell did a local news anchor afford an apartment in one of the most expensive neighborhoods in the world?

CHAPTER EIGHT
Sterling

I never should've let him come upstairs with me. I'd prepared for an argument when Denis came out of the bedroom, but he strode across the room to me, saying, "My apologies. I'm very sorry I upset you. I never meant to invade your privacy. It won't happen again."

"You're correct. Because this is the first, last, and only time you'll be in my apartment. You wanted breakfast? Here. Sit and eat, and then you can be on your way."

As usual, the damned man surprised me. "I think I've taken up enough of your time. I'll be on my way." He took his phone, wallet, and keys, and without further ado, walked out, slamming the door behind him.

"Son of a bitch," I muttered, now alone. After taking out all that extra food. Not to mention preparing a whole argument, ready to go at it.

I ate my breakfast, drank my juice, and steeped my tea. To clear my mind, I sat on a yoga mat facing the windows overlooking the park and tried to think pleasant thoughts. An endless blue sky, tranquil waters, birds chirping in the park. My feet hitting the ground while I ran.

The face of Denis Bouvier ruined my calm. Glittering black eyes, a wicked grin, and utter perfection of physical form had my heart topsy-turvy.

"No," I whispered in the stillness of my living room. "No. I refuse to let that pompous, overbearing sports junkie invade my personal space." Having lived with someone whose sense of self-worth was measured by ratings and reviews, I had no desire to waste my time with someone whose good looks were only exceeded by his ego and the need to be stroked every day.

Wait, no, I didn't mean that.

Drawing all the strength I'd mastered in my forty years, I closed my eyes and took a deep breath. And another. Soon I'd dismissed the unpleasant morning encounter and found my rhythm.

Twenty minutes later, I opened my eyes and got to my feet, ready to face the office. After my morning run, I opted for a car, and I walked into the newsroom energized and loving the *hum* of activity. This was my domain.

"Sterling, how's it going?" Rob DeVine, our news director, stopped to chat. He was a bit arrogant but shrewd as hell, and we had a good relationship. He and I would talk about the important stories of the day, and he allowed me to set the schedule of reporting and who to send out to get each story.

"Considering I just walked in the door, it's great," I joked, and he fell into step with me. "You look like you have something to say."

"I do want to talk."

"Why don't we go to my office?" I suggested, and we walked inside and closed the door.

We sat—me at my desk and Rob at the small conference table. I made a cup of tea for myself. Rob shook his head when I offered him one.

"What's up, Rob?"

"The summer was pretty slow in the city, as usual. Most people were out in the Hamptons or upstate, and if they don't have kids going back to school, they're still making their way home."

I made a face at the mention of the Hamptons. "Not my scene. Coming from Beverly Hills, I have no desire to hang out with the rich and beautiful people." I cracked a smile. "I prefer you guys here."

"Funny, Sterling. But there have been changes these past few years—you came on board, Adrian too, and we have Tag Gold, the new sports reporter."

"Bryan leaving surprised me." Not that I was unhappy about it. I'd always found him to be an obnoxious prick.

Rob made a noise in his throat. "He had an overinflated sense of self-worth. Guy was a good second-stringer, but he's no Louie. You've either got charisma, or you don't."

"And he didn't?"

Rob examined his fingernails. "Nah. You, Adrian, Tag, and Allie Brenner on the Queens beat...all of you have that 'it' quality—in different ways of course, but you get what I mean, don't you?"

"Yeah, sure, I guess." I lifted a shoulder. I didn't really, but personality deep dives weren't my thing. "Where is this leading? I know you didn't come visit to tell me the news has a low rating. I see the numbers. We've climbed into the number one spot finally."

"See? You're a cut-to-the-chase guy. I appreciate that. The powers that be came up with the idea to run small pieces on our reporters. The focus groups we met with over the summer have shown us that viewers love learning more about the people they tune in to see every night. Where they grew up, favorite foods, their pets, what they do in their spare time to wind down...you know, the warm and fuzzies."

My stomach went into free fall, and I forced a half smile. "That sounds like a terrible idea. Who wants to know about us? We're boring."

"Speak for yourself, Sterling. I've mentioned it to some of the staff, and they love the idea. As does Ed Riley."

My worst nightmare. If the station head wanted it, it was considered a done deal. "Well, who am I to be the lone naysayer?"

"Good. I was hoping not to have to twist your arm. You'll be first."

I blinked. "What? Why me?"

"Because you're the anchor. The face of the news and the main reason viewers tune in. Our focus group also showed that most people want to know about you. And in case you were wondering, it's split pretty evenly—fifty-two percent women and forty-eight percent men made you their first choice as the Channel 8 personality they'd most like to meet." Rob's smile was cunning. "We need to capitalize on both sides of the aisle. You keep your personal life extremely close to the vest. That makes you mysterious. And a man of mystery is a man whose layers people want to peel away to get to the core of who you are."

"What am I, an onion?"

Rob chuckled. "Was that a joke? I didn't know you had a sense of humor."

Maybe the hockey guy was rubbing off on me more than I thought. "I do if I want to."

"So think about what you want to say. Production will be in touch."

This wasn't going to work. I couldn't talk about my past—I never had. I'd left it all vague and had paid very, *very* good money to have all mentions of Dahlia and Marisel wiped from my background. With enough money, you could get anything accomplished.

"Are you sure about this? I'm not very exciting, you know. I don't have any hobbies or visit exotic places or even have a cute pet."

Rob shrugged. "I wouldn't worry. I'm sure there's something they can find to make you interesting." He cackled. "I'll see you at eleven for the morning news roundup."

After he left, I did a deep dive on myself to make sure my online history remained as sanitized as possible. About once a month I did a search on Dahlia. She hadn't done a movie in years—when she'd hit forty, she'd formed her own beauty company, and as of last year, she was one of the world's richest women, with a net worth hovering near one billion dollars. She'd started various foundations concentrating on women's issues—rape, domestic violence—which, considering what had happened to her, made sense. It softened me toward her, knowing she hadn't forgotten where she came from and was using her extreme wealth to help people. She'd never had any children with her three ex-husbands, and I remembered reading in gossip magazines about her decision to remain childless.

I wondered if she ever thought of me or regretted how she'd cut me out of her life to keep her traumatic past a secret. From the day I'd moved out for college, I'd neither seen nor spoken to her. Twenty-two years of silence. A punishment for a wrong I'd had no part in except being born.

Marisel too had walked out of my life and disappeared. Taken the millions of her payout and most likely was living in luxury somewhere. I couldn't blame her. I was a nobody in her life, a burden she'd never asked for but had benefited from.

I was the only stupid one who couldn't forget anything.

Nothing was getting accomplished by this morbid walk down memory lane, so I dove into my work. There were notes to prepare and clips to review. I ate a salad at my desk while watching the daily White House press briefing. For a few minutes, I closed my eyes and indulged in a what-if fantasy.

What if I'd let Denis tug my towel all the way off?

What if I'd taken off my clothes when he stood naked and sweaty in my living room and touched him. Gotten to my knees and—

Someone knocked on my door, and I rubbed my eyes. "Come in."

Adrian popped his head in. "Hi. I have that information about the city-council vote tomorrow. Do you want to discuss it?"

I blinked. "Oh, uh, yes. Please. Come in."

"Great. Apparently there's a bipartisan coalition that opposes the mayor, and it could get ugly." Adrian talked, and I listened and made comments where appropriate. He closed his notebook, and I waited.

"Something else? It sounds like you have it all covered and it could prove to be a rowdy meeting, which makes for a juicy news story."

"Uh, well, preseason starts this weekend, and I was wondering if you'd like to come watch the opening game. It's Saturday night."

"Why? I'm not a hockey fan."

"Yeah, I know, but I thought, well, it might be nice. You don't really know that much about it, and I thought maybe you'd like to see them play live. Neil can't come, and I hate to sit by myself."

"I don't think so, but thanks. It's not my thing."

"Oh, sure. Sorry to bother you." Adrian ducked his head, gathered his notebook, and hustled out of my office.

Had I been too harsh? "Dammit," I swore and left my seat to follow him to his cubicle. "Adrian."

He faced me with a bright smile. "Yes? Did we forget to talk about something?"

"No. I just want to apologize for being so abrupt. It wasn't very nice of me. But I'm sure you could find someone who actually likes hockey to go with you."

"It's fine. Don't worry about it. I just thought you might like to see it's not all brawn and no skill."

I wasn't about to argue with him. After all, he was married to a hockey player.

"Well"–I gave him a quick smile–"I've got stories to check."

"Denis mentioned to Rip he saw you in the park this morning?"

The confusion in Adrian's eyes matched my own.

Shit. Of course he would. My gut tightened, recalling him naked in my living room and how he'd touched me in my bedroom.

I rubbed my eyes. "It was odd running into him, but I guess it's one of those New York coincidences. The city isn't as large or anonymous as we think. Funny, right?" I attempted a grin.

"Yeah, I thought so too, especially since I know you're not friends. Anyway, I understand you're not a hockey fan. I'd better get my notes prepared for tonight's broadcast and get the clips from production."

I had no clue why I didn't simply agree with him and walk away. That would've been the smart thing to do. I couldn't fake interest in watching a bunch of grown men with big sticks, skating around an ice rink, fighting over a puck. From the little I'd seen, it could be a brutal, dangerous sport. I preferred my book and comfortable chair, with calming music in the background. My own company was all I needed. No one else could be trusted. And yet, I heard myself saying, "On second thought, I'll be happy to join you at the game." There was something so disarming and so damn sweet about Adrian that I couldn't say no to him. It would have been like kicking a puppy.

Varying emotions played across Adrian's face—shock, followed by excitement, and finally happiness. "Really? Are you sure? I don't want you to feel pressured or think you're going to upset me if you don't come. I sit alone at the games a lot. I mean, sometimes Seb's wife comes—or Neil, but I think it'll be fun."

The conversation was getting to be a bit much. "Sure. Thanks."

"I'll leave the ticket for you at the box office special event window."

"All right, then. I'll see you in the newsroom later."

I retreated to my office, closed the door, and with a great sigh, leaned against it.

"What the hell am I doing?" I shook my head in disbelief. "I'm making way too much of this. I'll go to the stupid game, and that'll be it. I'll have to make sure Denis doesn't see me. He'll think I'm there for him."

Yet suddenly I wished it wasn't Monday. Saturday night felt as though it were a very long way away.

CHAPTER NINE
Denis

Damn, it felt good to be on the ice again. I sometimes felt I was steadier on my feet there, with the cold air blasting and ferocious players rushing me at the net, than walking down the street. Even sex didn't match the high of fending off an opponent's shots on goal.

Maybe that meant I wasn't having sex with the right person. I'd seen the other men on the team with significant others, and they couldn't wait to get home to them after a game. Even when I'd lived with Rip or dated other men, I'd always been the one to suggest hitting up a club or having dinner. Anything to stave off the black cloud of loneliness that never faded, no matter who I was with. Looking at all the joy and happiness at Rip and Adrian's wedding, I'd realized my heart had never been privy to those levels of emotions. I had no idea what it meant to love someone with your whole self.

In the locker room, we all greeted each other as if it had been years since the last time we were together instead of at practice the day before. But knowing this was a new season electrified the air. We were in business. Seb had kept his beard, which made his normally badass expression even more fierce. With a smile, Rip strolled in, fit and serene. Marriage sure as hell agreed with him. I recalled something he'd said to me:

"Love is about finding that one person you don't need to compete with because they're your other half. They make you whole."

When he and I had been lovers, together or apart, we were the same. We'd never been each other's half of a whole, which was why we didn't work.

"Another season, another Cup, *mes amies*," I called out, and everyone roared with approval.

"You know it." Chitty bounced around fist-pumping. Ellis nodded to me, and I wondered if he was hoping to get more chances to play. I could be generous in the early days and give him extra ice time, but the net was still my domain, and I'd be damned if I'd let him take me away from what I loved.

It took me almost half an hour to get into my gear. I refused to rush, and taking my time with each pad and piece of protection gave me the opportunity to visualize how I would keep the puck from passing me. Finished with my prep, I put my helmet on, walked through the tunnel, and got on the ice. Some of the team was already there, and Coach waited until we were all present to speak.

"This might only be preseason, but it's our time to gauge what we'll need to concentrate on before the regular season starts. Any weaknesses that might've cropped up, or where we're out of shape from the off-season. Plus, we have to keep an eye on the other teams to see how we can exploit their deficiencies. Remember, we've now won the Cup twice in a row. Every team in the league will be gunning for us."

"Coach said it best." Rip stood in the center of our circle, something he always did prior to a skate. We were a family of sorts, and while I'd never admit it to anyone, these guys were the most important people in my life. They were all I had. "We're the team to beat. They know we're number one. So we need to stand together. Skate as a unit with the sole goal to protect our net and score on theirs. We are the champions, remember."

"Our *capitaine* is correct. And we are ready, *n'est-ce pas?*" I raised my stick in the air. "To a new season! *Allons-y!*"

I had three teammates stand in front, shooting pucks at me from all directions, and then I took shots on goal as they raced toward the net. I deflected all except one—outstanding for anyone else, but it pissed me off to have allowed even that. I prided myself on perfection and refused to accept anything less.

I came out in the crease to fend off more shots and Rip skated up to me, a grin on his face I could see despite his mouthguard. He spit it out.

"You can thank me later."

"What're you talking about?"

He tipped his head to the side of the bench. "I think you made a fan."

I skated to where he'd indicated, and in the lower bowl of the section, saw Adrian and...well, well, well. Who did we have here? Sterling Forest looking uncomfortable and out of place. Everyone was wearing a Blades jersey or T-shirt, aside from a random Icers fan. Everyone except for Sterling, who wore a button-down tucked into khakis. He was staring at me, but as soon as he saw I'd noticed him, he jerked his gaze away.

"He looks like he's going to the country club to play golf."

"Bouvier, back at it," Coach shouted. "You and Ellis take turns."

Without giving Sterling another look, I skated to the net, and we ran plays our offensive coaches gave us. We had a ten-minute break before intros, and while some players headed to the sidelines to talk to friends, family, and fans, I hustled to the locker room, grabbed an extra jersey from my locker, and returned to the ice. I skated up to the boards where Adrian was talking to Rip.

"Can you give this to your friend? He looks like he wants to sell a used car or something. Tell him to put this on."

Rip cackled while Adrian grabbed the jersey that I tossed over the protective plexiglass. "That's so nice of you. I don't think Sterling's ever been to a sports game. He asked me why everyone was dressed the same."

Of course he hadn't. That would be fun, and the man didn't believe in enjoying himself.

The game was frustrating, with the Icers constantly on me, but I forced some errors on them and managed to only allow one goal. We were a little slow on offense—to be expected after a break—and the game ended in a tie. Rip scored our only goal.

Coach wasn't happy and let us hear his displeasure. "Sloppy, lazy play. Unforced errors, missed opportunities. For fuck's sake, you looked like a team of rookies or a minor-league team. Not the two-time Stanley Cup champions. I'd better see more of an effort on Monday night when we play the Drifts."

I winced and saw that Coach's words hit everyone else just as hard. There was no joking around or laughter as we hit the bikes, then showered and dressed.

Rip and Seb had their heads together, but instead of excluding me as they usually did, Rip waved me over.

"Denis, c'mere."

I wondered what he had in mind and if it involved Sterling. "Yes? What's up?"

"Adrian and I are going to dinner, and we were wondering if you wanted to join us."

I quirked a brow. "And be a third wheel? I've done enough of that, *mon ami*. But thanks for the invitation."

"What if there was a fourth? Adrian said Sterling is coming as well."

"Is he? Well, in that case, I wouldn't want him to be the extra man and feel uncomfortable."

"You're a trouper," Rip drawled and shut his locker. "I said we'd meet them outside."

I grabbed my suit jacket, slipped my arms through it, and smoothed any wrinkles in my shirt. I could admit to being a bit of a fashionista and had even done some modeling in the off-seasons. I checked the mirror to make sure my hair was sleek. Rip, Seb, and I walked out, and after signing autographs and taking pictures with fans, found Adrian and Sterling waiting for us. Adrian's face lit up, and he and Rip kissed as though they'd been parted for days, not a few hours.

Sterling stood by awkwardly, and I had to fill the silence. "Young love, what can I say?" At his stoic expression, I tried again. "Did you enjoy the game?"

"I did. Thanks for having me."

I grinned. "I didn't invite you. It was a shock to me."

Pink bloomed in his cheeks. Was he pink everywhere? I hadn't forgotten touching him, my fingers teasing under his towel for even that brief moment. The skin of his belly was smooth, and I wanted more.

"You know what I mean. Oh, here." He handed me the jersey, and I frowned. "I didn't wear it."

"Why are you returning it?"

His expression ranged from confused to uncomfortable. "I don't—it's not like I wear these sorts of things. It'll just sit in my drawer."

Damn. Could the man be any more uptight? Plus, it was kind of rude. "Keep it anyway," I brushed him off. "I have a million of them. I give them away all the time." Untrue, but he didn't have to know that.

"All right. Thanks."

Arms around each other, Rip and Adrian had finished their lovefest, and Rip asked, "What do you all feel like eating?"

"I'm up for anything. And thank you for inviting me." It was gracious of Adrian and Rip to include me. None of my other exes even kept in touch with me. I'd like to think Rip and I would have been friends even if we weren't playing for the same team.

"Of course." Adrian's smile was bright. "How about Junior's? It's right over here, and they've got something for everyone. I know Sterling likes to eat pretty healthy, and I think they have salads and stuff you might like."

"Thanks," Sterling said. "I'm fine with wherever."

"No cheesecake for you?" I enjoyed poking at him. "Everyone needs a little indulgence once in a while."

"I try not to eat sugar. It's not good for you. I'm surprised you'd eat empty calories like that with your training schedule."

"There's all kinds of cake," I responded with a wink and his face flushed.

"Okay, let's go. Junior's it is." Rip took Adrian's hand, and Sterling and I followed.

We were seated at a table in the back of the restaurant, away from the crowd. That didn't stop people from taking our picture or asking for autographs while we walked through.

"It doesn't bother you, all the people asking for your time when you're just trying to eat a meal?" Sterling frowned.

I'd noticed several people had recognized him, whispering behind their hands and surreptitiously taking pictures, and wondered if he minded being linked with us.

Studying the menu, Rip shook his head. "Nah. It's part of the deal. Sort of what you sign up for when you choose to become a sports figure. But fans are cool here. They mostly give us our space."

This would be the perfect time to ask him about Dahlia Dumont, but I had to choose my words wisely. "You come from Beverly Hills, so you must've seen movie stars all the time?" I asked him.

"Yes, of course. But like here, we don't interfere with them."

"What was it like? Being surrounded by them?" I took a roll and buttered it. "I couldn't imagine sitting next to someone like, say...Dahlia Dumont. She's one of the greats. I must've seen that movie she won an Oscar for—*The Long Road*—at least five times." I watched Sterling carefully for his response.

Aside from a subtle tightening of his jaw and his eyes widening a bit, he remained calm. "I guess you get used to it, so it doesn't seem like they're any different than anyone else."

"*Mmm.*" I chewed and swallowed.

Our server came and took our orders. Sterling had a salad with grilled chicken and no dressing, and I made a face.

"With all the delicious food on the menu, that's what you get?"

"I like it." He glared at me. "Why is it your business what I eat?"

"It's not." I popped the rest of the roll into my mouth. "Just, every once in a while, you should let go. Live a little."

"I live plenty," he muttered.

"Who was the most famous person you've ever met?" I continued to question Sterling. "Did you interview lots of movie stars when you worked in Los Angeles?"

"I don't remember you being such a groupie, Denis." Rip chuckled, and I laughed along with him, but the truth was, we hadn't learned a lot about each other when we'd been together.

"Just making conversation. Lately I've been watching old movies. I like them better than the computerized, rehashed junk I see now."

"Don't hold back," Rip joked.

"And here I thought you were such a playboy, always at the clubs," Sterling commented, and it sounded like a condemnation.

"I've done my share when I was younger, and I make no apologies. But not lately. It's all boring now."

"What changed?" Adrian's question might be innocent but it forced me to delve deeper than I'd wanted.

I lifted a shoulder and drank some water to quench my suddenly dry mouth. "I guess me? I wasn't ready when I was younger. Even five years ago. Plus, I wanted to live a little—you know, single gay man in the big city. I didn't have that growing up." Staring out into space, I thought about my teenage years, when all I'd wanted was to play hockey and win. Now I'd achieved my dream. What was left for me?

"Where was that? Your hometown?" Sterling's question brought an almost wistful smile to my lips.

"A small town, midway between Montreal and Quebec City. Pretty rural, very charming for tourists who are into architecture and the like, but not so much for teenaged boys. For us, it was and always will be hockey."

"Was it hard being gay in such a small town?" Sterling's question hit like an arrow to my heart.

"Denis? You don't have to talk about it if it upsets you." Rip met my eyes, and the sympathy in their depths soured my stomach like curdled milk. Of course he'd remember our conversation at his wedding. I refused to give in and have them ruin my night, as I was sure they never thought of me at all.

Still, I trembled, and hoped no one would see my fingers shake as I gripped the water glass. "To answer you, no. It was not a problem since I told no one."

"I imagine that must've been harder than coming out. Keeping a secret like that."

A compassionate Sterling wasn't something I'd anticipated, but I was determined to drive the conversation away from me and my ugly past.

"Well, everyone lives with secrets, *n'est-ce pas?*"

Our food came, but I didn't touch my brisket. I wanted to see how Sterling would react, and at his pale face, I knew something more was going on there than an investigative report on Dahlia Dumont. I didn't miss the slight tremble of his hands as he dug into his bowl of lettuce.

"I agree," Adrian chimed in. "Everyone has things in their past they want to forget or avoid. God knows I do."

Oblivious to the tension between Sterling and myself, Adrian chattered on, and we all began to eat. He recounted some mishaps from his first few jobs, and soon we were all laughing and telling war stories. Adrian and Rip shared a piece of the famous cheesecake, but I passed, and—unsurprisingly—Sterling did too.

Over my coffee cup, I turned to Sterling, who was sipping his tea.

"So Adrian and Rip have told us about their most embarrassing professional moments. Mine was walking naked into a locker-room conference on a live feed. What was yours?"

His cheeks flamed, and he spoke directly to me. "I think you know."

Clueless, I searched my memory. "Obviously not, as I'm asking. What could I possibly know about your past? Plus, as far as I have seen or heard from Adrian, who sings your praises, you're perfect."

He ducked his head, then met my gaze. "Being caught on a hot mic, talking down about hockey players. It was wrong, and I know I apologized on air, but I need to tell you and Rip again, face-to-face, how sorry I am for what I said."

Rip gave a quick, reassuring smile. "Don't worry about it. Anyone can make a mistake."

I, of course, not being as nice as Rip nor so willing to let Sterling off so easily, decided to see how far I could push him.

"Are you sorry you said it or sorry it got picked up and reported?" I smirked. "There's a difference."

"Denis," Rip's warning came with a sigh attached, but Sterling put up a hand.

"It's a fair question. And at first, yes. I was simply sorry it got picked up."

The server came with the check, and I grabbed it before anyone else could. "So? What changed?"

"I'm not sure how much it has. I'm still not a sports nut, and I dislike the violence. I don't see why chasing a puck around the ice turns grown men into wild animals attacking each other."

"Is that your only takeaway? You don't see the skill and practice it takes? The strength?"

"Not when I'm looking at Rip, who's got scars all over his face from getting hurt."

"Unbelievable," I muttered. "You know, Sterling—"

"Denis—" Rip tried to cut me off.

"No. Don't shush me. I want to hear what Sterling has to say."

"I don't see that there's anything left for me to say. I'm sorry your feelings were hurt."

God, that calm, measured voice of his drove me crazy. I wanted to see Sterling Forest lose his temper and get mad. Raise his voice. Anything other than indifference. Like what I said didn't matter.

"My feelings?" I laughed. "That's what you think? You insulted every hockey player in the league, and all you care about is what you see on the surface. A few cuts and bruises. Because that's all that matters to you, isn't it?"

"That's not true."

"Come on, guys," Adrian pleaded. "Let's not ruin the evening. Why don't we go out for a drink?"

"That sounds like a good idea." Rip looked to Sterling and me. "Let's go have a drink."

"Thanks, but no." Sterling rose from the table, and I noticed he'd left most of his food—the diva probably thought he was too good for it. "I must get home. Thank you for inviting me. I had fun." Head up and shoulders straight, he walked away.

"How about the three of us?" Adrian suggested. "Come on, it'll be fun."

I finished my coffee and stood to go. I noticed he'd left behind the jersey I'd given him.

Pompous dick.

I grabbed the jersey and gave them each a swift kiss on the cheek. "No thanks. I'll see you tomorrow, Rip. I've got something to take care of. Night, guys."

More like some*one*. I wasn't finished with Sterling Forest tonight.

CHAPTER TEN
Sterling

"Pompous jerk," I muttered, entering my apartment and kicking off my shoes. "How dare he tell me I only care about appearances?"

I undressed and showered, then covered my face with a thin layer of antiwrinkle cream and moisturizer, taking care to check for age spots. A few more silver hairs had shown through, and I debated a second trip to the hairdresser or buying a kit—online, of course—and touching them up myself.

I pulled on a pair of sleep pants and settled on the couch for the late news. Another national scandal, protests, more singers behaving badly.

"Same shit, different day." I got up to make a cup of tea, when the buzzer rang. "Who the fuck is here at midnight?" I picked up the wall phone. "Zayn? Is there a problem?"

"No, Mr. Forest. But you have a guest. It's Denis Bouvier. The hockey player?"

Cold washed over me, followed by heat. I didn't miss the excitement in Zayn's voice, but the last thing I needed right now was a confrontation. "Please tell him it's late and I'm going to bed. Thanks."

I didn't wait for an answer and hung up. The worst mistake I'd ever made was allowing that man into my apartment the first time. I wasn't about to be that foolish a second time.

My bell rang, and my heart kicked up. I strode to the door, first peering through the peephole, but Denis was so tall, all I got was his chin, so I opened it a crack. "What the hell are you doing up here? Why did Zayn let you up? He knows better."

"Don't blame the poor guy. I made it impossible for him."

"Why am I not surprised? Anyway, go away. It's late."

"We're not finished with the conversation from dinner."

I laughed. "Oh, yeah we are. Good night." I closed the door, but he began to relentlessly ring my bell. I ignored him, but he began to knock and call my name. Bastard. I stomped across the floor and flung the door open. "What are you *doing*?" I hissed, unwilling to have a public scene. "I have neighbors."

"I said I wanted to talk to you," he stated, that deep, husky voice raising goose bumps up and down my arms.

"I already told you, it's late and I have nothing to say."

He leaned on the doorframe, gazing at me. I hated that he was so tall and had that advantage over me. "But maybe I have something to say to you." That wicked grin I hated because it made it hard for me to breathe curved his lips. Once again I found myself unable to resist. He moved closer, and because I stepped aside, he took that as an invitation to enter.

"Fine. Now you're here. What is it?" I stood my ground, waiting by the door so he wouldn't think it would be a prolonged social visit.

"You're a snob." He pointed his finger at me.

That wasn't what I expected, and my jaw dropped. "What?"

"You think you're better than everyone else. It's why you didn't eat your food. It's not from some fancy restaurant."

"That's not true," I sputtered. "It was late, and I don't like eating after six. It's not good for digestion."

He rolled his eyes. "You've got to be kidding me. That's the lamest excuse I've ever heard. Plus, your response about hockey players was bullshit. *Merde.* Scars, bruises...so what? We're not pretty boys, dressed up for the camera, not a hair out of place. We're men who play hard."

Oh, I knew that. Denis's golden hair lay in waves around his face, his cheeks shadowed with late-night stubble. Thick biceps bulged against his dress shirt, and powerful thighs strained the fabric of his slacks. My dick knew it too, as it was rock-hard. I stayed quiet, letting him rant, hoping he'd run out of steam and leave.

"You think because we play sports, we're all just dumb lunkheads who get off on beating each other up."

"If the skates fit."

"You think you're funny."

I lifted a shoulder, and my mild response only seemed to anger him further. His face grew dark, his lips drawing back from his teeth in a feral snarl. Maybe I wanted to see how far I could goad him because I was hoping for something more. I smiled up into his face.

"What should the public think when they see grown men punching each other because of some game? You're not changing the world or—*mmmh.*"

My head bumped the door as he slammed his mouth on mine. My hands clutched his shoulders, and I meant to push him off me. And I would. In a minute. First I had to taste him. Suck that thick, wet tongue in my mouth. My fingers twisted the thin fabric as I pulled him closer, and I heard a tearing sound. The overhead light faded as my vision blurred. The press of his solid dick to mine nearly sent me to my knees. An arm steadied my waist while his other hand held my face as his lips moved over mine. Slow and intimate. Breath for breath. I burned and wondered how I wasn't lying in a heap of ash at his feet.

So long. It had been so long...

"*Mon cher. Je t'adore.*"

His whispered endearments ghosted across my jaw as he continued to kiss me, and I clung to him. Denis palmed my ass, then slipped his hand inside my pants and briefs. My heart seized, and I froze as he slid his large, rough finger into my cleft.

"*Je veux te baiser,*" he almost growled, and I didn't need to understand French to know what he meant.

How had I let this happen? I never lost control. My slowly melting brain kicked in, and I shoved him off me. "What the hell are you doing?"

Lips red and kiss-swollen, Denis brushed the hair off his face. Damn the man, but he was barely affected while I struggled to remain upright and draw air into my lungs.

"You have a problem recognizing the obvious. I was kissing you."

"I never said you could." I scowled and wiped my mouth on my sleeve, and Denis's eyes narrowed.

"Because you were too busy kissing me back." He grinned and winced. "Can a tongue be dislocated? I think yes, with how hard you were sucking mine."

I saw red. "You bastard. You didn't ask or give me a chance to do anything."

"What do you expect from a lunkhead hockey player?" Those clever eyes glittered, and I itched to smack that beautiful face. "Besides, you were talking nonsense, and I needed to shut you up. My mouth on yours seemed the best way."

"Get out. Now." I opened the door, and the fucker was laughing as he passed by me.

"You ripped my shirt. You know, because you didn't want me to kiss you."

Frustrated and embarrassed, I slammed the door and locked it quickly, afraid I'd open it and ask him to come finish what he started. Because if I switched off my brain that was exactly what I'd do. Thank God I wasn't ruled by emotions.

It took three cups of chamomile tea to settle my racing nerves before I could go to bed. Tomorrow was Sunday, and I could relax and forget all about Denis Bouvier.

The morning dawned fair but not hot, and I completed my first lap, this time choosing the reservoir as my route. I released a sigh of relief. I had some crazy notion that Denis would be waiting for me outside my apartment or in the same spot in the park where he'd met me last time, so I changed my routine. My sneakers pounded the cement path, and with each yard I advanced, I imagined Denis's face underfoot, me squashing him like a bug.

I'd lain awake half the night, angry at my inability to forget about the kiss. Each time I recalled how needy I'd been, how I'd wanted to climb him like a fucking tree and wrap myself around him, the burn of my humiliation scalded my blood.

The worst part was, I'd acted as if I'd never been kissed. I was no virgin. I'd had sex in college and enjoyed it, but I'd never made demands for a relationship. I couldn't take the chance of anyone finding out who I really was, so I'd go to parties and find someone. Some kissing and touching, followed by sex, and it was finished. A towel for the wet spot. Rarely any conversation or even much talking beyond, *On all fours or on your back? Yeah, right there.* Showers and good-byes. No numbers exchanged, no expectations. Nice and uncomplicated. Never any thrusting tongues or ragged breaths. No ripped shirts and a desperate longing to be dragged and thrown on the bed. No wanting to give up control.

Denis had unleashed something primitive in me, and I didn't like it. I couldn't allow it to happen again. I slowed my pace for a cooldown and drank deeply from my water bottle. I checked my watch and saw with satisfaction I'd beaten my best time by a full three seconds. I exited the park and walked home, planning a day of skin-and-hair treatments after my shower. I needed to rest and rejuvenate to look good for the week ahead.

Denis Bouvier was clueless. He could get hit in the face, and the fans would cheer every bruise and scar he carried, but not me. He thought I was shallow, but his job didn't require him to look forever young while under harsh, unforgiving lights. I knew what the camera picked up, every line in high definition, and I had to appear as if I was aging in reverse.

I entered my lobby and stood for a moment, my eyes closed to enjoy the cool air flowing over my warm skin. The first thing I planned to do upstairs was to peel off these sticky clothes and get into a cool shower.

"Bonjour, *mon cher.* How was your run?"

My eyes flew open, and my stomach bottomed out. "Wh-what're you doing here?" I struggled to maintain my composure. I wanted to punch him. I wanted to kiss him. I took a step away.

"I brought breakfast." He held up a bag.

"I told you. I don't eat bagels."

"I know." He fluttered his lashes. "I am here to make peace. *Une trêve.*"

"It's fine. I forgive you. Now go away."

"Forgive me? For what?"

About to speak, I could see we'd drawn somewhat of a crowd. Being hyperaware that my personal life was about to be exposed, I gritted my teeth. "Fine. Come upstairs. But only for a little while. I have things to do."

"As do I." He trailed behind me, and we didn't speak until we got inside.

"Okay. I need to shower, so let's make this quick. What did you come to say?"

"I want you to admit you're wrong."

Truly baffled, I gazed up at him. "Wrong about what?"

"Hockey players. Me."

"I can*not* believe you're still hung up on that one comment. Let. It. Go."

"Would you like it if someone called you a grinning suit who just parrots the words people write for you?" He arched a dark brow as I gaped at him in shock before anger flooded me.

"What the hell? I write all my own copy. Research my stories. Nothing goes through the newsroom without verification."

His lips curled in a slight sneer. "Who would know that? All the public sees is what's on the screen."

"Because I'm telling you. That's why."

With his arms folded, Denis leaned against the wall. "You mean, like I tell you that hockey is not mere brute force? That it's a master game of psychological warfare, plus strength, endurance, and teamwork."

"Warfare?" I wrinkled my nose. "See? It's dangerous."

"So is walking out of your house in the morning."

Despite how annoying he was, my lips twitched. "You've got me there. Listen, I really have to shower. Can I trust you to wait out here?"

"*Mon ami.* You wound me. Of course. I am like a Boy Scout."

His smirk morphed into a charming smile that almost made me like him. Shaking my head, I left him to wash up. When I returned, I stopped in my tracks.

On my kitchen island were two place settings. A platter of cut fresh fruit sat between the two plates. There was a package of homemade granola from my favorite bakery, Dominique Ansel, along with a container of plain Greek yogurt, also in my preferred brand. In a small vase was a single pink rose.

"What is this?" I couldn't stop staring at what he'd done. For me.

"You know, you have a very bad habit of asking obvious questions." The kettle whistled, and he poured me tea. Loose-leafed in a strainer, not bagged. "Let that steep and come sit. The yogurt won't stay."

But I remained where I was. "Why me? This is something you do for a close friend. Something I'm not."

"That's debatable." He crunched some of the granola. "You eat this every day? Bah." Making a face, he shrugged. "No offense, *mon ami*, but give me a bagel with a schmear any day."

I couldn't help but laugh. "I think you just like saying schmear." I wouldn't tell him, but even Yiddish sounded sexy with his slight French accent. "This is whole grains and protein. Fuel for my body."

"I prefer eggs and meat in the morning to give me fuel. Not something I might crack my teeth on."

I sat and spooned yogurt into a bowl, poured some granola, and arranged the fruit. "How did you know what I eat in the morning?"

He popped some grapes into his mouth. "I saw the granola bag on the counter the last time. And you mentioned you eat yogurt."

"Why are you really here?" I asked as I ate. "I have things to do to prepare for work tomorrow."

"Because of yesterday," he said, and my damned traitorous body leaped to life, remembering. Wanting.

Mon cher. Je t'adore.

His tongue in my mouth. Hands on my face.

Did he want to continue? I knew where it would end up. Me under him. I couldn't allow that.

Could I?

Deciding to play it cool, even as my blood boiled with lust, I ate another spoonful of yogurt.

"What about yesterday?"

His teeth flashed in a smile. "You never admit when you're wrong, do you? I can see you know I am more than who you thought when we first met, yet you won't say it." He leaned across the island, coming dangerously close to invading my personal space. "Say it. Three little words: *I was wrong.*"

My tea sufficiently strong, I removed the strainer and sipped. "I have three other little words: *no, I'm not.* And why do you even care what I think? We're not friends. If it wasn't for your connection with Adrian, I wouldn't even know who you were."

A flash of anger lit those dark-brown eyes. "So you'll continue to be rude and obnoxious even when I offer peace. That says a lot more about your character than mine."

"My character is just fine, thank you. And I didn't ask for this, or want it. You came to me and basically bullied your way into my home, uninvited. I'm not interested in friendship. Why don't you go find someone who'll be enamored of your star power? Because you won't find him here." I pushed away from the island and walked to the door. "Time to leave."

"Bullied? Those are dangerous words to casually say." His face red, Denis strode to me but stopped before leaving. "You're right. I don't know why I bothered. We're not friends, and one gorgeous kiss doesn't make us lovers. I can find that anywhere. Be alone. That's what you want."

He slammed the door behind him, and I stood there stunned.

I returned to the kitchen to eat my breakfast, but the apartment seemed so empty now that Denis had left. His personality brought energy, and he'd taken all that life with him.

"Stop mooning like an overgrown teenager."

An alert beeped on my phone: *Interview on Wednesday for your personal profile story.*

Time to get to work and figure out how to make sure my childhood stayed out of the picture. But no matter how I tried, all I could think of was Denis Bouvier and that kiss. And I didn't know what to do to make it stop.

CHAPTER ELEVEN
Denis

We'd finished the preseason with a 5-2-1 record, which was typical for us, and now, a few weeks into the regular season, we were leading the division. My days were filled with practice, exercise, and physical therapy to keep me limber. Being the champions rested a heavy weight on our shoulders. It also put a target on our backs for other teams, plus the fans had come to expect us to not only be in the postseason, but to win it all.

I knew it was foolish of me, but even after so many weeks of silence, I looked in the stands during home games, wondering if Sterling would show up again. Blades Arena held twenty-five thousand people, and I hadn't left him a

VIP ticket, so why I thought I'd spot him was beyond me. Maybe he'd exude a pompous-ass, don't-touch-me aura that would surround him, making him easy to find. Today, though, I didn't have to think about it, as we were playing an away game.

It also didn't help that Rip constantly questioned me about him. Tonight was no exception. As we were getting ready to take the ice, he sat by my locker while I put on my gear.

"Why don't you call him?" he asked as he examined his stick to make sure it was taped and ready.

"Call who?" I strapped on my skates.

"Don't be dense. I saw how you looked at Sterling that night when we had dinner. You like him."

"What I'd like is to stop talking about this. The man is not my type. Too rigid. He probably wears a suit and tie to bed. Plus, he still thinks we're all just a bunch of ignorant jocks."

"So? Prove him wrong. The Denis I know would take it as a challenge."

But you don't really know me.

"I don't have his number." I strapped on my ankle guards, then the blockers.

"I do. You want it?" His eyes danced.

"No. I don't." I slid the chest protector over my head. "I'm not chasing anyone. Besides, that one is way too much trouble."

"Trouble can be a good thing."

Exasperated, I glared at his smirking face. "Why are you all up in my love life anyway? You're a newlywed. Shouldn't you be more concerned with keeping your man satisfied?"

His grin widened. "Trust me, I have no problem in that area. We both satisfy each other completely."

No denying that. I'd never seen Rip as content, and he was playing at the top of his game. "So now you've moved on to tormenting me?"

To my surprise, Rip didn't volley another smartass remark at me. "I care about you, Denis. We were close once, and I want you to be happy. Right now, I don't think you are."

Unexpected tears stung my eyes. "But I am. I have two Stanley Cups, all the money in the world, and a beautiful apartment. I have a great life." Like many other players, I'd secured a long-term contract front-loaded with salary, and with my off-ice endorsement deals, even if I stopped playing now, I'd never have to work again for the rest of my life. "We've done well for ourselves."

Somber, Rip nodded. "We have, but that's not what I'm talking about. All that is material stuff. You joke about being the playboy, and you've gone out with tons of guys, but I know you. Maybe better than you know yourself, because you won't admit the truth. You want someone steady to come home to. Someone who loves you."

"Well, unfortunately for me, you've already taken the perfect man."

A slight smile tipped up the corner of Rip's mouth. "Damn right. But the man who's perfect for you is out there as well. Just don't make a mistake and look past him."

"One thing I'm curious about. Adrian is always friendly to me."

Rip shrugged. "He's a nice guy."

"You never told him about the time I suggested the threesome, did you? I hope not."

"Actually, I did. We have no secrets. He also knows I threw you out."

My cheeks flamed. "Not one of my finer moments. I don't think I ever properly apologized for that apart from everything else. I knew you wouldn't go for it. I was lashing out."

He clapped me on the back. "I know. I don't give it a second thought, and neither should you."

Coach came in and gave us our pregame directives. I knew the Icers would be after our asses. When Gordie and I had been together, his teammates were friendly, but now that we'd broken up, they'd made it their mission to come at me with a vengeance. I was definitely enemy number one in their minds, and I'd best be on top of my game.

We tramped through the tunnel and onto the ice. We were in Icers territory and booed as soon as we skated out. I ignored the name-calling and concentrated on getting comfortable in front of the net. Ellis and I practiced taking shots, and I had to admit he was good. Fast, instinctive, and smart.

The game began, and right away I could see the Icers had changed tactics from the previous seasons. Now they were heavy into forechecking, less about finessing the puck and more about strong-arming and playing physical. Caught off guard, we had to adjust, but they ran with the puck, and their center, Ray Sorenson, came up in my face in an attempt to smash right through me.

"Motherfucker, that's not how this is going to play out," I snarled and made the save. Ray grinned and shoved his stick at my face.

"Yeah? We'll see about that, asshole."

We regrouped after a time-out and came out ready to bust through their new tactics. By the end of the third period, we were ahead, 4-2. Several fights had broken out, and even Coach had been ejected from the game for arguing with the refs. With two minutes left, Rip and Sorenson took the face-off and fought it out on the boards. Seb and Chitty muscled the puck out and passed to Varhov, who took a shot but missed. It was picked up by the Icers, and they tore down the ice. I was facing a five on one, and though Seb was right there and the others were catching up, it was left up to me to face those bastards.

"Fuck you, Bouvier," their defender, McLucas, yelled, attempting to draw me out, but I was too canny to fall for that trick. I knew exactly how far I could come in the crease without getting called for a penalty.

Their shot on goal went wide, but instead of going after the puck, McLucas skated into me and rammed me with his stick. It slipped under my padding, and my leg twisted in a position I knew right away was going to be a problem. Pain rocketed up my groin through my side, and I collapsed, yelling in agony.

"Fuck, fuck," I screamed, holding my side. Whistles blew, and Hutch, along with others from the medical team, ran out. I couldn't walk and was helped off the ice to cheers, Rip holding me on one side and Chitty on the other.

"What the fuck was that all about?" Hutch and Coach both fumed as I was taken to the medical suite.

"They were gunning for me. From the start. All because of Gordie. McLucas came into the net deliberately. He wanted to hurt me. *Salopard, connard,*" I swore.

"My guess is a groin injury. Hopefully you didn't tear anything. We'll know more after the MRI."

"Son of a bitch, coward," I continued to spew curses as they helped me undress and change. I was taken to the hospital and waited for testing. I lay on a narrow bed, feeling more alone than I ever had in my life.

When I was finally taken to a room, Coach, Hutch, and Rip were there waiting for me. It was so good to see familiar faces that I almost broke down and cried. Instead, I put on a brave face and gave a thumbs-up.

"*Mes amis,* what is the good word?" The pain meds were wearing off, and my entire body throbbed. I winced as they moved me to the bed, and I didn't miss the anxious looks Hutch and Coach exchanged.

"How do you feel?" Rip asked, standing by my bedside.

"Like I had a stick shoved from my balls up to my ribs."

"They're going to expedite reading your results, so we should know soon how bad it is." Hutch's grim face didn't make me feel better.

"I'm sure it'll be fine. A bruise on my nuts. I'll rest and be ready for the next game." I forced a smile. "It's not as if I'm getting any action anyway, so no loss."

My joke fell flat. The doctor entered the room, and everyone shut up and waited. I didn't breathe.

"Mr. Bouvier, I'm Dr. Raskin. You've suffered a groin injury somewhere between mild to moderate. You'll need to stay off it for at least two weeks, possibly a month, apply ice, do physical therapy, and rest it. If you don't improve, could be six weeks."

A month? Six weeks? "Impossible. I have to–"

"Rest. You listen to me because if you don't and you exacerbate the injured area, it'll become weak, and the next time it'll tear and you'll be out for the entire season." He fixed me with a disapproving glare. "If you take care and follow instructions, you won't suffer any lasting effects."

I fell back on the pillow. "Fuck." Three sets of eyes watched me, and I rubbed my face. "I can't believe it. Those bastards got what they wanted."

"It's treatable, Denis," Hutch said. "A common injury. You know that. We'll get you home and begin a regimen for your recovery right away."

"Goddamn right, we will."

My attempt to get out of the bed had me seeing stars from the pain, and Rip put a hand on my shoulder.

"Don't move. We're gonna get you set up to come home with the team."

Hutch nodded. "Yeah. I'm gonna stay with you through-out your transport so you won't have to worry."

"Not worry? I can't fucking walk." I clenched my fists. "Sorry. I don't mean to take it out on you. I'm glad you're all here."

Rip patted me on the shoulder. "I'm gonna go to the hotel. Do you want me to pack your stuff up for you?"

I carded my hands through my hair. I hadn't cleaned up or showered and felt like a broken mess. Careers had ended on injuries like this, but I wasn't ready to give up. They'd have to carry me out feet first before I'd walk away.

"Please. And Hutch?" I turned to him. "I promise to do everything you ask of me. I'm not planning on being a hero. I'll be playing again soon enough."

"I know you will." He squeezed my shoulder. "I'm going to talk to the doctors. You get some sleep, and we'll be here in the morning to pick you up."

Easier said than done, as the staff came to check on me every hour to change the ice pack on my body and check the compression bandage wrapped around me. Machines beeped incessantly. When Hutch and his assistant showed up early in the morning to bring me home, I could've kissed them both. I didn't remember the last time I'd been so tired.

"Get me out of here. I'm ready to lose my mind."

I didn't have to wait long, and within the hour I was chock-full of pain meds and on the plane with my team. They all greeted me with cheers and fist bumps of encouragement, along with vows of revenge for the cheap shot I'd taken.

"No, no." I grimaced as I tried, and failed, to get comfortable. "The best revenge is winning. Ellis, come." I waved to the young goalie, and he approached with trepidation.

"Denis...I hate this shit. You're gonna get better and come back stronger."

I clasped his nape, feeling like a father giving advice to his child. God, was I really getting this old?

"Listen to me. I know you didn't want it to happen this way, but you're the man now."

Fear entered his big brown eyes. "I-I don't know if—"

I tightened my hold on him. "You can. And you must. You've got the raw talent, the skills and instinct. And you're a team player. We're counting on you. After practice and me seeing the doctors, you and I will sit and talk. I'll teach you, but when you're out on the ice, you must rely on two things: this"–I tapped my head–"and almost more importantly, this"–I put a hand over my heart.

"Thanks, Denis. I'd like that. I won't let the team down."

"I have no doubt."

That done, all the energy drained from me, and I closed my eyes and slept. Upon arrival at the airport, the Blades had a car waiting for me.

"Go home, rest a bit, and we'll send a car for you in a few hours for you to come to the arena for a more in-depth medical evaluation and treatment plan," Hutch informed me. "We'll see how much mobility you have. And we're arranging for someone to be with you during the day."

Rip volunteered to come home with me to get me settled. Strange, but I felt awkward having my old lover alone with me.

"I don't think that's necessary. Besides, I'm sure Adrian is looking forward to seeing you. You should get home and be with him."

"Shut up," he said with such affection, my heart squeezed tight. "Adrian's meeting us there."

True to his word, when the car pulled up, Adrian was waiting in the lobby with several bags. At the sight of me hobbling and in obvious pain, he rushed to help.

"Oh God, Denis. Does it hurt really badly? I'm sorry. Of course it does. I stopped off at the supermarket and brought some things for you so you wouldn't have to worry."

Rip hugged Adrian and gave him a kiss. "You're the best, babe."

"Yes, you are. Thank you very much." It must've been the medication coupled with the injury that made me so damn emotional, because I had to turn away in case they saw my eyes grow wet.

"Come," Rip told me, then motioned to the concierge. "Could you see these get brought up to Denis's apartment?"

"Of course, sir."

He put his arm around me, and where once his touch had felt natural on my body, now it was nothing more than friendly. "We'll bring you upstairs and see you get settled. Remember what Hutch said: ice and keep off your feet."

I nodded, and they helped me into my apartment, put the refrigerated items inside, and left. I stared in the mirror, balancing on one leg to brush my teeth. I looked like crap. Pouchy dark shadows sat under my eyes, and fucking hell if there weren't gray flecks in my beard. I sighed and splashed water on my face, then shaved that shit away.

I had little appetite but knew to put food in my stomach because my entire body was one hurting unit and I had to take my meds. Sitting in my empty apartment was making me itch with nerves. I wanted to get a medical evaluation as soon as possible, so I called Hutch.

"When can I come in?"

"I'll send the car for you and meet you at the arena in an hour. The driver will help you."

"Okay."

It took me nearly that length of time to dress. Even with painkillers, I couldn't move without a deep ache not only in my leg, but my entire body. I managed to wiggle into some sweats and a T-shirt and stuck my foot into flip-flops.

"Better get some sneakers without laces."

The driver came upstairs to help me, and I was off. Once in the arena, my anxiety escalated. Things I'd once taken for granted—stairs, long walkways—now seemed insurmountable. The crutches hurt like hell, but I pushed through and waited in the therapy suite for Hutch.

How the fuck did this happen to me?

One minute I was on top of the world, the next I was facedown in the dirt.

"Okay. Stop feeling sorry for yourself." I sat and gave myself a pep talk. "You've got the best trainers in the world and the best doctors."

Hutch entered with another man, about forty, balding, and with wire-rimmed glasses. Chad, our head exercise therapist, followed.

"Okay," Hutch said. "Let's see what we've got. This is Dr. Young. He's a sports injury specialist."

Chad waited as Hutch and the doctor examined me and looked at my MRI results. "How are you feeling?" Dr. Young asked, and my lips thinned.

"Like shit. But I'm ready to start therapy or whatever this afternoon."

Dr. Young's gaze sharpened. "Rest is the only option right now. Your injury is borderline Level One, but if you aggravate it, you can do more damage, and that'll take it to a two, which might take you out for the season."

My stomach dropped. *What the fuck.* About to argue, my muscle twitched, sending such a sharp pain through my entire body, I thought I'd pass out. The doctor noticed and nodded.

"Spasms will happen on and off in the beginning. I know they hurt. That's why you need to stay put for a while. In a few days you'll come back, we'll reevaluate you, and hopefully the swelling will have receded and you can begin physical therapy."

"So I just sit and do nothing?"

A faint smile came and went. "No. But you need to not overextend yourself. This isn't the same as trying to build up a muscle. Right now, ice it, as it's still swollen, and keep your leg elevated. The crutches are only for a few days, and then you should be able to walk normally and put weight on that side without pain. The aide will change your ice packs, check the swelling, and assist you in the shower and getting dressed."

"Good." My lips twitched. "Make sure he's good-looking."

"Glad to see you haven't lost your sense of humor. They'll help with PT as well." Hutch sat next to me. "It's going to be okay. I'm amazed you've never had this injury before. It's common for goalies. You'll get through it and be on the ice in no time."

"Yeah. Thanks. Like I said, I'm not trying to be a hero. I just don't want to let my team down."

He squeezed my shoulder. "You won't. Let's get you home and set up. The driver is waiting, and he'll help you upstairs to your apartment."

"Okay."

"I'll stop by tomorrow to check on you," Hutch said, and he and Chad gave me their hands to help me stand. It was a little easier to maneuver and walk, and I made it to the car without much trouble. Once inside my apartment, I sent the driver home. I had no desire to have someone hanging around when I was at my weakest.

My phone was filled with texts from the team giving me words of encouragement. I called my agent.

"Ezra?"

"Denis, crap. How are you feeling? Can you walk? That fucking McLucas. He should be suspended for that dirty hit. I'd like to ram a stick up his ass, stupid bastard."

I chuckled. "So bloodthirsty on my behalf. I love it. Physically, I'm hurting. I just came back from my medical eval, and they want me to take it slow. I hate hearing that, but the consequences if I push it would make it worse, so I'm going to be a good soldier and listen."

"And mentally? How are you holding up?"

"Like shit. I feel like I'm failing the team, disappointing the fans. Plus…" I sighed. "Eh, never mind. I'll be fine."

"Denis. You aren't. Your team and the fans love you, and the only thing you have to do is get healthy. Athletes get injured all the time. You'll heal and have a great season. I know it's hard to sit on the sidelines and watch everyone else play. But it's only temporary. You'll be stronger than ever."

"Thanks," I whispered.

"Do you need anything? I'll stop by later to check on you."

"That'd be great, but I've got everything I need."

"Cool. I'll text you."

It was only the afternoon, yet a lifetime had passed since the game the night before. I flicked on the sports channel, and of course they were replaying my injury, the commentators having a field day talking about the hit. Ezra had thought I was upset about not playing, and what I said was true, but there was something more. Something that surprised even me.

Had my parents heard the news? Did they see it on television and change the channel to watch another show, or did they simply not give a damn that I was hurt? The buzzer sounded. My aide.

"God, now I'm going to have someone sitting here and watching my every move." But I needed to shower, and I couldn't risk slipping. Plus, I had to keep off my feet. I hobbled over and picked up the house phone.

"Denis?"

"Yeah, Joe, just send him up. I'm expecting him."

"Oh. Okay."

"Thanks."

I waited by the door, the ache blossoming up my thigh to my lower abdomen. Damn, I needed to sit down. Finally, the bell rang. I opened the door—and blinked.

"Sterling?"

Big blue eyes, warm with sympathy, held my gaze. "Hello. Can I come in?"

CHAPTER TWELVE
Sterling

From the first time I'd learned his name and watched him play, Denis Bouvier had projected a larger-than-life image. It wasn't merely his height or pure physical perfection. Most athletes I'd met during the course of my career were big and strong.

Something in his overall attitude, that brash cockiness or air of arrogance he carried with him, made him eminently frustrating and annoying as hell. Unfortunately for me, it also sparked something else I hadn't been willing to recognize or accept. As much as I hated to admit it, the total package—looks, talent, ego—also made him unforgettable.

Desirable. So damn sexy that I hadn't been able to put that kiss we'd shared out of my mind.

I was home as usual on Friday night and searching for something late to watch. I'd decided to stop on the hockey game, and damned if I hadn't gotten caught up. Of course I'd focused on Denis and appreciated his quick reflexes and his strength. I'd winced at the fights that broke out among the other players.

But nothing prepared me for the sheer horror of seeing him lying on the ice, writhing in pain after getting slammed into the net so hard, it became dislodged from the ice. I sat transfixed, watching as two players had to help him walk because he couldn't put weight on one leg.

"Fucking hell," I whispered and switched around to find the sports news, assuming it would be a top story and they'd have an update. I found a press conference with their coach, where he announced that Denis had been taken to the hospital for evaluation.

"Son of a bitch."

Knowing Denis's fierce competitive spirit, I couldn't even imagine his state of mind. I paced my apartment, waiting for an update, and when it was revealed it was a groin injury and he would be on the injured roster for maybe a month, I hurt for him. Denis lived for hockey, and to have that stripped away was like cutting him off from his identity.

I had to find out what was happening. Was he staying in Chicago for treatment or coming home? Adrian would know. Without taking time to think that it might seem odd for me to ask, I sent him a text, and to my surprise, he responded immediately.

I spoke with Rip, and he said Denis is coming home with them. He'll be examined by the Blades medical team.

Thank you.

That didn't tell me much beyond what I already knew. I should be satisfied.

I wasn't.

Saturday afternoon, after my yoga, run, and shower, I sat in my kitchen and drank my tea, wondering if Denis was home and how his evaluation went at the hospital in Chicago. Frustrated, I shook my head. I had work to do, and thinking about a hockey player wasn't going to get it done. Surely Denis had friends on the team who'd check up on him. And if not, they would arrange something. He was one of their superstars. They'd take care of him. He wouldn't be alone.

Would he?

After an hour of staring at the same page of notes, I threw my hands up and spoke to the ceiling. "I'm a dumbass, aren't I?"

I grabbed my keys, wallet, phone, and left my apartment, making one stop on my way to Brooklyn. The doorman let me up, so I was confused when Denis opened the door and his eyes widened with shock.

"Sterling?"

"Hello. Can I come in?"

With some difficulty, he shifted, allowing me to pass, then closed the door. I held up a shopping bag. "I heard the news late last night and thought maybe you'd need some things."

God, he looked like hell.

"Adrian and Rip brought some stuff, but thank you."

I walked to the kitchen, and he followed, slowly. Knowing how athletic and strong he was, to see him in this condition hit me hard. Harder than I'd anticipated.

"I'm so sorry this happened."

He leaned the crutches against the island and eased himself onto a chair, wincing with every movement. "Are you? Well, that's nice to hear. But you didn't have to come all the way down to Brooklyn to tell me."

"I'm trying to be nice."

"Why?" He shrugged, not meeting my eyes. "As you said last time, we're not friends, and I bullied my way into your apartment, uninvited. Yet here you are, weeks later, after total silence, and nothing's changed. We're still not friends, and now you showed up to *my* home, uninvited. Do you want to gloat?"

Horrified, I dropped the bag on the floor. "What? No. Of course not. I…I saw what happened, and I felt bad. I wanted to make sure you weren't alone." I bowed my head. "I apologize for my poor choice of words. I didn't mean them."

"Whatever." He waved a hand in the air. "The team is sending someone to help me, so you don't have to concern yourself with that. He'll help me keep ice on it and check the compression bandage."

It all sounded extremely uncomfortable, and my sympathy outweighed my earlier annoyance. "That's good. But they're not here yet?"

"No. They'll be coming sometime today. Look. It's very nice that you came, but—"

"I'll stay until they get here," I blurted.

He raised his head, those dark eyes narrowed. "Why? The only thing I really need to do is take a shower." His lips curved in that rakish smile. "Are you offering to wash my back? And front?"

I rolled my eyes. "Very funny. And no. But I can help you walk or get comfortable. Change your ice packs."

"Again, why? Isn't that something a friend would offer to do?" He arched a brow.

"You're fucking impossible. You know what? Fine. I'll leave."

His phone buzzed, and he pulled it out of his pocket to answer. The motion triggered something, and I watched his face whiten. The phone dropped from his hand and landed on the floor. Lines of pain etched deep grooves in his cheeks, and he groaned and swore.

"Fuck, fuck, fuck."

I raced to his side. "What's wrong? What can I do to help?"

"Don't fucking know," he panted. "Just...please...help me to the couch."

I slipped my arm around his waist, and with him leaning heavily on me, we slowly made our way across the living room.

"Can you sit?"

"I'll try." Sweat poured off his brow, and I could almost hear the grind of his teeth. *Shit.* This was no joke.

My anxiety spiked, and I held one of his elbows as he lowered himself to the cushions. I exhaled a sigh of relief when he made it.

Still pale, he lay still with his eyes closed. "Can you do me a favor?"

"Of course, what is it?"

"I have a special ice pack in the freezer. Could you get it and bring it to me, please?"

"Yeah, sure."

I left him and hurried to the kitchen. I found what I assumed to be the ice pack—a large contraption with Velcro strips. Upon my return, I stopped short. He'd pulled his sweats down to his knees. Instead of briefs or boxers, he wore a skintight pair of athletic shorts with a bandage wrapped around his right thigh and groin. Unfortunately for me, it did nothing to conceal the fact that Denis was extremely well endowed.

My mouth dried as my stomach tumbled. "What are you doing?" I rasped, looking everywhere but at his exposed lower half.

"What do you mean?" He looked as innocent as a child caught with their hand in the cookie jar. And just as naughty if the twinkle in his eyes was any indication.

"You took your pants off."

His gaze dropped to his lap. "*Bien sûr.* You have to put the ice pack directly on the area. How else could that work? My pants would get wet. That wouldn't be comfortable."

My lips tightened. Denis spoke simply, as if I were a child. While his explanation made sense, I couldn't get past the feeling that I was being played. Only I couldn't figure out how.

"Me? You want me to put that on you? Can't you do it yourself?"

"No. So if you wouldn't mind, I'll lift up and you can slide it underneath me."

"Won't that hurt?"

"I'll be okay. Could you, please?"

While I came to help him, touching Denis so intimately hadn't crossed my mind, but I could hardly refuse. There was no faking his injury. With reluctance, I nodded, and he braced his hands on the couch and raised his hips. I leaned close and placed the contraption on him. My fingers brushed his leg.

"Sorry," I muttered and closed the strap.

"I'm not." His hand closed on my wrist, and I stilled. A muscle ticked in Denis's jaw. "I lied. It hurts like a bitch."

"Then let me go."

His grasp tightened. "I have a high tolerance for pain. But zero when it comes to having you near me."

My breath caught as he tugged me close, and I wanted to pull away, but for some reason, at his touch, I became immobile. This was madness. The man was injured.

"You should let me go," I whispered, my voice fading as his fingers skated up to my elbow. The hairs on my arm rose.

"I should do a lot of things I don't," he teased, and I wondered if everything was a game to him.

The buzzer sounded.

I came to my senses and yanked away.

"Can you get the house phone, please?" he asked, maddeningly serene. The bastard.

"I-I have to get going. Things to do. Work to catch up on." I sounded like a babbling fool and almost ran across the room to the intercom. "Hello?"

"Dane, the aide for Denis, is here?"

"O-okay. Let him up."

"You don't have to leave," Denis called out and spread his arms wide on the couch.

Oh, yes I did.

"Tell your aide to put away the things I brought—there's probiotic yogurt, supplements that are good for inflammation, and some other things." Denis had become way too much of a temptation. I had to resist him.

At the sound of the bell, I flew over to the door and opened it. In walked a god of a man—tall, square-jawed, thick blond hair, and eyes so green they looked unreal.

"Hey, how are you? I'm Dane."

"I—he's on the couch."

Dane's brows drew together. "You look familiar. Have we met?"

"No. Never."

I wanted to leave, but I waited as Dane crossed the room and greeted Denis.

"Dude. How's it goin'? What the hell, man? That was a royally fucked-up hit."

"C'est *la vie*. If you're as big a player as I am, you're always a target on the ice."

My stomach churned watching them kiss hello. It was obvious the two of them knew each other beyond hockey player and sports therapist. Dane reminded me of the surfer guys who posed on Venice Beach, their sleek, tanned torsos oiled and gleaming.

"You know it. The Blades are paying me to take care of you, so I'm at your disposal. I'm here for whatever you need."

I'll bet he was. And from the way Denis smiled up into his eyes, I could only imagine what services Dane would be performing.

Denis glanced at me. "Oh, I didn't know you were still here."

My face flamed at the slight. "I was just leaving."

Denis shrugged. "Thanks for stopping by. Dane works in the physical therapy division for the Blades. He helped me out once when I rolled my ankle on my skates and gives the best massages. This is Sterling Forest, the newscaster."

"Oh, yeah? I don't listen to the news. Too depressing. I only catch the sports and flicks. I'm a movie buff."

Why was I not surprised that a friend of Denis's wasn't interested in the world they lived in?

"The door locks behind you, so don't worry," Denis called out. "Have a great night."

Shaking with anger over being dismissed like a delivery person, I finally forced my feet to move and got the hell out of there. The door slammed behind me, and I had to wait for my head to clear.

Damn it. I clenched my hand in a fist. Why was I such a fool? Denis was an incorrigible flirt and didn't care who his intended target was—if the man breathed and had a pulse, Denis Bouvier would make a move.

"The man is a walking hormone. He can't take anything seriously. Good thing I got out of there. I might've done something stupid I'd regret."

But judging by my inability to work the rest of the day and a restless night filled with dreams of Denis and our almost kiss, my real regret might've been walking away. And that was the scariest thing of all.

CHAPTER THIRTEEN
Denis

Dane brought me my meds and unwrapped my bandage to check for swelling and bruises. I winced as he prodded my inner thigh, his gaze laser-focused on my body and reaction to his touch.

"Ow, damn, that hurts."

"No shit. You have an injury." With expert hands, he rewrapped me and replaced the ice pack. "When I told Olivia I was taking care of you, she said to give you a hug and kiss and to get your pretty ass back out on the ice ASAP."

I chuckled. "Your wife is a doll. How're the kids?"

Dane pulled out his phone to show me. "Marnie is four and taking ballet. Tali is two and wants to do everything

Marnie does, and Rosie is just beginning to open her eyes. One month and counting."

"Three little girls." I cackled. "Gonna try for a boy?"

"Dude. If I even mention sex, Olivia gives me a side-eye and tells me to keep my baby-making dick away from her. Like it's all my fault."

"Horny bastard." I winced, and he carefully lifted my leg with a pillow to elevate it farther.

"You gay guys are lucky. Sex without worrying if you're gonna get your partner pregnant."

Oh, yeah. We're lucky as hell. It's always fun to lose your family because you were caught kissing a boy. I'm one fucking lucky guy.

"Anytime you want to broaden your horizons, let me know." I held up my hands. "Just kidding. I know you'd never cheat on your wife."

He snorted. "Got that right. She's perfect. Why would I look anywhere else when I've got her? I mean, you're hot, but it ain't happening. Plus, your friend would have my balls for dinner."

"Who?"

"The newscaster. Man, he was giving me the stink eye. I felt it all the way from where he was standing."

Now that was interesting. "Tell me more."

Dane shrugged. "Not much to tell other than that. You two banging?"

I laughed out loud. "I think his head would explode if he heard you say that. Sterling is a little…"

"Uptight? Stiff?" Dane's eyes twinkled. "Totally not your type. Except the stiff part." He patted my knee. "Let's have something to eat, and then I'll give you a shower, 'cause you're kinda rank, dude. No offense."

"None taken. Listen, Sterling said he brought a few things that need to be refrigerated. Could you do that for me?"

"Yeah, of course." Dane rummaged through the shopping bag. "This is some good shit. Salad, cold-pressed juices, turmeric shots, probiotic yogurts. Supplements too. This stuff is primo." He stuck them all in the refrigerator. "I've been after you and the guys for years to change your eating habits. Guess it takes a hot guy to make you change your mind."

"Don't be jealous, baby. You're still hot as fuck."

Dane made a muscle. "I know."

"So how'd you meet him?"

I drank down the rest of my juice. I had to hand it to Sterling; it was tasty.

"Who?"

"Sterling. Come on. Don't hold out on a buddy."

"Why? You're not getting any at home, so you need to hear about my love life?" He gave me pathetic, puppy-dog eyes, and I sighed. "Honestly? There's not much to tell. You know Adrian, Rip's husband?" At Dane's nod, I popped another grape into my mouth. "They work together at Channel 8. Sterling is the anchor, and Adrian's the political reporter."

Dane stacked the plates in the dishwasher. He'd made us salads from the food Adrian and Sterling had brought. "Like I said, he's not your usual type, is he? What's the deal?"

"What's my usual type?" I was curious to hear.

Dane gripped my elbow as I managed to leave the chair without pain. "Easy does it." Tough guy that I was, I didn't think I'd need someone's help, but I was exhausted from the simple effort of fighting the deep-seated muscle ache and spasms that came and went without warning.

We made it to the couch, where I took up the spot I feared would become my permanent residence for the next few weeks.

"Go on, Dane. Tell me more."

Dane stretched out his long legs, and I envied him the ability to do so pain free. "Dude. Come on. You love the athletes—muscles, maybe some tats. A little bit of the bad-boy image."

I brushed that off. "All surface stuff."

"Yeah, but you're going from one extreme to the other. That Sterling guy? He's like the country-club type. Not preppy, but someone whose clothes never get wrinkled. I bet he wears old-man pajamas to bed." Dane snickered.

"I wouldn't know."

"So you're not doing the deed? That's got to be a record, huh? Usually you've got them in the sack first or second time out."

"Tell me again why you're obsessed with my sex life, and don't give me that shit about you not having one. The baby's only a month old. I haven't been with anyone in...damn. It's been so long, I can't remember." My first real dry spell. Rudy had fucked me up for sure. Now that it had been months since we'd broken up, I could see we had nothing in common other than sex. We'd never talked except to make plans for dinner or the weekend. Come to think of it, that seemed to be the trend with all the men I'd been with, including Rip, my longest relationship. He'd tried to get closer, but I'd pushed him away, afraid if I opened up and showed any vulnerability, it would be seen as weak. And I'd had to be strong for a very long time. There was safety in hiding behind those inner walls.

"It's not your sex life. We've known each other a long time. I've seen you go through guys like Skittles, and for the most part—Ripley Tremaine excluded—it's been wham, bam. In and out."

"I was engaged to Gordie, you know." That part of my life was less real than my time with Rip. I barely remembered what he looked like, now that he'd retired last year.

Dane snorted. "That was a mistake, and you know it."

"Yeah." I folded my arms behind my head. "You're right. He was too...sweet. Too eager to give in. I like a challenge."

"So that's what turns you on about this Sterling guy? That he doesn't want you?" Dane's brow furrowed. "That's kinda twisted, isn't it? Why make shit so difficult? You wanna fuck him? Just turn on the charm, use that sexy-as-fuck French accent, and get him. It's never failed you."

Until now. Sterling Forest had been a complicated man who didn't allow his emotions to take control. And, as crude as Dane had put it, what I wanted from Sterling was more than sex. I didn't know what or why, and that was part of the reason I'd held back. It was easy to spar with words. We could keep it fun and light. I wasn't sure I knew how to go deeper. Or maybe I was afraid if we did, he'd find out everything and see me as weak.

"It's not as easy as it sounds. We tend to get on each other's nerves. He thinks I'm nothing more than a dumb hockey player, and I've called him out on it. He can be a pompous dick sometimes."

Dane arched a brow, and his lips quirked. "Sounds familiar. Well, good for you on telling him to shove his snotty attitude. But I'm telling you, man. I feel like I've seen him before."

"Has to be the news. You never watch Channel 8? Or maybe you've seen the promo he does for them?"

"Nah. We really don't watch any regular TV. Once the kids are asleep, I'm not gonna sit and listen to a bunch of depressing shit. Only movies, sports, and reality shows."

"I wouldn't mind a movie right now. Maybe it'll take my mind off this." I gestured to my leg. "Not sports ones, though."

"All righty, then. Let's hook us up." He rubbed his hands together. "I can stay late today, so we've got plenty of time. I'll make the popcorn, and we'll be good to go."

The first movie was some comedy I didn't find all that funny, and the second was an action hero that wasn't much better. As a kid I'd loved the movies, but the classics, not the computer-generated crap spit out now.

"Give me something with depth. Something not mindless."

Dane searched through the listings. "Here's one, but it's, like, twenty years old. A suspense. It's one of Olivia's favorites. I think it won the Oscar or something."

"Or something," I joked. "Only the biggest award in movies. You're too much. Let's watch it."

"Let me get us some dinner. How about a bunch of grilled chicken sliders and sweet potato fries?"

"Damn, you can make that?"

He chuckled. "No, but the diner can."

"Go for it."

While we waited for the delivery, Dane checked out my injury again.

"Swelling is down considerably. You might be able to start exercising tomorrow or the next day. Nothing strenuous, just gentle stretching and some other things I'll show you."

"Thank God. Much as it's nice to have the time to myself, I hate sitting around. We play Monday night, and I plan to be there with my team."

Dane finished wrapping my thigh. "You will be."

The bell rang, and he went to get the food. The movie came on, and after the first scene, Dane slapped his knee. "That's it. Now I know."

"Know what?" I was interested to watch this because Dahlia Dumont was the lead actress. And speaking of, I'd never found out why Sterling was interested in her.

Dane picked up the remote and froze the movie with Dahlia's face in full view. "Huh."

"What?" I took a bite of my slider.

"Nothing, except it's weird how much that guy looks like Dahlia Dumont."

"What guy?" My antennae buzzed.

"Your newscaster friend. Don't you think so?"

About to take another bite, I set the slider on the plate and stared. The eyes, the shape of the face and mouth. Yeah. It was obvious now that I saw it in front of me.

Was this the secret Sterling was keeping, and if so, why?

CHAPTER FOURTEEN
Sterling

I was driving myself crazy for a man I didn't even like. But what was it he'd said to me?

"You don't have to like me to want me to fuck you. You know how good it will be."

And from the way my body responded every time that damn man came near me, I was afraid he was right. Even worse, I didn't know how to handle it aside from ignoring it, and so I spent the rest of the weekend buried in work, researching stories our reporters were working on.

In moments of weakness, though, I thought about Denis.

How the hell had I gotten to this point where I was lusting after a man? An athlete. *Him.* A tease and a flirt who no doubt would use me and forget me as soon as it was finished.

But was that such a bad thing? I didn't want a relationship with him. The thought was absurd. This was about pure unadulterated desire.

"I can't believe you're even thinking about this. You're an idiot," I told the mirror, then went to bed.

Monday morning, I sat in my office, waiting for Adrian to walk by. I heard him before I saw him, as he always stopped to say hello to each of the staff.

"Adrian, how was your weekend?" I asked when he got to my door.

"Well, Rip's home for a few days in between games so it's always good." He blushed. "But the team's concerned about Denis."

"I'm sure he's getting the best care."

"Oh, definitely. And they have someone with him at home to make sure he doesn't get hurt."

My lips curled. "Yes. I know." And instantly realized my mistake watching Adrian's brows shoot up.

"You do?"

I pulled myself together. The last thing I needed was for Adrian to find out I went to Denis's apartment. "I mean, I assumed they would. He's a superstar. I'm sure the team will do anything they can to help him."

"*Hmm.*" He shot me a look, but I kept quiet. "Well, he'll be at the games even if he can't play. Not the away games, but tonight's at home."

"Adrian, why are you telling me this? In case you've forgotten, we work at night. And for the last time, I'm not interested in being friends with Denis Bouvier."

Which was kind of the truth. I didn't want to be friends with him. I wanted him to fuck me. Two entirely different things.

"Fine. I'll leave you alone."

"Good. Because you have work to do. There's a city-council hearing this morning, and you need to be there. It's about the new development they want to build on the West Side. Lots of opposition, so it promises to be pretty raucous."

"I'm on it. I did some research on the development company—Steele Properties. They're pretty good from what I've heard."

"Write it all up, and we'll go over it this afternoon."

He left, and I opened my browser to read the morning round-up, but instead I searched the sports news for any stories about Denis. There were a few, some downgrading the Blades' chances at a three-peat of the Stanley Cup or even winning the division.

"It's not only Bouvier's lightning-quick reactions and skill at the net that makes him one of the greatest of all time. He possesses an innate ability that can't be taught, to always anticipate where the puck will land. Bouvier has proved he's unsurpassed in the league when it comes to low-scoring games, and he's been one of the keys to the Blades' success."

I couldn't help but be impressed. Denis was held in high esteem by his peers. He was a leader among his teammates. Was I allowing myself to feel something now that he'd proved he was worthy? Did I think I was better than him because I went to college? Was I a snob?

I huffed. "No need to ask. It's pretty obvious."

For someone whose life had been hidden in the shadows, I was loath to step into the firestorm a relationship with a professional athlete would bring. And yet I needed to do *something*. This craving for Denis's kiss...to touch him...feel him inside me...it all ate at me like a fever burning through my blood. It was unacceptable to have it infringing on my work, and it needed to stop.

"Use that self-control, dammit. It's gotten you through worse."

I closed my eyes and imagined my sixteen-year-old self in that hallway, hearing the two most important people in my life bargaining over how much it was worth *not* to be my mother.

I must've lost my damn mind because I downloaded a sports app that allowed me to watch hockey on my phone. In between my anchor duties in the evening, I watched the Blades, not to see them play, but in the hope I'd get a quick look at Denis on the bench. Whenever the camera panned to him cheering for his teammates, I caught an unguarded glimpse of his wistful face and devastated eyes. It might not be career-ending, but I couldn't imagine the mental toll this injury was taking on him, and sympathy chased away most of my anger toward him.

What the hell are you going to do about it?

A month passed before I broke. By that time, I was watching every game the Blades played and was happy to see him occasionally replace the backup goalie for a few shift changes. For some reason, Adrian believed it was necessary to report to me that Denis had progressed so well that he was scheduled to play in the Saturday afternoon game.

"If you're interested, I can get you a ticket. We could sit together."

"Why?"

Adrian's face fell, and though I felt a twinge of remorse, no way in hell I'd go on this double date.

"Trust me, I'm not trying to set you two up. I don't think it would be a good idea. I just figured it could be fun. Forget it."

He rushed out of my office, and we were polite but no more than cordial during the newscast. When we were finished for the night, I stopped by his office. He was packing up his leather bag to go home.

"Adrian?" He stopped and faced me. "I apologize for being short with you earlier. I didn't mean to be so abrupt. I'm just a very private person, and I keep my personal life to myself." I also wanted him to expand on why he didn't think Denis and I would be good for each other, but that would be hypocritical. If I didn't want to be set up, it shouldn't matter.

His head dipped. "I'm sorry. Would you ever come for dinner? If it's not just the four of us?"

My smile was faint. "I don't really socialize that much. I'm pretty drained after the week and use the weekend to recuperate and recharge. But thank you for thinking of me."

"I understand. Well, have a nice weekend, whatever you do. I'll be at the arena tomorrow, cheering for the Blades."

"Good luck."

At home I thought that lately I'd been going to bed so late after watching the games that I'd neglected my self-care, so it was time to remedy that. I did a full detox—body and skin. I could feel the sluggish enzymes and molecules draining from my pores, lightening all the ugliness I held inside. I grimaced at the ever-encroaching silver hairs and dyed my sideburns, which solved that problem. I used a face mask and performed some at-home teeth whitening. I took a melatonin and went to bed.

In the morning, I decided on a totally new route for my jog and ran down to Riverside Drive. I came home, showered, and ate my yogurt and granola. I paced the apartment, its walls closing in on me.

Why do I feel like I'm going to regret this? Before I could stop and think, I went online and bought a ticket to the Blades game. I grabbed my phone, keys, wallet, and ran out of my apartment to the train. I emerged in Brooklyn, getting caught up in the crowd. I stood out as one of the few who didn't wear a Blades sweat shirt or jersey. *I've come this far. Might as well go all out.*

I held out my phone to be scanned and headed to the Blades shop, where I bought a jersey with Denis's name and number. "Why am I not surprised he'd have Number One," I muttered to myself as the cashier handed me the item. "Egomaniac."

"It's old-fashioned. Used to be lots more goalies wore Number One. Now they're mostly in the thirties, but sometimes twenties or forties."

"I didn't know there were rules for numbers."

The kid stared at me. "Not a hockey fan, huh?"

I tucked away my credit card. "Not really." I pulled off the tag and tugged the jersey on.

"It's his first game since he got hurt. We need him. Lost four games without him, and now we're second in the division."

Not knowing how to answer that, I nodded. "Thanks."

I picked up an obscenely overpriced water and found my seat in the lower half of the stadium. I scanned the rows and saw Adrian's blond head. He was talking to other people, so it looked like he didn't miss me.

The row I was in was occupied by a group of men in their midsixties. They kept side-eyeing me, and finally the man next to me tapped my arm.

"You're that guy who does the news on Channel 8, ain'tcha?"

"Yes."

"Wow. Me and my wife watch you every night. Hey, Charlie, Ed, Morty. It's that guy who does the news on Channel 8. My name's Larry."

The whole row peered over at me and waved. While inside I cringed, I managed to put a smile on my face and waved back.

"You're a Bouvier fan?" Larry asked and drank some of his beer.

"What? Oh, because of the jersey? I've met him, so I figured why not?"

"Thank God he recovered fast. Blades dropped too many games without him. Their other goalies are good, but Bouvier is the GOAT. He'll get 'em on the right track—he's in a league by himself. You'll see."

"GOAT?" I wrinkled my nose.

"Greatest of all time."

"Cheap shot from that fuckin' player. Glad they suspended him."

I hadn't heard. "I'm glad too. It's not right to win by hurting someone else."

The players came on the ice for the practice skate, and I picked out Denis immediately. The crowd did as well, with a huge roar of approval. Everyone stood and clapped, and as it would look odd for me to remain seated, I joined them.

He skated to center ice, raised his stick in acknowledgment, and put a hand to his chest and blew kisses to the crowd. It tugged at my heart, and as much as we clashed, I was happy he'd recuperated and was ready to play again.

The first period flew by, and I could see the other team—I didn't even know their names or care that much—trying to play on what they thought would be Denis's weakness, but he stopped every shot on goal. Meanwhile, Rip and his teammates scored a total of four goals, and I couldn't help smiling at Adrian's fist-pumping and clapping for his husband.

During the second intermission, I finished my water and watched all the people in the stands. The big jumbo screen flashed random pictures of the fans as well as some celebrities.

"Crap," I muttered to myself and ducked my head to check my phone, but I wasn't quick enough. The crowd began to whistle and clap, and I peeked up, my heart sinking as I saw my face up on the Jumbotron. Twenty-five thousand seats in this damn arena, and they picked mine. *Fuck.*

The guys in my row leaned in close to me, waved and laughed, while I kept my eyes on Adrian. He stood and scanned the crowd, and when he found me, his face lit up like Rockefeller Center at Christmas. He waved with an excited smile, and I gave a halfhearted one in return.

The players returned to the ice, and I saw Denis take his stance in front of the goal, but I could've sworn he knew I was there and faced my section before settling in for the last period.

My phone began to buzz with text after text. Adrian, of course.

I'm so glad you're here.

Why didn't you tell me you were coming?

Please change your mind and come to our place after.

Isn't the game great?

It was as if I had a personal Blades groupie.

I decided to wait to answer because Denis was besieged by the other team, and I held my breath as he kicked away one puck only to have them slap it right in his face again. He deflected it, and my row mates started yelling. "Come on! Take the pressure off!"

Finally, someone from the Blades got the puck, and the action moved to the other end of the rink. It all happened too fast for me to keep track of, and I didn't understand why some players got penalties and others didn't, but in the end the Blades won 4-1, and Denis was back.

And I had to figure out what I was going to do. I couldn't leave now without looking like a complete asshole, so I waited for Adrian, and he ran over to me after he got off the towering escalator.

"I couldn't believe it was you. What made you change your mind? And you should've told me you were coming. You could've sat with me."

Adrian was a sweet man but tiring.

"It was spur of the moment."

"And that jersey?"

My cheeks grew warm. "I saw everyone was wearing one and didn't want to stand out. Turns out it didn't matter. They found me anyway." My smile was wry. "Maybe they recognized me from the news."

"Yeah, they do that. When they have celebrities at the game, they always pick them out and put them on the Jumbotron."

"I'm hardly a celebrity."

Adrian waved at me. "Come on. We'll wait for the guys outside the locker room."

"I-I don't think I should stay."

"You have to," Adrian insisted. "Denis knows you're here. And what're you going to do, go home and have dinner by yourself? Come on. It's not only Denis. Other guys from the team are coming, and I invited Tag too. He filled in for me on *Playing the Field* when I was on my honeymoon. We're getting barbecue from Hometown."

Tag Gold. Another happy-go-lucky person. He reminded me of a golden retriever—big brown eyes, lots of blond hair, and always smiling. And barbecue was so not on my diet.

"It all sounds good, but—"

"But nothing. It's no big deal. I know you don't like to socialize, but it's only dinner. If you're really against it, you can leave, but at least come and have something to drink. I even have green tea."

My lips twitched. Adrian was so nice, you felt like a shit saying no to him.

"Okay. Only for a little while."

"That's great. Are you still busy with that story about the mayor's residency?"

I breathed a sigh of relief. Work I could talk about. "Definitely. But I can't seem to get anyone willing to lay it on the line to verify information for me. Frustrating as hell, but I'm hoping to find something."

"I can do some digging if you want."

"Sure. You're the political reporter, after all."

We walked down the corridor to the locker-room area. I could hear voices and the music blasting.

"They should be out soon. They do a little press, ride the bikes to cool off, shower, and get dressed."

"Like you said, it's not like I've got anything else to do." Adrian snickered.

A few moments later, the doors opened and the players poured out. I recognized a few from Adrian's wedding. Finally, Rip appeared, followed by Denis, who walked steadily albeit slowly. A grin spread across his face, and his eyes glittered. "Well, who do we have here? I thought I saw you up on the screen."

"Glad you're back in action."

Rip greeted Adrian, and Denis fell in step beside me, leaning in close. "I can show you some real action later if you're interested."

I met his gaze. "Maybe I am."

CHAPTER FIFTEEN
Denis

I'd been planning a quick exit from the dinner, but now everything changed. Today had been a day I'd waited a month for. The roar of the crowd set my blood singing, and when I skated out, the cold air blasting in my face, it was like coming home. This was all I needed. My team. The fans.

Or so I'd thought. Because walking out of the locker room and seeing Sterling wearing a jersey with my number—a jersey I knew he'd bought—I realized I missed him and his crabby attitude. Our sniping and verbal sparring got my juices flowing, and I hadn't gotten laid in ages. Now

I was hoping that might change. I itched to have him under me, maybe wearing nothing but my jersey.

After the night Dane had pointed out the similarities between Sterling and Dahlia Dumont, I'd spent the following weeks watching and rewatching all her old films. Then Channel 8 had run a profile on Sterling, and I'd sat engrossed, watching a younger Sterling revealed in school graduation pictures and his rise from reporter to anchor in Los Angeles. He'd matured, but one thing that had never changed was the haunted shadows in his eyes. There was no doubt in my mind—the two of them were related. But from everything I'd read, Dahlia Dumont had never had any children.

All that had to be put on the back burner for the moment because I was not going to fuck up this opportunity. Sterling had come uninvited to one of my games, my first since the injury, and was wearing my jersey. He'd waited for me afterward, and was coming to dinner. It was Saturday, so he didn't have the excuse of work the next day. If all went as I hoped, he'd be naked in my bed by midnight.

We arrived at Rip and Adrian's, and though I'd known Rip had changed the furniture, it had been remodeled completely—a totally new apartment. I understood why. I got myself a glass of wine and a juice for Sterling. As others from the team arrived, I maneuvered him to the stretch of windows overlooking the river. We watched the boats and the Staten Island Ferry chugging across the gray expanse of water.

"Is it awkward for you to be here?" he asked me.

"It's been years, and the apartment underwent a complete remodel. And as I said, we're very different people now. I feel nothing for Rip but friendship."

"Strange, isn't it? Considering you were once in love."

I sipped my wine. "I'm not sure we ever were. I barely remember us being together."

He gazed up at me. "I guess if you don't know, most likely it wasn't."

"I have a feeling being with you would be unforgettable."

His lashes lowered, but he stayed silent.

"Dinner," Rip called.

Everyone gathered at the giant island where the feast had been set out and tore into the food, except, of course, Sterling. He took a small piece of chicken and some vegetables. I was starving and demolished half a chicken, some ribs, and a big dollop of mashed potatoes.

A blond man showed up with a full plate and a young woman on his arm. "Hey, guys. Great game, Denis. Not sure we've met. I'm Tag Gold, the new sports reporter for Channel 8. I work with Sterling and Adrian."

As pretty as he was to look at, I had little desire to act on the vibes I was receiving from him. I'd had enough of men who'd bend over backward to give me anything I wanted.

My only interest was in the stiff-necked man at my side who fought me at every turn. It wasn't a game between us any longer. I hungered for him physically yet also wanted to know what in his life had made him so unyielding and afraid. I had a feeling it all revolved around Dahlia Dumont.

Oblivious to it all, Tag continued to chatter. "This is my sister, Nora. She's a huge fan of the Blades."

As bubbly as her brother, Nora tucked her hair behind her ears and clasped her hands. "Hi, so amazing to meet you. I watch you all the time on the news, Sterling, and I'm your biggest fan, Denis. There's something so...larger than life about a goalie."

Her enthusiasm was sweet, but I wanted them both to go away so I could keep talking to Sterling. I prepared to make small talk before shooing them off, but then Sterling gave me the ultimate surprise.

"I think Denis needs to go home and rest. Playing his first game after his injury, I'm sure you'll understand he's a little tired."

"Oh, of course. We completely understand." Tag nodded like a bobblehead. "You took a ton of shots on goal tonight and handled them perfectly. No lingering issues from the groin pull?"

"None," I responded pleasantly but with enough bite in my tone to indicate I wasn't interested in being interviewed at the moment. This person would not be allowed to get in the way of my goal.

"Definitely go home and go to bed. You need to unwind."

After they left us and mingled with the others, I caught Sterling by the elbow. "You heard them. Go home and go to bed. Are you coming with me?"

"Is that an invitation?"

"If we weren't with other people, I'd drag you out the door," I growled, and heat flared in those luminous blue eyes. I wanted to see them catch fire when I moved on top of him.

"Maybe you wouldn't have to drag me."

Considering how the two of us bickered all the time, I was a little taken aback by him embracing the idea of us having sex, but I didn't care. It was going to happen, and judging by that one sizzling kiss we'd shared, it promised to be explosive.

We found Rip taking some beer out of the refrigerator. "I think I'll be going. I'm a little tired and want to rest. Go to bed early."

Rip nodded, but I could see the gleam in his eye. "Completely understandable. You should get off your feet."

"I intend to, *mon ami*."

Sterling cleared his throat. "Thanks, Rip. Tell Adrian I'll see him Monday."

"I will. He's around here somewhere, being the perfect host. Make sure Denis doesn't overdo it. We need him ready for the next game on Tuesday."

Sterling nodded, but his neck was red. Even though we were in the hall waiting for the elevator, I brushed my fingers along his nape, and he shivered. I bent to press a kiss right above the edge of the jersey.

"You blush so easily. Are you red everywhere?"

He twisted away as the doors opened. "Not here."

Amused, I kept my hands and lips to myself, and we walked the half mile to my apartment. I was pleased that I suffered no achiness or pain from the injury. I wanted nothing in the way of enjoying Sterling.

Once inside, I kicked off my sneakers and stripped off my hoodie. Watchful eyes met mine, and I held out my hand. Waiting. Hoping. For the first time, unsure of a man's desire. Would he run a second time? Was I about to be the victim of the consequences of my actions?

He took my hand, I went weak with relief.

"Come."

Our fingers entwined, we walked into my bedroom. My bed was custom-made—plenty of room for the two of us. We sat and I cupped his cheek and touched my lips gently to his.

"I'm very happy you're here tonight."

"I think I should make something clear." He shifted a bit away from me, and my hand fell from his face. "I'm not looking for a relationship, Denis. I just...I want to have sex with you and get it done. It's been hanging over our heads for several months now, and I figured if we do this, we'll get it out of our systems and move on."

Unsure whether to laugh or tell him to get the hell out, I did neither. I rubbed my chin. "*Get it done...move on...mon cher*, these are not words that should ever be uttered when I take someone to bed with me. Usually it's *yes, please*, *more.*" My lips twitched as his face burned bright red. "Why do I have the feeling you've never been properly made love to?"

He made a face. "That's not important."

Torn between pity and anger, I took his hand. "Ahh, but it is. It's very, very important. And I assure you, after tonight, you will know what true lovemaking is."

"I don't—"

Enough with the talking. I settled my mouth on his and held him firmly. He stiffened for only a moment before softening and opening to the pressure of my tongue. The velvet heat of his breath pulled me into a vortex of lust and desire, and I sucked and licked. Hard nails dug into my shoulders, and I pushed him on the bed and straddled him.

"You have too many clothes on." I yanked at his jersey, deciding I needed him fully naked. "Take this off."

I watched as he dragged it over his head, the flat ridges of his muscled abs flexing and bunching. Finally he lay under me, chest smooth except for the points of his brown nipples. I lowered my head and licked one, loving how he squirmed and hissed. If nothing else, Sterling Forest was going to lose control tonight.

I tugged at his pants, pulling the waistband past his thighs. A thick cock bulged from his black briefs, and I smiled.

"Have I ever told you that black underwear is very sexy? I love the contrast with your skin." My fingers played along the elastic, and he shifted, bucking his hips. "Do you want me to touch you?"

He didn't answer, eyes wide, tongue playing with his bottom lip. It didn't matter. We didn't need words between us. The passion we were about to share was enough.

"You have no idea how long I've waited to have you like this."

Sterling remained silent but held my nape to crush our lips together. I pressed kisses to his jaw and neck, teasing his earlobe. A hard groan split the quiet, and my fingertips skimmed the hard dips of his quivering body, stopping at his underwear again. I leaned in close, took it between my teeth, and pulled. The rich scent of his desire filled my senses, and I finished removing his clothing, freeing his beautiful cock. I took the head between my lips and sucked, but I concentrated on his face. I wanted to see him fall apart in my bed.

"Oh, God." He sighed, and I smiled around the shaft, licked its straining length before taking him fully to the back of my throat. "Fuck!" Sterling slapped the bed, his fingers curling on the sheet. "Please," he gasped, the normally hard lines of his mouth soft and slack with need. "Please."

To have this strong-willed man so weak with desire that he pled with me to make love to him was an aphrodisiac. His taste consumed me, his smell soaked into my skin. I wanted to swallow him whole, take him inside me so I carried him with me for always. I nuzzled his groin, the hairs rough, while my hands and mouth continued to play with his dick.

"Denis," he whispered, tremors racking his body, and the sound of his broken voice hurt me to my soul. Who had made him so afraid to let go and enjoy life?

"*Je te désire.*" I kissed his knees, sliding my tongue up his leg to lick the precome gathered at the tip of his dick. "I want in you. I need to feel you holding me tight."

He gripped his shaft, stroking himself hard and fast. I reached for the condoms and lube, stopping to capture a kiss from him. The unexpected wetness on his cheeks sent shockwaves through me, and I raised my head to meet his gaze.

"I'm okay," he responded to the unasked question in my eyes. "It's…it's been a while."

I nudged his nose with mine. "For me too, *mon cher*. We'll take it slow. Savor each other. Pleasure like we will be giving each other should not be rushed." I licked my finger and reached down to play with his rim.

His mouth fell open as I slipped in farther and added another finger. "Denis, oh please, Denis. More."

I could've kept him there all night, touching him, kissing him, drowning in his eyes. He was everything beautiful. And he was mine.

"Are you ready for me?" I brushed my lips to his.

"I have a feeling I'll never be fully ready for the storm that's Denis Bouvier." A teasing smile curved his lips, and the years fell away from his face.

I rolled the condom on. "Maybe we'll have to keep trying to make sure. But for now?" I guided the tip of my throbbing cock past his rim and sank in slowly, trying to be gentle. Feeling his walls clasp me tight was both perfection and torture, but I'd gladly live with this pleasure-pain forever. He wrapped his legs around me, driving me in deep, and I lost control, thrusting into that silken fist. The sting of his nails scraping across my shoulders only heightened my lust, and I sank my teeth into his neck, then kissed the reddened spot.

"You are incredible. Perfect. I have to have you. All of you. Give yourself to me." The ache in my balls grew, my heart thundering until I was certain it would burst. Sterling drove me wild and incapable of any coherent thought, except to hold him and never let go.

"Take me, oh God, Denis." Sterling's head thrashed on the pillow, and he writhed against me. Warm stickiness spread between us. A harsh cry escaped him, and we kissed, my tongue plundering his mouth. I soared high, then plummeted to earth, waves of desire engulfing me. Nothing and no one had transcended anything before this moment.

My lips were buried in his hair, and I was covered in sweat. Sterling's heart pounded in sync with mine. When I'd put the pieces of my brain together, I lifted off him and pulled out. After I got rid of the condom, a wave of exhaustion hit me, and all I wanted was to sleep.

"*Mon cher*, come with me. We'll shower and go to bed."

Hazy eyes met mine, and he rose from the bed. We stood under the hot water, and there was a special kind of intimacy in washing Sterling's hair and soaping his body. As tired as I was, I looked forward to having him again. I wanted to fall asleep with him naked and warm by my side. We'd wake up and make love while the sun rose over the river. The dawn of a new day. A new beginning.

I chose to wear a compression bandage still, to keep from aggravating the newly healed injury, and went to fetch it from the drawer. Upon my return, Sterling wasn't waiting for me under the duvet, but stood in the middle of the room, half-dressed.

"What is this?" I asked, sensing his withdrawal with each second that passed.

"I'm going home." His head disappeared under the jersey and popped out through the top. "Like I said, we got it out of our systems, and that's that. I'm glad you're feeling better now."

He put on his socks and stepped into his loafers.

My anger rose. "That's that?"

He tipped up his chin to meet my gaze. "Yes. Have a good night." He opened the door and walked out.

Angry and hurt, I lashed out and called after him, "How are you and Dahlia Dumont related?"

He froze, then took off, sprinting down the hallway and vanishing from sight around the corner. It confirmed my hunch that there was some relationship between him and Dahlia Dumont.

"You can run, but you can't hide from me. I'll see you soon."

CHAPTER SIXTEEN
Sterling

Luckily, I made it home before I got sick.

Our perfect night—and yes, I called it that but only in my mind, never to be spoken out loud—had been ruined as soon as Denis asked me about Dahlia.

"How the hell did he find out? How much does he know?" Wild with panic and anxiety, I'd become physically ill, and couldn't stop the pain shooting through my stomach.

I changed into pajamas, but sleep was a faint memory, though it was after one in the morning. I paced my living room, frantically replaying the words he'd flung at me.

"How are you and Dahlia Dumont related?"

"Okay, okay. So he doesn't know anything. He's fishing. Somehow he'd made a connection between us. It couldn't have been the profile piece on me—I made sure to clear it with production. If I say nothing, he'll get bored and forget about it. Denis only cares about hockey and sex."

It would be harder to forget what happened tonight between us. If I'd had a hint I'd become this panting, sweaty mess of need the moment he touched me, I would never have agreed to sleep with him. For weeks, my brain short-circuited from our single kiss. That alone should've been the first clue that Denis would be trouble.

"Who are you kidding?" I muttered. "You wanted it as much as he did. More, even." Denis showed me tenderness. A sweet gentleness I hadn't known he possessed. I'd thought we'd have sex and I'd walk away. Instead, I found passion, and somewhere in the muddle, I lost my peace of mind, while strugglingly valiantly to hold on to my heart.

Growing up in Hollywood, sex had been everywhere. Dahlia was always falling in and out of love with her leading men, and Marisel would bring boyfriends to the house if Dahlia was making a movie and was away on location. No one ever thought about the young boy wandering around the giant house in Bel-Air, hearing and seeing things not meant for a child's ears and eyes.

I figured I was strong. Never easily swayed by the physical. I could appreciate a good-looking man. Sex was nice, but it had its place. The rare times the tension built up from working too hard without a break, I'd find someone from the discreet service I'd joined. I'd rent a hotel room, and they'd come for the night. The men had served a purpose, and I'd been set for another few months.

So why did Denis have to be the one to turn me on my head? My plan should've worked. I'd had it all figured out—sex with Denis would be like with every other man I'd been with. One shot and good-bye.

Instead, I wanted to hold Denis tight and never let him go. Even as I dressed and walked away, my body ached to remain in his bed, wrapped in his powerful arms. I wanted the kisses that made me weak and that sexy French accent whispering in my ear. The wicked grin that melted my bones and turned me into a puddle of desire.

I couldn't even use the excuse that I was drunk, like I'd been at Adrian's wedding. I'd initiated this—practically threw myself at him. Of course he'd be happy to oblige. What man would turn down sex when offered?

I sank into a chair with my head in my hands. I never imagined a man like Denis Bouvier could be such a generous lover. He could have anyone he desired. He'd been voted one of the most eligible men in sports, handsomest hockey player, a gay icon of the league. He'd modeled in Paris and walked in New York Fashion Week.

My humiliation was complete. I'd made it so damn easy for him. Everyone at Adrian's party knew we'd left to have sex—would Denis brag about how I couldn't keep my hands or lips off him? I squeezed my eyes shut and clenched my fists. *Stop thinking about him. It's only sex.* More important was what the hell to do with Denis's question about Dahlia.

I could make light of it, tell Denis he needed glasses or that I should be so lucky to be related to one of the most famous faces in the world. The fact that we both had dark hair and blue eyes was a pretty flimsy connection.

My best option? Ignore him completely.

It was three a.m. before I finally closed my eyes, and I didn't wake up until close to noon. I checked my messages and had three texts from Adrian—the first saying he was sorry he didn't say good-bye, a second asking if I'd had a good time, and the last asking if Denis and I were now friends.

"Friends." I couldn't help but laugh. "How the hell do I answer that?" My body still hummed from his touch, and my ass was sore, but I loved it. *Of course we're friends. He fucked my brains out, but I ran away because I was scared of how he made me feel. Oh, and he mentioned my mother who no one knows is my mother because she won't admit she ever had a child.*

I laughed so hard I cried.

"God, I'm a reality show in the making."

My phone pinged, and by this time I was afraid to look, so I decided, sore or not, I needed to ignore everything, get out, and keep to my routine. Half an hour of mind-clearing yoga, plus a good run, would reset my focus.

I winced at my reflection in the mirror. "Late nights are terrible for the skin." I'd retained enough of the Beverly Hills mindset to be vain about my appearance and vowed to spend the afternoon giving myself a much-needed facial and skin treatment.

Feeling more rejuvenated with these decisions made, I did my half hour of yoga and could feel the knots of anxiety melt from my shoulders and neck. I laced up my sneakers, grabbed a water bottle, and set off for my run. Forty-five minutes and five miles later, I returned home, a sweaty mess but with my self-control on the right track. I showered and ate, planning to watch some television.

I sat on the couch, the news playing in the background, but my thoughts were on Dahlia. In a way, I felt sorry for her. I couldn't imagine growing up in such an insular community, then being forced to run away from everyone I knew to keep my freedom. She could've left me behind or given me up. Nowadays single actresses routinely had babies without being married, and had high-profile adoptions, but forty years ago the industry wasn't as open-minded and enlightened. Did I have a right to judge her decisions?

But immediately, I rejected any sympathy for her. Growing up, she'd barely been present in my life. Her lovers had received more attention than I ever did. I'd never received a single birthday or Christmas present. No one had shown up to my school plays. Dahlia steadfastly refused to acknowledge my existence and would rather pay me off than admit I was her child. People could claim she'd taken care of me, given me food, clothing, shelter, and medical attention, and it was true. But there'd never been a good-night kiss or someone to hold me when I was sick. No family pictures of me growing up—at Christmas or any holiday. Rejection was a hell of a hard pill to swallow, and five million dollars couldn't make up for wanting a mother's love.

"Why couldn't either of them at least have pretended to care?"

None of this reminiscing was getting my work done for the week. I read through production reports and made notes. The city was gearing up for an election next year, and it promised to be an ugly one.

Later on, feeling claustrophobic, I went for a walk, heading down to Riverside Park. I stood, watching the gray waters of the river flow past. I wondered what Denis was doing. I wondered why I cared. I was happy he'd left me alone. Obviously, he had no desire to run after me, since here I stood alone. It was what I wanted.

Wasn't it?

I'd only worn a sweat shirt and shivered. Time to go home.

I turned the corner to Central Park West, and my heart leaped seeing Denis under the awning, chatting up the doorman. A shopping bag dangled from one hand, and I watched as Denis pulled out a sweat shirt and cap and handed them to him.

I strolled up. "Bribing my doormen, Denis?"

He turned the full force of that charming smile on me, and damned if my traitorous body didn't respond.

"No, Mr. Forest, he wasn't," Carmine protested, and I shook my head.

"I'm only joking, don't worry. Thanks." I walked through the door Carmine held open for me.

Of course Denis followed, and as much as I wanted to tell him to get the hell away from me, I couldn't form the words. Now that I'd tasted the forbidden fruit, I was addicted and craved more.

"I wanted to make sure you were all right. You ran away so quickly last night."

"You're so kind and considerate." I pushed the elevator button.

He put his hand on my shoulder, and I gazed up at his surprisingly serious face. "I am. What made you leave?" His voice dropped to a husky rasp. "I thought it was special."

I bit the inside of my cheek. Hard. "It was good." The doors slid open, and I entered, Denis coming with me.

"Good?" He crowded me into the corner, and I couldn't move. All that thick golden hair lay in long waves to his shoulders, and he skimmed his fingers across my cheek. "It was better than good. You felt it too. I know you did."

I forced my lips to a smile. "I bet you say that to all the guys. I've heard the stories."

Anger turned the gentle warmth in his eyes into hard chips of onyx. "I thought you were a legitimate newsman. Don't you know not to believe everything you read on the Internet?"

We reached my floor, and I took out my keys. My damn hands shook, and to my utter horror, I dropped them when I tried to unlock the door. He picked them up and did it for me.

Without a word, I opened the door a crack. "Thanks. But you can't come in. I have work to do."

"You mean reading more lies about me?" His eyes glittering, he loomed over me, and my heart thudded so loudly—how could he not hear it?

"Not everything's about you."

His lips kicked up in a sinful grin. "In my world it is. And that world includes you. So unless you want to give your neighbors a free show, you'd better let me in, because I'm going to kiss you."

I should tell him to go away. That I didn't want him. But my hands were already reaching for his face, and he pushed the door open as we stumbled inside my apartment. I opened my mouth to his tongue and sucked it greedily.

"Don't run from me again. I promise I'll come find you."

I couldn't speak, too caught up in need and want. I sank to my knees and yanked his sweats to his ankles. He wore compression underwear that highlighted every bump of his gorgeous dick. I peeled it off, freeing his cock, and I hummed with pleasure as I took him in my mouth. He was large, thick, and hot, and he filled my throat to the point of gagging, but I didn't care. I wanted it, wanted him to make me feel.

"*Mon dieu*," he cried and flung his head back. He held my head lightly as I bobbed up and down, swirling my lips on the wide head. His hips rolled and thrust gently. "I can't stop."

I ran my hands up those tree-trunk thighs to his balls and rolled them before sliding my fingers past his taint to the cleft of his ass. "Do you like that?" I whispered, coming off his cock to rub my cheek against its steely length.

"I like everything you do."

I wet my thumb and slipped it past his rim. "How about that?" I took him between my lips.

"Fuck," he shouted and came, his hot seed filling my mouth. I swallowed as much as I could, wiping my chin from the overflow. Still on my knees, I looked up at his flushed face, and his steady dark eyes bore into mine as he pulled his clothes up.

"Come here," he demanded, and I rose, a bit unsteady on my feet when he grasped me by my nape and kissed me. I gripped his sweat shirt in my hands, drawing him close. "I want to taste myself on you."

We continued kissing, and he backed me up until we reached my couch. He pushed me down, and I twisted my fingers in his hair as he removed my clothes. I was in so deep, I didn't care that I lay naked and vulnerable in my living room. At that point I'd let him do anything he wanted just to feel him again.

"Fuck me, you're so perfect." He smoothed his hands over my chest, tweaking my nipples, and I moaned softly. "Know what I like?" I clenched my fists as he nibbled and sucked at one, then the other. "Watching you under me."

I couldn't answer, couldn't catch my breath. He lowered his mouth on my cock, and I was so on the edge, I knew I wouldn't last.

"Denis," I whispered, and he met my gaze even as his tongue worked me. I couldn't keep from crying out. My body throbbed, and my skin burned. "Don't stop," I begged. "Don't ever stop."

To my dismay, he pulled off and dragged my legs apart. "Too quick. I need to make you last."

He buried his face in my ass, his tongue thrusting into my hole. Denis held me open and licked and sucked my ass, and I screamed for release.

"Fuck me, please. I can't take it. *Denis.*" I flailed, my nails scraping his shoulders.

He returned to my leaking dick, and I couldn't hold off anymore. I came so hard, I must've passed out. I opened my eyes and he was next to me on the couch, holding me close.

"*Le petit mort,*" he murmured. "The little death. A beautiful sight to see."

My head rested on his shoulder, and I sighed into his neck. "Are you cuddling me?" His arms tightened, and I grinned. "Big, tough Denis Bouvier a cuddler. Who knew?"

His lips brushed my hair. "No one, *mon cœur*. Only with you."

I rolled my eyes and squeezed out a laugh. "Now I know you're lying."

He shoved me. "Liar? You'd better look me in the face when you insult me. Otherwise you're a coward."

I turned my head away from him instead. "This wasn't supposed to happen again. I thought it would be a one-time thing, and we'd forget about it."

Long, rough fingers tipped my chin up. "Is that what you want?"

"Yes...no...I-I don't know." Why couldn't I shut up? This happened every time Denis came near. I went from a strong, self-possessed man, to a hormone-driven teenager who couldn't stop thinking about sex.

"Yes, you do. Be honest for once, goddamn it."

"You should go," I said through numb lips.

"I'm not going anywhere until you talk to me."

"About what? The fact that we're sexually attracted to each other? Fine. I'll admit it. Now will you leave me alone?" Aware I was naked, I scrambled away from him and threw on my clothes. "I need to prepare for work tomorrow."

"If you want to lie to me, go ahead. But what I can't figure out is why you're lying to yourself. And not just about us. If you keep too many secrets, you might forget the truth." He got to his feet and dressed. "I hope you figure it out."

I kept my head down as he walked out the door.

CHAPTER SEVENTEEN
Denis

Monday morning practice started off with me annoyed as fuck. Sterling was messing with my head, and I didn't like it. My focus had to be on hockey, not some guy. But Sterling wasn't just any man, and he'd invaded my dreams, disturbing my normally untroubled sleep, and I came into the arena pissed off. I stood in front of my locker and merely grunted at the team as they greeted me. I'd always been able to separate my personal life from my professional career, and hockey had come out on top every single time. But now with Sterling first on my mind instead of the upcoming game, I was massively irritated with myself.

I was stripping out of my clothes to get changed when I heard a whistle from across the room.

"Damn, bro. You get attacked by a wild animal this weekend or what?" I turned to see Seb's dancing eyes, and Rip stuck his head into his locker, but it couldn't drown out his cackling.

Idiots.

"Or what," I snapped and set out my pads and shields.

"So closemouthed," Rip said. "But Seb's right. Those scratches look like it was either hand-to-hand combat or fun as hell." Having recovered from his hysteria, Rip shut his locker and sat to check the tape on his sticks. "Normally you love talking about your conquests."

"Why, are you jealous? You can't already be tired of the gorgeous Adrian." I knew that would get a reaction from Rip, and I was right.

"Don't be an ass. I'll never get tired of him. But how was the rest of the night with Sterling? You two officially dating now?"

"No." I strapped on my chest protector and slipped the jersey over my head.

"Just fuck-buddies, huh?" Rip side-eyed me with amusement. "So what you're saying is nothing's really changed. You're still embracing the bachelor life. Well...I guess if you're not involved, I should tell Adrian. He likes Tag. The guy might be good for Sterling. Lighten him up."

"That golden retriever?" I snorted. "Don't be ridiculous. Who could put up with his annoying, perpetual smile and corny jokes? And what's with your husband? Is he a reporter or a matchmaker?"

"I don't know about that," Rip mused, ignoring my question. "I could see them together. They'd have that whole grumpy-sunshine thing going on."

"What the fuck is that—grumpy sunshine?" I stared at him. "Are you on edibles? You must be. Sterling would never be interested in a guy like Tag."

"Why?" Seb slammed his locker. "He likes playing with your stick too much? You put the biscuit in the basket yet?"

I growled, and next thing I knew I had Seb by the throat and pushed up against the row of lockers. "Don't talk about him like that. Would you want someone thinking about you and Jolie having sex?" Seb's eyes flared with anger, but after a moment he dipped his head.

"You're right. That was both rude and crude." The entire room had gone silent, and breathing hard, I released him. We locked gazes. He stuck out his hand. "I'm sorry. I apologize."

We shook, and I glared at everyone else standing around. "Don't you all have anything better to do? *Idiots*," I snapped and stomped away on my skates toward the tunnel. Rip caught up with me before we hit the ice.

"Hey. I'm sorry too. I didn't realize."

"Realize what?"

"That you really like the guy. I won't tease you again."

"I don't know what you're talking about. And why are you so up in my business? You didn't care so much when I was with Gordie or Rudy."

"That's not true. But we weren't in a good place when you were with Gordie. And I knew Rudy wasn't long-term."

"You did? How?" Surprised, I glossed over my failed engagement, not wanting to bring up the foolishness of my past.

"I'm not sure." He shrugged, and we set out on the ice. "You're more intense about Sterling."

"We're not together. But you're right. I am more intense—I've never met anyone so damn frustrating and annoying in my life. He makes me want to punch a wall."

"Must make for some great sex. Just sayin'." He popped in his mouth guard and took off.

"You have no idea," I muttered to myself, but Coach called to us and I put Sterling out of my mind. I wasn't some teenager mooning about a boy. The last time I'd done that, it had cost me everything. I was an adult now, and I had room for only one love in my life. Hockey. Everything else came in second.

Tuesday was an away game, and on the flight to DC, I sat across from Rip. I was still angry with Sterling and didn't expect to hear from him. I sure as hell wasn't about to get in touch with him. I didn't run after men. They came to me.

"Want to hear something funny?" Rip asked.

"Sure." I was reading an old article on Dahlia Dumont to see if I could glean anything pertaining to their connection.

"Remember how I mentioned yesterday that Sterling and Tag should get together?"

A sour taste rose in my mouth. "Yeah."

"Adrian jumped on it all on his own and went ahead and arranged a double date. The four of us are going to dinner Thursday night."

"You're full of shit." I laughed, but Rip remained serious, and I set the magazine aside.

"No. Adrian thought he'd have to convince Sterling, but he agreed right away. Maybe he really does like the guy."

"And you're telling me this, why?" A red haze filled my vision. It made no sense that Sterling would agree to a date with him yet push me away.

"Because you were so sure Sterling wasn't into Tag."

"Thank you for your need to point out all my incorrect assumptions. But I don't give a fuck who that man dates. And I'd like you to stop bringing up his name. Understood?" I picked up the magazine again.

"Yeah. I understand." Something that looked like sympathy rested in Rip's eyes, and it made me furious that I'd allowed myself to lose control.

The short flight landed at noon, and after dumping our stuff at the hotel, we went to lunch, then headed to the Snow Caps arena to practice before the game. I felt good—strong and quick. Ellis skated over to me to change shifts.

"You're playing better than ever, Denis. I know I failed the team when you were out." He hung his head in defeat. "My parents came to watch me play, and of course it was a game I lost. They tried to tell me it didn't mean anything, that everyone loses, but they worked so hard to give me my shot."

Years ago I would've built up my own ego by tearing his down, but I didn't need to spread negativity.

"Nonsense. Do you think we've never lost games before? In my first few years, I was booed on the regular. The key is to never give in to self-doubt. Take the anger you feel at those losses and turn it to the game. You've got the talent, Ellis. You're gonna get your shot."

"I'm not like Lindy who thinks he's better than Rip. I want to be the best, and I know I can learn from you."

"You will be. And your parents are proud, I'm sure."

"Yeah. I mean, I'm sure yours are too, about your success."

There was no way I could truthfully answer that, so I just shrugged.

"We're champions. What more could anyone want?"

We skated to the bench for pregame instructions. The Snow Caps were division rivals and always played us hard. This game was no exception, and we ended up with a tie, which always annoyed me, but it wasn't a loss and kept us in second place. On the plane ride home, I wanted to block out the conversations around me, but I'd forgotten to charge my headphones, so I was forced to listen to Rip and Seb gossip.

"Adrian and I are going out with Tag and Sterling tomorrow night. Wanna come with us? You and Jolie can get a sitter."

"Wish I could, but her brother's introducing us to his new girlfriend. I didn't know Sterling and Tag were dating."

The words of the article in front of me blurred as I strained to listen.

"Adrian said Tag asked him if Sterling was seeing anyone. Guess the strong and silent type is having a moment."

I grinned to myself. Sterling wasn't so quiet when I was inside him. Then I remembered how he couldn't wait for me to leave the last time, and my good mood vanished. I closed my eyes to concentrate on listening to Rip and Seb. I had zero fucks to give about eavesdropping.

"Anyway, Adrian said he was surprised Sterling agreed. When Adrian first came to the station, Sterling seemed standoffish, but he's warming up."

"Looks like it." Seb chuckled. "Guess he's making up for slighting hockey players and sports in general. First Denis, now Tag."

"Adrian was never pushing Denis and Sterling. He's still a little upset about some things that happened between Denis and me and has a hard time letting go. He likes Denis, but I don't think he trusts him."

I winced but could hardly blame Adrian. That three-some I'd proposed to Rip would forever haunt me.

Rip accepted a glass of water from the flight attendant. "As much as I care about Denis, I'm not sure he's capable of being with one man for long. And Sterling appears to be a pretty quiet, private guy. Not his usual type. I'm guessing he's not a partier or someone who'd enjoy being one of many. Denis might've tried, but in the end, he's just not the type to settle down."

I supposed I deserved that. Rip had seen me at my worst, and because I respected Sterling's wishes to keep our encounters private, there was little reason for him to think I'd changed.

By the time we landed in New York, my mood had turned black. I picked up my overnight bag and didn't hang around for anyone else—my car was waiting, and I took off for home. In the old days, I might've hit up a club and partied a little, but it was late, and I was exhausted. Once in my apartment, I thought sleep would come easily, but instead, the river view called to me. I sat on my couch and stared at the lights twinkling in the darkness.

My talk with Ellis had unexpectedly reopened the old wounds of my parents' betrayal. My father's whole life revolved around hockey—surely he'd known I'd been out for a month. No one from my family had acknowledged my two Stanley Cups, being named MVP of the series, or my three Vezina trophies.

All because twenty years ago, I'd kissed a boy.

My sleep sucked, and I was up early the following morning, drinking cappuccinos and checking my calendar. Practice in the morning, PT in the afternoon. My evening was empty.

Unlike Sterling, who'd decided I was only good as a fuck-buddy and was busy with a new boy toy. Guess the tables had turned, as I wanted to see him, but he'd obviously moved on.

Fuck that.

Practice was intense as the upcoming game would be a matchup of last year's Cup final. At PT, I pushed myself to where a concerned Hutch took me aside.

"You all right? There's no need to go to where it gets painful."

I swept the sweat-soaked hair off my brow. "I'm feeling good—great, in fact. I want to make sure I can go past the point of no return. Every team is after our asses this year. I need to be better than ever."

"You're at the top of your game. I don't think you need to worry. You're one of the greats, Denis. You've won so many awards. Don't knock yourself out. You've got nothing to prove."

I nodded, but my mind was on what he hadn't said. I had professional success but nothing else in my life. People like Rip and Seb, they'd managed to have it all. They were the best in the game and had someone to share that with. I came home to a world-class view I stared at alone.

Tonight was Sterling and Tag's date. I didn't begrudge Tag his angling for this—if I had a chance to be with Sterling, I'd snap that up in a heartbeat. But that didn't mean I was about to lie down and give it up. I hadn't gotten where I was in life by waiting for others to tell me what to do. I made my own rules.

That was why, at eleven that night, I was at Sterling's apartment building, waiting in the lobby. I'd already greased the wheels by bringing signed jerseys and pucks for the concierge and doorman to let me sit.

What the hell was wrong with me?

Sterling was the first man I was with who didn't care about my fame and actively disliked it. He fought our attraction at every turn and had no issue kicking me out even after sex so intense, I had trouble catching my breath and remembering my own name.

The thought of Sterling bringing another man to his apartment or even kissing him good night was unacceptable to me. This Tag fucker better not make a move, or I'd make sure he was dead to the Blades.

"Denis? What're you doing here?" Brows knitted, Sterling stood in front of me, and I rose to my feet.

"Where's Tag?"

"Why? What business is it of yours?"

I covered his mouth with mine, shoving my tongue past those frowning lips until he sagged in my arms and kissed me back.

"Everything about you is my business. Now, am I coming upstairs or not?"

CHAPTER EIGHTEEN
Sterling

I wanted to be strong.

Really.

But it had been an interminable evening of pretending, and I'd had enough. Tag had told me about how they'd had to cut half of his profile report because he'd talked too much and how he'd loved watching mine. I'd cringed at that. He was a sweet guy—gorgeous, funny, and said all the right things to show he was interested in me. Any man would jump at the chance to be with him.

Any man except me, apparently.

Because for some reason, I was hung up on an egotistical, annoying as fuck, sexy as hell hockey player. Tag had suggested a nightcap but I'd begged off, saying I had to prepare notes for the next day. He'd kissed my cheek and said he understood.

"Maybe another time?"

My smile had been halfhearted at best. "Yeah, sure." I didn't wait for a car, waving good-bye to him and hustling to the train station. It came relatively quickly, and less than half an hour later, I was walking into my lobby to see Denis sitting there. He stood as our eyes met.

"Where's Tag?"

"Why? What business is it of yours?"

Denis's answer was to pull me into his arms and cover my mouth with his. For a moment I thought about resisting, but I lost my ability to think straight when he pushed his tongue into my mouth. My fingers curled, clutching his shirt, holding him close. I tried to keep my brain from scrambling, but that battle was lost.

He ran his nose down my cheek and whispered, "Everything about you is my business. Now, am I coming upstairs or not?"

I wanted to say no. What were we doing here? I had too much to hide, and Denis seemed to be poking his nose where it didn't belong. But dammit, I was tired of being alone and lonely. Tonight had proved that even forcing myself to be with someone else couldn't stop me from thinking of Denis. I didn't answer, but holding on to him, walked to the elevators.

Once up in my apartment, Denis didn't take me to bed. He cupped my cheek in his large palm and kissed me, gentle and sweet. "I wondered if you'd go home with Tag or bring him here."

"What would you have done if I showed up with him?" His warm mouth pressed kisses along my jaw, eyes, and brow, and I wanted to rub on him like a cat marking its territory.

Mine, mine, mine.

"I would've asked you to send him home." He smiled against my lips. "I can be very persuasive."

"I know. But why are you here?" With each passing second it was becoming harder for me to speak. Denis's body heat soaked through me, whipping up an inferno that threatened to explode, and I was seriously doubting my mental state as all I wanted was to get naked in the middle of my living room. "Do you think you can just show up and have sex with me anytime you want?"

Obviously my body thought that was a stupendous idea because I was hard as a rock. Denis rested his hands on my shoulders. "No. Of course not. But you were the one who told me to leave last time. I wanted to talk because we never do."

"Talk about what?" My heart thudded.

"I know nothing about you."

"Didn't you watch the profile about me on the news? You could've found out what you need to know."

His grip tightened. "Is that what you think is right? For me to watch the news to discover who you are? I'm your lover, not a viewer."

"My lover?"

His eyes flashed. "What do you think we're doing here?"

"Having fun?" I shrugged. "It's casual sex. We're not exclusive or a couple."

His fingers bit into my shoulders. "Is that so? Tell me. Why didn't you end up with Tag tonight?"

"Because I don't sleep with every man I have a date with."

"Or maybe he doesn't turn you on like I do. *Hmm, mon cher*? Is that it?" He slid his hands over my throat, coming to rest on my chest.

That sexy accent was going to be my undoing. That, and his touch, his smell. *Fuck.* Everything about this man turned me on.

Denis kissed my neck at the point where it met my shoulder, and I couldn't stop my fingers from sliding through his hair to anchor him in place. I'd give anything to be able to stop time and keep this moment locked away forever.

"You don't want to feel this way, but you can't help it, can you?" He sucked my earlobe into his mouth, and I moaned, swaying toward him. "You don't want to want me, but you do. Say it. Tell me you want me."

I stayed silent, but it didn't matter. The rapid pump of my heart gave it all away.

He chuckled, low and deep, and rocked his hips against mine. "I'll say it first because I have no shame. I want you more than anything. I have to have you. All of you."

"Denis," I whispered.

His fingers made quick work of my belt and zipper, and he sank to his knees, taking my clothes with him.

"Plain white? You didn't wear that sexy black underwear for him. Good. Because it's only for me." The tip of his tongue traced the head of my cock and licked the slit. "This is mine too. No one else gets to touch you."

I hissed when his hot mouth sucked me fully and his tongue swirled up and down my aching shaft. "Please," I begged, my hips pumping. "Please."

He clutched my ass, his lips wreaking havoc on my rock-hard length, and I tangled my fingers in his hair and came so violently, I lost my footing and stumbled into his arms.

"It's okay," he crooned, holding me tight. "It's going to be okay. I've got you."

His lips met mine, and I tasted my bitterness. He stroked me, and I waited until the fog cleared from my mind to speak.

"I've never been with anyone I've wanted to see more than once. Except you. And I don't know why or what to do or say..." I hung my head, but he tipped my chin up with those long fingers. I gazed into his solemn face.

"Sometimes we don't need words to speak what's in our hearts."

My lips quirked in a smile. "That's very profound."

His eyes danced. "I can be deep." He kissed me. "And I feel the same. No one has intrigued me as much as you. I find everything about you fascinating. I want to know more. Teach me about you."

"There isn't much to tell."

His brow furrowed. "Why are you holding back?" He smoothed the sweat-dampened hair off my brow. "I know there's some connection between you and Dahlia Dumont. You look so much like her. Your eyes and the shape of your face." I stiffened and tried to pull away, but he held on to me. "Don't run away from me, please. I won't tell anyone. Are you related? What hold does she have over you?"

"None," I said, but couldn't face him. "It's nothing."

"What are you hiding?" His eyes widened. "You're her son. That's it, isn't it?"

"I didn't say that. And you should leave."

Of course he ignored me. "Why would you need to hide that she had a child?"

"Not America's Sweetheart," I burst out. "She got her start in Hollywood playing the young, beautiful, virginal teenager, then the woman every man wanted as their wife. No room for the bastard child she had at fifteen." My ugly past, hidden for so long, spilled out. "I would've ruined everything. My whole existence was wiped out and recreated for her benefit."

Denis gathered me to his chest, and my arms naturally came around his waist. How long had it been since someone had held me?

Forever.

I pushed away from him and fixed my clothes. "I shouldn't have said anything."

"Why? It all makes sense now."

"Because I'm not allowed to speak about it. It was part of the agreement we worked out."

Sympathy clouded his face. "Agreement? Like a settlement?"

"Yes. Can we sit? It's a long story."

At this point it made no difference if I told him everything. I finished my story, he sat for a long time without saying a word. After so many years of silence, releasing the weight of my secret was like a rebirth of sorts.

"You did the best you could, being alone in the world from when you were a child. It's not easy to make it, but you did."

My smile was wry. "The millions of dollars paved the way."

"She didn't get you your jobs at news stations, did she?" Denis frowned, and I shook my head.

"No. I started out doing radio news at school, then working in local stations until I graduated and applied for reporter positions. I worked my ass off—first as a stand-in for late-night reporters, weekend anchors, and the morning news. I finally got my chance at prime time five years ago."

Denis played with the ends of my hair. "But you moved here. Why?"

I nibbled on my lip. "Funny enough, Dahlia was promoting her makeup line, and someone from my station commented that I looked like her. I brushed it off but freaked and decided to move as far away as possible. Hence, New York City."

"Wouldn't it be better if you weren't the face of the news?" he asked, and it was a fair question.

"Yes, but I'm not going to be a national anchor. I've chosen to never push for that, even though it was once a dream of mine."

Surprising me, Denis grasped my arms and came nose-to-nose. "You should absolutely go for it. What your mother did to you was horrible, and you owe her nothing. Why should you lose your dream so she can live hers?"

"She gave me life when she could've ended it. And she did take me with her."

"I can't figure that out."

"Neither can I. A shred of decency knowing what would be in store for me? Perhaps. But she did, and for that I have to give her credit." I shuddered, imagining a life so restrictive and wondering how gay Amish teens survived. If they did. Maybe that was a story that needed telling. "And there's our agreement."

"I'm certain if you show it to your attorney, they'd agree with me."

Ashamed, I couldn't face him. "I've never let anyone see it. It's in my safe-deposit box at the bank."

"*Merde*," he cursed under his breath. "And you say hockey players are stupid. You have a lawyer, I'm sure. If you want someone very discreet, I can recommend mine. He handles many pro athletes and celebrities."

"Maybe...I don't know..." I sounded as weak as I felt. Like a child who'd lost their way home and didn't know which street to take.

This night was full of surprises as again, Denis drew me close. "You're afraid, I can see. And I understand. Your whole life you've lived as someone else wanted. And you don't have to expose Dahlia if you choose not to. Although you owe her nothing at this point, in my opinion. But I hate to see you give up on your dream."

"It wasn't one I actively pursued. But my agent has been approached by several cable networks, which could be a way for me to get my foot in the door."

"Maybe try that and see? You are lucky in that respect. When a team wants to trade you, there's no asking. They just do it, and you're like a chess piece—swept off one side of the board and taken to the other."

I sensed bitterness, and because I'd had enough talking about myself and my issues, was ready for Denis to take center stage. Or ice in his case.

"Do you worry about being traded? Don't they have to ask you first?"

His chuckle rumbled through his broad chest, and I had to admit it was nice lying with him in the semidarkness, simply talking.

"Si *seulement*." He sighed, and I nudged his cheek with my nose.

"Translate, please. I only took high school Spanish," I said with a smile.

"It means 'if only.' And I'll teach you some French, *mon cœur*." He nuzzled my neck. "As for the game? The teams can trade us when they no longer want us. Meaning, if we get too old, too slow, or someone better comes along."

Sadness hung over his words. I never realized how terrible it must be to give your whole life to a team only for them to replace you once they deemed you expendable.

"I'm sure the Blades wouldn't do that to you. Not after how well you've played these past years."

His huff left no doubt he disagreed.

"Well, I think they'd be fools to consider it, and I doubt you have anything to worry about."

"I always worry. Getting injured means vulnerability."

"Even you?"

He stared off into nothingness. "Even me. No one is irreplaceable."

I put a tentative hand on his shoulder. "Are you actually concerned? You're the best goalie in the league."

"A compliment? Did I hear correctly?"

My cheeks warmed. "I'm repeating a statistic Tag told me."

"Don't mention him." A growl escaped Denis's lips. I never imagined I'd find the caveman thing sexy, but I kind of liked it.

"I might've watched a few games."

A brow arched high. "You've been following the Blades, *mon cher*? Or me?" His lips curved in that wicked grin that never failed to make my bones weak. "Does that mean you maybe like me? *Un petit peu*? That means 'a little,' in case you didn't know."

"Maybe a little," I conceded, and he pressed a warm kiss to my lips.

"*Hmm*. How can I convince you to make it more?"

I gazed into his hard face and met those glittering eyes, like bright chips of onyx.

How had we come to this point where I was revealing life-long secrets to a man I once couldn't stand to be in the same room with?

"You know my secrets. Tell me yours."

CHAPTER NINETEEN
Denis

This wasn't going as planned. I was shocked by Sterling's secret—it was much worse than I'd imagined, and I could understand how it still haunted him. For all the things my parents had done to me, at least for the first sixteen years of my life I'd known their love.

But now he wanted the very part of me I'd worked so hard to hide. Something no one but Gil knew. Not even Rip or Gordie. And if I chose to say nothing or brushed it off, Sterling would walk me to the door and slam it in my face, ending this tentative peace between us, and I couldn't let that happen. He'd find someone else, and I'd have to hear about his dates and run into them at Rip's house, where that nameless, faceless man would touch and kiss him. My stomach turned to knots at the very thought.

Sterling deserved my truth, if only because he'd given me that piece of himself he'd never shared before. Something deeply powerful to his soul. I knew I'd treasure not only what he revealed, but the fact that he'd chosen me, unwittingly, as a kindred spirit. A child who understood betrayal so visceral and permanent, it was burned in my veins.

If holding on to my past meant letting go of Sterling, the choice was clear.

"I had a wonderful childhood. Small town in Quebec, which meant hockey all the time. My father and uncle...we were always together. And when I showed hockey promise as a child, I was their hope. Their chance to have a pro in the family, playing in the league."

"Was it your dream or theirs?"

"Both," I admitted. "Here your sports icons are baseball or football players. In Canada, it's hockey. It's every boy's dream."

"I get it. Go on."

"I was in a junior league, and so was my neighbor, Georges. I was in school with his sister, and everyone believed we were boyfriend and girlfriend. But it wasn't Thérèse I wanted."

"You had a crush on Georges."

No matter that it happened twenty years earlier, it might've been yesterday the way my emotions roared to the surface. "I did. I was hopelessly in love with him. Georges was older and on his way to the NHL. So when he invited me one afternoon to skate, I was overjoyed. Excited."

Sterling remained silent, but his hand circled my nape, and now it was him offering a soothing touch. I leaned into it.

"It was after...he said he wanted to show me all the trophies in his room. He was leaving soon, and I jumped at the chance. No one was home, and we were upstairs in his room...he kissed me. I couldn't believe it happened. Then he touched me, and after I got off—embarrassingly quickly—he said he'd teach me how to suck him, since I'd never done it. He said he'd do m-me." My voice caught, and a rush of tears burned my eyes. Horrified, I pinched my eyes together.

Sterling kissed my cheek. "It's okay. Don't worry. I'm here."

I sniffled. "I was on my knees and his mother walked in. Georges told her I came on to him, called me a filthy pervert. They screamed at me to get out of their house. That night at home..." Again, I had to pause. "My father was always thinking of hockey. He wouldn't physically touch me because he might hurt me and that would ruin my chances to play."

"Small comfort," Sterling muttered.

"That entire night he got in my face, screaming about what a filthy animal I was. A disgrace, a molester...the usual hateful comments. No son of his would be a man-fucker, as he called it."

"Where was your mother?"

I choked out a laugh. "She ran to the church to pray for my soul. Guess her plan failed."

"Did...did they hurt you?"

"Only my heart...to think they were my parents and yet could turn against me because of who I want to love."

"What happened after?"

"For the next six months, every night they locked me at home after hockey practice and subjected me to my father's rants and my mother's praying. I was told I was a disappointment as a son and worth nothing other than playing hockey."

"They wanted to punish the gay out of you?"

I nodded. "And they tried very hard. It got so bad that it began to affect my play. In Canada we have a major junior league, where we get drafted from, and it didn't take long before my coaches noticed I was off my game." Bittersweet memories flooded my mind.

"What is it?" Sterling asked, and I put my arm around him. "Why are you smiling?"

"My coach, Gil Girard. The man was—still is—a legend in the game, and you knew if you were lucky enough to skate for him, you had the best. Anyway, he was the only one I confided in as to what was going on at home. The next day, he came to my parents' house, sat them down, and told them I was leaving and moving in with him and his wife. I'd finish off the school year living with them and until I was drafted. And unless they changed their attitude, they were banned from seeing me and coming to my games."

"And they agreed?" Sterling sounded aghast. "They were willing to let you go? All because of hockey?"

I lifted a shoulder. "I told you. Hockey is king. They gave me up so they'd get to brag I played in the league. Gil and Mary, his wife, saved me."

He rubbed my back. "It was a good thing Gil did, to get you out of that atmosphere. It must've been intolerable living at home."

I rested my head in my hands. "I was going to run away. Or kill myself. I didn't know what else to do. I couldn't take it anymore. You can't imagine how awful it was to live with someone constantly telling you you're abnormal, sick. A freak. That no one will ever love you and you'll be alone forever. Gil and Mary saved my life."

Sterling pressed his wet cheek to mine. "Thank God you had them. Do you still keep in touch with them?"

"Mary died about eight years ago. Gil has coached many players, but I'm the only one still active, and I wanted him to come live in New York when I got traded here. At first he refused, saying he didn't want to leave Mary, but he finally relented and moved into an assisted-living facility in Westchester." I laughed at the memory. "He refused to live in a big city, so we compromised."

My parents' daily torment had taught me to never let them see you cry or fall apart. Losing control of your emotions meant weakness. And the one way I'd learned to survive before Gil rescued me was to remain stoic and unbending. But at some point the weight becomes too heavy and you break.

Telling my story was my breaking point, and I let Sterling comfort and hold me. After several minutes, his lips brushed my hair.

"And what about your parents? Have you had any contact with them?"

"No. And I have no desire to, ever again. They know where I am, and in all these years, they've made no attempt to contact me. As far as I'm concerned, they're dead."

A shiver ran through Sterling, and something occurred to me.

"You've only talked about Dahlia. What about your father? Did you ever try and contact him?"

"I found out he spent four years in jail for statutory rape since my mother was only fifteen and he was twenty-seven. I heard that Dahlia's brothers and some of the other men in the community roughed him up, and when the police came, he admitted to having sex with Dahlia, so they arrested him. He's married now, with a family of his own. I doubt he'd be too thrilled to have me pop up on his doorstep, claiming him as my father." Sterling's cheek rested on mine. "I'm better off letting things stay as they are."

Ours were two of the many sad stories out in the world. Sterling and I were each lucky to have escaped a life that could have ended up very badly.

"I wouldn't mind you popping up on my doorstep," I teased, hoping to break the somber mood. "Or anywhere else."

A tiny smile kicked up the corner of his lips. "Is that so?" His hand cupped my stiffening cock. "I think it's you who's popping up."

"I can't help it. Whenever you're near, I get hard."

Wicked fingers traced the outline of my erection, and my breath grew short.

"Guess I'd better not come to any of your games. Wouldn't want you to walk around with this monster trapped in a jock."

Hearing Sterling, who'd always spoken so proper, call my dick a monster had me busting out laughing. "A monster? Are you calling it ugly?"

"No." More solemn than ever, he ghosted his fingertips over my jaw, cheeks, and eyes. "Everything about you is perfect," he whispered. "Even the scars from your fights on the ice. And the ones on your heart, now that I know what happened." He ran his hands through my hair, tangling them, holding my face, and gazing into my eyes. "Thank you for trusting me with your story. I know it couldn't have been easy to share."

"I've never told anyone the whole truth. Only you."

A siren sounded outside, then several police cars followed, but nothing could drown out the thundering of my heart.

"Why me?" he asked.

"I don't know." But maybe I did and was too afraid to admit it. "You asked, and initially I thought I'd give you the same story as always. Instead, I wanted you to know everything. The real me, not the guy you see on the ice."

"He's pretty amazing."

"So are you. I think we've come a long way since you called me an uneducated hulk."

He grinned. "Not you personally. And you've taught me some things."

"Like what?"

"How to take a chance. Let down my guard and not be so judgmental. Go after what I want…"

The air grew thick with tension. "What do you want, Sterling?"

His fingers tightened in my hair. "You. I want you."

I captured his mouth. "*Mon cœur, mon amour.* You have me."

The time for talking had ended. I needed him with a frightening intensity. We rose to our feet, still kissing, and made it to his bedroom, where we stripped out of our clothes and fell on the bed naked, hot and hard.

"Denis," he moaned. "I need you."

Pain grew in my chest—no one had ever said that to me. Plenty of men had said they'd wanted me, and a few had even said they'd loved me, and I'd accepted it and even repeated it, but something had always been missing. Now I knew. There'd never been this fierce, overwhelming desire to protect and claim a person and never, ever let anything or anyone hurt them. The mere thought of Sterling with anyone else set my blood boiling in my veins. No one could touch him. Ever. He was mine.

"Take me. You have every piece of me, including my heart." I rolled him under me and kissed him until we both gasped for air. "I need you. I want you. I have to have you. All of you. Your body. Your heart. Tell me. Tell me you want the same thing."

His eyes widened with shock. "What are you saying?"

Nose-to-nose, I pinned him to the bed. My cock was hard to the point of bursting, but this went beyond the physical release. This was an emotional mountain I'd scaled alone, but now at the pinnacle I'd found the person to share this moment of glory with, and everything else beyond.

"I'm in love with you. I can't sleep at night because I'm wondering where you are and who you're with. I want you by my side for my wins and losses. When they see your face, they need to know you're the one who's taken my heart prisoner and I've gladly thrown away the key." My chest rose and fell rapidly from my unexpected outburst, and I waited for his response.

"Tonight, when I agreed to go out with Tag, it wasn't because I wanted to spend time with him. I accepted, thinking if I could see other men, I might find someone to drive me out of my mind. There had to be another man whose kisses would drive me wild. Who frustrates me no end, yet is the only one who makes me laugh. But it didn't work. No matter how hard he tried, he wasn't you." His eyes shone in the pale moonlight illuminating the room.

"I have been called one of a kind," I teased, so full of love and hope that my head spun.

"You are. You're *my* one. Only months ago, I couldn't bear to look at you, but now?" His smile turned tender. "Now I can't bear the thought of never seeing you again. Is that love? I want to believe it is, but how can I be sure? I've never known what it means to be loved."

"You've come to the right place. It will be my mission to make sure you know what love is. Because being loved by me is like nothing else in the world." I kissed him and pulled him on top of me, then grabbed the bottle of lube I'd spotted on the nightstand and held it up with a grin. "Did you use this and think of me?"

This adorable man, so strong and determined in his everyday life, ducked his head and nodded. I coated my fingers and slid them down his cleft to play with his rim. His beautiful dick stood up between us, firm and glistening.

"Touch yourself," I demanded, and he bit his lip and ran his palm along his shaft, pumping fast. His head fell back, and I pulled him up by the waist to slip two fingers inside him.

"Oh, fuck me, Denis," he groaned, and I sped up my movements, pressing against the hot walls of his ass. "More," he whimpered. "It's not enough."

I withdrew and pawed at the drawer to open it, found a condom, and rolled it on. "Jesus," I hissed, almost coming from one touch.

"Don't you dare," Sterling ordered and squeezed me at the root. He rose on his knees, and with a blissful sigh, lowered himself onto my throbbing cock. "Oh God, you're splitting me in half."

"You kept me and my monster waiting." My fingers gripped his pale skin as I thrust up. "It's the price you pay."

"Take...all...my...money." He rode me hard, his hand flashing on his dick. I rolled my hips and spared him no mercy, holding him as I drove up deep. "Oh my God," he cried out and came, splattering over my chest and his, even hitting my chin and nose.

"You're perfect," I panted, hammering him hard through his climax. He lay on top of me, twitching and boneless, yet with enough strength to squeeze my dick in his passage. I wrapped my arms around him, thrusting several more times. My climax hit and I broke apart and came, my body flushed with heat.

"So are you," he murmured a while later and kissed my neck. "Except I don't think I can walk." He winced, and I slipped out of him, still half-hard. "Or move."

"You have all night to recover. And I don't have a game until Saturday."

"So it's all about you, *hmm*?"

I threw away the condom and returned to the bed. I held him and tangled my feet with his. "Not anymore. It's all about us."

CHAPTER TWENTY
Sterling

I woke up before Denis and stretched, wincing with each move. Bruises littered the lower half of my body, which I didn't have to worry about as they could be hidden. If I had to admit, I kind of liked them. If I thought to question whether Denis and I were sexually compatible, I only had to touch the fingertip marks on my hips where he'd held me down as he drove in deep, all the while whispering in my ear in that sexy accent that drove me wild. I'd had sex, but Denis gave me the passion, lust, and desire I'd been missing to understand why wars had been fought and lives lost for love.

In the bathroom, I peered in the mirror and grimaced. Bite marks scored an angry red on my neck, and I knew it would take time and effort to hide them. I couldn't walk into the office like this. I sighed and stepped into the shower.

Once out and dried, I began my daily regime of skin care and was halfway through when Denis came in. Bleary-eyed, he barely gave me a glance, but after he finished, he stopped to kiss my shoulder, then paused. In the reflection, I watched his jaw drop.

"*Mère de Dieu*. What in the name of all that is holy is this crap?" He reached out to pick up my Vitamin C serum and my squalene-and-peptides lotion. His eyes narrowed as he read the bottle. "What are you doing with this stuff?"

I finished dabbing serum on my neck, and with my jaw set, folded my arms. "Unlike you, whose career is solely based on physical strength, speed, and athleticism, being on camera means not only do I have to read the news properly, but I have to look a certain way."

"Like how? A greased-up bobblehead? Ow!" He rubbed the spot where I whacked him.

"I'm forty years old. I have to be on the lookout for someone younger coming in and taking my place."

Denis shook his head, that thick mane of hair falling in front of his face. "*Non, non, et non*. You are gorgeous as is. You don't need to look like one of those plastic-faced people." He tucked the tangled strands behind his ear. "Please tell me you haven't had any of those ridiculous surgeries." Long, rough fingers skimmed along my cheeks. "Promise me you won't touch these." He kissed my eyes and fluttering lashes. "A life well lived and loved should be celebrated, not erased."

Embarrassed, I patted at the cream he'd smeared. "You don't understand. It's a competition. Like you said, the players under you might be faster and stronger and you worry. It's the same for me."

"But people don't want silly young faces reading them the terrible news of the day. They want a person they can relate to. Someone who sounds and looks empathetic, warm, and knowledgeable."

Denis's adamance surprised me. "You're really upset about this." I screwed the top on the jar of my stupid-expensive wrinkle cream and hoped he didn't open the linen closet where I stored my red-light mask.

"I am. Very. Do you think we don't grow old and wear the scars of our wins and losses on our faces? There's beauty in those lines. I think you fell for all that bullshit in Hollywood, where someone's looks mean more than who they are." He tapped his chest. "In here."

I smiled. "You're a romantic."

"I am French Canadian," he stated as if that explained everything. "We worship love and hockey."

"I want what you said. To be the face people trust and will turn to in a crisis. Growing up, I only knew what I lived with, which was youth and beauty and excess. My mother made her name in the movies not only for her acting ability, but for her beauty and youthful appearance. She amassed her fortune by selling that dream to everyone. I guess I'm as foolish as anyone for falling for it."

He pulled me into his chest. "You're not foolish. But now you have me, to tell you what's real."

I shook with laughter. "Says the man with the massive ego."

He cupped my ass and rubbed up against me. "My ego isn't the only thing that's massive. I want you," he growled, and I nearly swooned at his possessiveness. "You're going to be away until late, and you'll need to remember who and what you have waiting for you."

"I can hardly forget, considering I can barely walk straight. And you can wipe that smug look off your face."

"Who, me?" He snickered, and I wanted to smack him again, but he pulled my towel off and put his hands on me, and I lost my ability to think. "I wish I could keep you like this all day," he whispered in my ear, and his touch had me quivering and ready to do whatever he wanted. "Naked and so close to the edge."

Oh God, he's going to be the death of me.

"I should be doing yoga right now." I sighed as he backed me out of the bathroom toward the bed.

"You can downward dog on me."

I was almost late for work. Denis had lain in my bed, looking way too good for the morning. Who knew I had a thing for long, messy hair and eyes so large and dark, they appeared to hold the secrets of the universe in their depths?

"This is all your fault," I grumbled, slinging a tie around my neck. "Now I won't have time to fix those marks on my neck. I'll have to do it in the office."

"*Désolé, mon cœur.*" Denis's grin negated his words. I wanted to be annoyed with him, but with my body still recovering from his lips and tongue, he'd rightfully call me out as a liar.

And God help me, but I loved every damn second of it.

In my office, I carefully applied the skin-tone cream, making sure I put a napkin between my shirt and skin to not have it bleed all over my collar. I thought I'd done a decent job, and I knew Patty in makeup would touch it up before we went on air. Someone knocked, and I swept the mess on my desk into the drawer and whisked the napkin off my neck.

"Come in."

The door opened, and Tag stuck his head in, that perennial smile beaming from his handsome face. "Hey. How are you this morning?"

I felt bad for brushing him off, but after the emotional night I'd had with Denis, there had been no doubt I was with whom I was meant to be.

"I'm good, thanks. How about you?"

"Just wanted to check in and make sure you got home all right. I texted you, but you didn't answer."

I winced. "Sorry. I, uh, got caught up in stuff when I got home."

"Can I come in?"

"Yes, sure." I beckoned to him. "I didn't mean to make you wait at the door."

He took a seat at the conference table by the window overlooking Midtown. The view was a sign of my status as news anchor. I joined him and waited with clasped hands for him to speak.

"Did I do something wrong?" Tag asked. "Last night, I mean."

Shit. I should've known he'd want to talk about it.

"No, of course not. I had a nice time."

He grimaced. "Ouch. Nice is the kiss of death on a date. I was hoping you'd felt something. Like I did."

Fuck. This was one of the reasons I'd shied away from relationships. All this messy personal stuff. Then I remembered holding Denis, feeling him trembling in my arms as he recounted the story of his parents' behavior, and I knew I'd do everything in my power to help him become whole again.

"You're a great guy, Tag. And I enjoyed myself, but…to be honest, no. I didn't."

"Is there another guy?"

Damn, he was pushy.

I met his frank question with my chin up and no regrets. "Yes. There is. But I don't discuss my personal life. You and I had a nice time at dinner, but I'd like to keep it as friends. If you can't, I guess there's nothing more to say."

For the first time since I'd known him, Tag frowned. "I'm fine with being friends, but for me that goes beyond a casual hi and good morning. If you don't want that, I'll stay out of your way." Without waiting for my answer, he left and closed the door behind him.

I cast my eyes up at the ceiling. "This is why I shouldn't get involved with people." As if to taunt me, there was another knock at my door. I counted to three before I answered.

"Come."

This time Adrian's blond head popped in. "May I come in?"

"Be my guest. Not like I'm getting anything done this morning."

I was prepared to argue with him about me and Tag, but Adrian surprised me. "I know we have the end-of-week meeting soon, but I wanted you to know that I spoke to an informant and he said one of his buddies saw the mayor in Jersey last weekend, coming in and out of a house. When I ran the address, it came up registered to an Angela Barnetti."

My jaw dropped. "As in the Barnetti crime family? Angela is the daughter of the boss. Damn. I don't know which is a bigger scandal—the mayor not living in the city, or him being involved with a mob boss's daughter."

"I know, I know," Adrian agreed, his head bobbing up and down with excitement. "He wants to talk, but only to you."

My pulse spiked, and I remembered Denis urging me to go for my dream and push to report on the national news. Surely this story would make the cut.

"Good. Arrange it. Today, even. We can meet him for lunch anywhere he wants."

"Great. I'll set it up."

When he didn't leave, I knew what was coming. "Anything else? I need to read through the morning reports."

"Well, uh, yeah. How was the rest of your evening with Tag? He's such a nice guy, and I know he really likes you—"

I put a hand up. "Adrian. I think maybe because I came to your wedding and your home a few times, you believe it means I'm going to spill my heart out to you. But I'm not that kind of person."

His face fell. "Oh. I thought we were becoming friends. But I get it. No worries. We can keep it strictly business." He rose from his seat.

Dammit. I didn't want to hurt Adrian's feelings. He was being nice and only trying to help me. I had to take a leap of faith and start letting people in because the loner thing hadn't worked too well for me. Adrian had been the first to crack open the door—and then Denis had barreled right through and taken what he wanted.

I waved for him to sit again. "No, please listen. I've never been the type to open up to people. But you're right. We *are* beginning to be friends, and I'd like it to continue."

Adrian's face shone with happiness. "I'm glad. Because Rip and I enjoyed having you and Tag over for dinner. I thought the two of you were getting along?"

He waited expectantly, but this was a tricky situation. Denis and Rip had been together for years, and Denis's cheating had resulted in a public, ugly breakup. On the surface now, they seemed fine, but was that reality or only for the game?

"We did. He's a nice guy."

Adrian's smile faded. "Okay, I know what that means. Nice isn't what someone wants to hear on a date."

I chuckled. "I wouldn't say that. You're a nice guy, and Rip adores you."

His cheeks pinked. "Well, yeah, but it was hard work to get him to see past that facade."

"So you're not really nice?" I joked. "But you know what I mean. There has to be a something there. And Tag and I don't have it."

"I'm sorry." Adrian looked crestfallen, which led me to the decision to tell him the truth.

"It's okay. I...I've kind of been seeing someone else."

Immediately, he brightened. "You have? That's great. Why didn't you say something? I wouldn't have tried to set you up with Tag." He waited. "So...? Anyone I know?"

For the first time I felt unsure and younger than my forty years. I'd interviewed senators and governors, yet talking about my personal life made my skin crawl with embarrassment. Like I was undressing in the locker room before gym class in front of the jocks, and they were laughing at my less than muscular body. But Adrian deserved to know because if my being involved with Denis would cause a problem, we'd need to find a solution.

"Yes. It's Denis." I waited for his reaction.

"Oh." He blinked. "That's...unexpected. I didn't know you were that friendly. You might've thought I'd been trying to push you two together, but I wasn't."

"I recall you telling me you didn't think it was a good idea, but I didn't pay much attention because at that point we weren't even friends." No need to reveal how close we'd become.

"Right. I figured it was for the best. You're...uh...very different."

"I'm aware. But you seem uncomfortable with what I told you. Is it because he and Rip were once together?"

Adrian nibbled on his lip. "No. We're well past that now."

My head began to throb with all of Adrian's verbal gymnastics. "You're not a politician, Adrian. You can tell me the truth and leave out the word salad. Reporters give facts, not opinions or personal beliefs."

"I'm sorry. It's just that Denis can charm a peanut out of its shell. I don't know how much of it is real or just show for that playboy image he likes to project, but..."

"What is it?" I grew impatient. "Spit it out already."

Adrian was as stubborn as he was sweet, and he ignored that, forging on. "I'm not telling you this because Denis cheated on Rip. You know that. There isn't bad blood anymore between them. Both of them now realize they never loved each other and they're better off as friends."

"Adrian..." I warned.

His blush deepened, and he huffed. "Okay, so. When Rip and I were dating and Denis was still engaged, he proposed a threesome to Rip—him, Gordie, and Rip. I never said anything before because you two kept arguing all the time and I didn't think you'd ever hook up. But now you have, and I think you deserve to know the whole story. I don't know if I could ever fully trust Denis."

That startling information sent shockwaves through me, and I didn't bother to explain that I didn't "hook up." Was this something I had to look forward to? Denis had been so possessive. So insistent that it was only the two of us and he wanted me and only me. Sharing didn't seem to be in his makeup. "I...see. Thank you for letting me know."

"I hope I didn't upset you. But as your friend..." He trailed off, eyes anxious, a worried crease to his brow.

"I appreciate it. It's time for the meeting. We'd better get going."

All through the morning, my focus was only half on the news of the day. Had I made a mistake and gotten in over my head with a man ruled by his hormones and who only gave a damn about sex? Was Denis exactly whom I initially thought him to be?

CHAPTER TWENTY-ONE
Denis

"Hey, Denis. How's it going? How was your night?" Rip was sitting on the bench, strapping on his pads.

I pulled my jersey over my head and secured my hair in a tight bun. "Pretty damn good. And yours?"

"We had Tag and Sterling for dinner."

"Oh? How'd that go?" I buckled on my chest protector. "Tag's very...cheerful." The look Rip gave me told me all I needed to know, and I suppressed a smile. "The man is on a perpetual high. Always in a good mood."

"God, I hate those kinds of people," Rip groused.

We snickered, and a warm feeling settled in my chest. I sat beside Rip and nudged his shoulder. "It's good, you know. You and me, I mean. I'm very happy you didn't hold my bad behavior against me and we're now friends."

Rip's eyes softened, the lines around them more pronounced than when we first met. Then again, I wasn't a young stud any longer either.

"I'm glad too. People make mistakes, but they deserve a second chance. I learned that with my father."

"Sometimes they do, *mon ami*. But there are some mistakes one can't forget or forgive. They create scars that never heal."

Solemn-faced, Rip stopped putting on his equipment and set it between us on the bench. "Is that what happened with you and your family? I know there must be reasons why you never mention them. The only one you keep in contact with is your old coach, Gil."

My lips formed a brittle smile ready to crack at any moment. "As far as I'm concerned, I have no family."

The rest of the team walked by us, getting ready for practice, their voices rising and falling as they put on their equipment. Music played in the background, but Rip and I remained oblivious, and he reached out and squeezed my wrist.

"How come we never talked like this when we were together?" he asked, and I patted his cheek.

"I don't know. You never told me about your father either. Neither of us was forthcoming. We shared a bed, but that was all. Eventually, it wasn't enough."

"Our timing was wrong," Rip said, rueful but quiet.

"Perhaps," I conceded. "Or maybe...I didn't know who I was yet to admit I wasn't ready to be with one person. I'm just sorry to have hurt you in the process."

"It takes courage to say that." Rip tilted his head and regarded me with thoughtful eyes. "You've changed recently. You're more self-aware. A little more humble."

"Don't make me out to be a paragon, *mon ami*." I snickered. "I'm still the best in the league. And faster than you on the ice."

"The hell you say, you bastard. Them's fightin' words."

We finished suiting up, and Ellis and I took to the net, taking one-on-ones and pile-ups in front. We practiced with the whole team, and afterward had lunch and watched films of the Drifts. Coach went over the plays for the upcoming game, stressing where we were weak and the Drifts liked to come for us.

I hit the gym for a hard workout followed by PT. Hutch checked me out, prodding my groin area and ribs.

"No pain or stiffness?"

I winked. "Only when it counts."

Hutch rolled his eyes. "You're a real comedian, Denis. Do us all a favor and stick to your real job, just sayin'."

"Hey. Use it or lose it."

"Say that to my wife's face," Hutch teased.

"No way. She'd cook my balls for dinner. How is Carole?"

"She's great. Sends her love. My little boy, Michael, says he wants to be a goalie like you."

"Not a *docteur* like his *papa*?"

Laughing, Hutch shook his head. "Nope. He wants a goalie stick for Christmas, and we've promised to send him to hockey camp. He's pretty fast already and is doing great in the Hockey Tots League. He's ready to move up now."

"I'd better get ready. He's coming for me. Next time you bring him to the game, make sure you come see me, and I'll have something special for him."

"Thanks, I will." He collected his instruments. "I'd keep the compression shorts on for at least another month, and make sure you continue with the PT. You're doing great."

"Thanks. See you tomorrow."

Late in the day, I left the arena for home, and where I'd once hit up the clubs, now all I wanted was a nap.

"Maybe you are an old man after all," I muttered and climbed into my car. Downtown Brooklyn traffic was its predictable snarl of pedestrians, cars, and buses, and the ten-minute drive turned into twenty-five before I walked through my front door. "Damn, next time I should walk."

I called in for dinner and ate without tasting. Alone, it didn't matter much what was on my plate. I used food for fuel and nothing more. To properly share a meal, I'd wait for the weekend–Saturday night after the game, to be exact–to sit across the table from Sterling.

Between my injury and spending time with Sterling, I'd neglected checking in on Gil. The years of playing hockey had wrecked his knees and hips to the point where arthritis had made it too painful for him to walk. No operations had helped him, and he was mostly confined to a wheelchair now. On the days I visited, I took him for walks to the pretty lake on the premises.

I stretched out on the couch for a nice chat. "Gil? *C'est moi, Denis. Comment ça va?* How is it going?"

"*Bien, bien.* So good to hear your voice, *mon fils.* I've been watching your play since your injury. It's all good now, eh?"

"Yes. *Tout va bien.* I'm sorry I haven't called in a while." In the off-season I drove up to see him every week. Arthritis had taken away his mobility, but his mind remained sharp, and he had his cronies with whom he could play cards and talk hockey.

"You're a busy man–road trips and television. A superstar."

It was one thing to boast among your peers, but hearing Gil say the words made me cringe. "Not quite, but I'm happy with how we're playing. I think with this next stretch, we can regain first place."

"I think so too. Although those pesky Drifts have been your nemesis, *pas vrai?*" He chuckled, and I joined in.

"You are correct. They love to play the spoiler. Time to teach them a lesson once and for all."

"That's the spirit. I have to say, I'm very impressed with how quickly you came back from your injury. I'm glad you listened to your doctors."

"Someone once told me to play hockey, not the hero. A very wise man, in fact." We shared a laugh. "Now enough about me. How are you feeling? I'm sure you're taking your own advice and doing what your therapists tell you to."

"Bah. I'm an old man. They should let me live out my days in peace."

My heart squeezed. "You have many years ahead of you. Plus, I need you around for when we win our third Cup in a row. I expect you to be in the stands." He stayed silent for so long, I thought we'd gotten disconnected. "Gil? *Es-tu là?*"

He grunted. "I debated whether to tell you or not, but you should know. Your parents...they called me after your injury."

My voice stayed steady even as my stomach cramped. "Did they? How did they find you?"

"*C'est pas pertinent.* They asked what I knew and if I'd spoken to you. How you were recovering."

"And you said what?" I tried to remain nonchalant, but it was hard to catch my breath.

"I told them they should call you if they wanted the answer."

"I received no calls. So they weren't too concerned." I found myself unable to sit still, and started pacing.

"They obviously watch your games."

I choked on the bitterness of my laughter. "How nice for them. They can brag about their son the hockey player out of one side of their mouth, while telling me I will burn in hell from the other side." I stopped in front of the window and placed my forehead against the cool windowpane.

"Twenty years, Gil. Twenty years of silence. Am I supposed to care that they called?"

A sigh filled my ear. "*C'est affreux de détester tes parents, mon fils.* But it was a terrible thing you endured, and I understand."

"I'm not sure you do. I held back from telling you the worst of the abuse–the constant slurs, how week after week they forced me to sit and read from the Bible well past midnight until my eyes burned from lack of sleep. My father would sit face-to-face with me and say I was going to burn in hell. That I was dirty, wrong, a disgrace. And *Maman*, she let it happen. She'd sit and pray on the rosary all night long. You saved my life, Gil. You and Mary were more parents to me than my own flesh and blood. They didn't ask me for my side of what happened in Georges's bedroom. They believed him, and that was it. I was condemned and judged."

"I am so sorry."

"It is fine. I am fine now." Chest heaving as if I'd run miles, I gazed out the window. Twinkling lights popped up in the lavender haze of twilight in the city. "I live a wonderful life. I have the career I'd dreamed about, a beautiful apartment, and good friends."

"And love? What of that?"

"Always the romantic," I said with a smile, almost echoing what Sterling had said to me that morning. It would be late by the time he finished work, but it didn't matter. I had to see him, needed to, and made a mental note to text him whether it would be his apartment or mine.

"Love can do wonders to heal the heart."

I had to remember this was Gil and not snort in his ear or call him a fool. "Even a lover can't help when some things are broken beyond repair."

"You are too wonderful a person to be alone all the time."

I didn't think it was necessary or that Gil would appreciate hearing about all my bed partners or failed love affairs. He'd liked Rip, and I knew he'd hoped we'd stay together. In contrast, he'd never thought much of Gordie. And now there was Sterling. A man completely different from any other I'd ever been with. The only man to whom I'd bared my heart as well as my body. And because I wasn't sure where we stood, I said nothing to Gil. I didn't want another failure.

"Thank you for the compliment, but at the moment all my focus has to be on regaining first place and winning games. We want to win three Cups in a row."

"I think you can do it, but it won't be easy. Trades and drafts have made other teams stronger than last year."

"Ah, Gil." I sighed. "I wish you'd come live closer to me—my building even. You could attend all the games. You could have anything you wanted."

"*Non, mon fils.* I need the quiet and serenity, not the hustle-bustle. I'm not far away. You have been as beloved to me as if you were my own blood. No matter what happens with your parents, you will always have me."

I wiped my face. "*Je t'aime, Papa.*"

"We will talk again soon. Have a good night."

"Sleep well."

I watched night fall over the river. From my perch high above, I followed the twisting ribbons of taillights on the highway as they traveled across the sparkle of the Brooklyn Bridge necklace. At one point it had filled me with awe—so many people living so many different lives to form one city. I had to go, do, be part of it, or else I'd be missing out.

But now? I wasn't ready to give up playing hockey, but I was tired of the scene. I'd had my wild nights. Now I wanted a place to call home and someone who looked forward to seeing me walk through the door.

I checked my phone and frowned at Sterling's silence. But knowing how his focus was strictly on work, I shouldn't be surprised. My conversation with Gil had cut into news viewing time—a.k.a. Sterling Forest—but I could still catch the end.

I hit the remote and flicked until I came to Channel 8. Sterling's face filled my seventy-five-inch screen, and I grinned. "*Mmm*, looks like you managed to cover all my love bites. Should I take that as a challenge for later?" I sat and listened to his deep baritone, admiring his handsome face.

"*It's time to turn to sports, with our own Tag Gold. What do you have for us tonight, Tag?*"

The golden-haired man bopped his curly head up and down. "*Thanks, Sterling. Our Brooklyn Blades are off tonight, but they're gearing up for what promises to be an intense game against the Portland Drifts, a team that always seems to give them a hard time. They need to make up wins for the weeks their superstar goalie, Bouvier, was out with his groin injury.*"

"You think so, Sunshine Boy?" I scoffed. "Why don't you try skating in our shoes one night and see?"

He finished off the rest of the segment without any further digs at us, and Sterling took over again. "*Coming up tonight at ten, Adrian Hunt will be reporting on a city-council vote to ban outdoor fruit markets, as some call it a health hazard.*" Sterling gazed straight into the camera. "*This is Sterling Forest. Have a great evening and an even better tomorrow.*"

I cleaned up, did some stretches, and took a shower. Another check of my phone, but my messages remained empty.

"What the fuck? I'm sure you have some time to acknowledge me."

I decided to hell with it and packed an overnight bag for his place. Around 10:15 I called for a car, and a half hour later, it let me out in front of his building on Central Park West. I no longer had to guess how Sterling could afford such a pricy address. Obviously, it was part of the money his mother had given him. *Neither of us won the parent jackpot for sure.* I settled the strap on my shoulder, and after greeting the doorman, walked inside. The concierge was the same as the previous night, and his brows shot up as he recognized me.

"Oh, hello, sir. Mr. Forest isn't here."

"I know." I flashed an easy, buddy-buddy smile, as if we were compadres. "I was hoping you'd let me sit and wait. I'm a bit early."

"Sure, sure. No problem." He waved me toward the lounge area, and I sat on the overstuffed velvet couch, facing the door.

Fifteen minutes passed before Sterling walked in, greeting the doorman. I rose to my feet, and he met my eyes even as the concierge announced my presence.

"Mr. Forest—"

"Thanks, Leon. I see."

I met him halfway. "Hey. I texted a few times, but you didn't answer."

He evaded eye contact. "Yes, well, sorry, it was a busy day."

Something was definitely up. "Can we go upstairs?"

"I don't know if that's a good idea. It's late, and—"

"And unless you want to have this discussion in your lobby, I think we're going up because I'm not leaving until you tell me what the hell is going on." This bullshit wasn't going to fly with me.

Sterling's face remained impassive, but he gave me a sharp nod, and I followed him to the elevators. We entered his apartment and I dropped my bag on the floor, folded my arms, and stood in front of him.

"What's wrong?"

He couldn't even meet my eyes, his head hung low, and his voice was a shadow of the strength he'd projected on screen. "I'm not sure we should keep seeing each other."

CHAPTER TWENTY-TWO
Sterling

It had been a miserable fucking day.

Or, I should say, after Adrian's shocking story about Denis, I'd been a miserable idiot, snapping at people, shunning phone calls. I'd ignored Denis's texts, which I never did, but I didn't know how to respond. I was afraid I'd say something I'd regret. Then, out of left field, I received a call from Charles Fox, the headhunter who'd found me the position at Channel 8.

"*Sterling. One of the big cable news networks is looking for an anchor to take over a spot. Are you interested?*"

I told Charles to send me the info because I was too busy to talk. A half-truth because all day, throughout meetings and running the script before the six and ten p.m. broadcasts, the only thing I could think of was Denis propositioning Rip to have sex with him and another man. I cringed at the thought, my entire body rebelling that this was the same man who claimed I held his heart.

Was that where his seduction of me was leading? It was hard to reconcile that person with the sensual man whispering sweet words in my ear as he made love to me. He'd said he loved me, and in doing so, had woken me up from sleepwalking through life. I was so close to giving away a part of me I'd never known existed, but I was no damn Sleeping Beauty waiting for a kiss from Prince Charming, no matter how much he'd made me care.

And goddammit, I did.

So when I saw Denis waiting for me in my lobby, I had to restrain myself from flinging my arms around him and letting him take me upstairs, where I knew one kiss from him would make me tumble into another night of bliss. But I hadn't lived this long on my wits to be dazzled by a beautiful face or seduced by a smile and a big dick. And Denis wisely kept quiet and stood in the center of my living room, waiting for me to speak first.

"I talked to Adrian today."

Eyes wary and face pinched with concern, he nodded. "All right. And?"

I ran a hand through my hair, undid my tie, and tossed my jacket onto the back of the chair by the kitchen island. "He revealed something...troubling."

"About me?"

"Yes."

"Will you tell me so I can defend what I supposedly did, or have you already made me a condemned man?"

"Let's sit." I walked to my giant sectional and sat. Denis trailed after me and sat at the opposite end, far away from me, intuiting how upset I was.

"*Dites-moi.*" He clasped his hands.

"I don't want you to be upset with Adrian. What he said was out of concern for me as his friend."

"Funny. Here I thought he and I were friends as well." He waved his hand. "Don't worry. I understand. I am the outsider in the threesome of your friendship with him and Rip. Continue."

"Before you and I...got together, I understood you had a history. Not only with Rip, but with many other men. I put that aside because I believed you when you said you'd changed and were satisfied and wanted only me."

"And so? You're still the only man I want to be with."

"For how long?" The words tasted bitter on my tongue, and I watched his confusion war with anger on his face.

"What did Adrian say?" he asked, voice calm but tense. "Obviously it's something bad about me."

"No, not bad. But...he told me of a time when he and Rip were dating and you went to Rip and—"

"Asked him for a threesome." Red spots burned high on Denis's cheeks, and he bowed his head. "Not my finest moment, I will agree."

"So it's true." A sour taste rose in my throat.

"Will you allow me to explain or condemn me outright?"

I undid the cuffs of my shirt and a few buttons down the front so I could breathe. "Go ahead."

I might not have known Denis very long, but he was not a man to be at a loss for words or fumble what he had to say. Yet he sat chewing the inside of his cheek, hesitant, and it made me second-guess my fear and ugly thoughts. He wasn't brushing me off with sarcasm and trite jokes, nor did he get defensive and snappish. So I kept my mind and heart open and listened.

"That afternoon when I spoke to Rip, I wasn't in a good place. I knew that Gordie and I had rushed our engagement and it wasn't right, but I didn't want to admit it. There I was, again, in another failed relationship. Plus"—he ducked his head—"I was jealous."

"Jealous? Of what?"

"The two of them. Rip and Adrian were so stupid in love and perfect for each other. It came so easily to Rip after he and I broke up."

"Because of your cheating."

"I never denied that," he said quietly. "It was a mistake."

"Another one. So that's two when it comes to Rip." My lips twisted in an ugly excuse for a smile. "Are you sure you're just not over him? That you're not still in love with him?"

"That would only be possible if I was ever *in* love with him. Which I wasn't. And I'm not. We tried to make it work, but we were too different, and I wasn't ready to be with one person then. I had something to prove."

"To whom?"

"Myself, the fans...who knows?"

"I'd like to," I urged. "Talk to me."

"I was young and living in New York City all by myself. Rip was gorgeous, a little older, the captain...I wanted him. I'll never deny our sexual attraction, but it was really all we had in common. When that burned out pretty quickly, neither of us wanted to be the first to walk away from such a public relationship. So I decided to be the bad guy."

All this still didn't address my main concern. "I'm aware of your past relationship. I knew from the start you weren't a saint. But the threesome?"

"*Je suis donc bien épai.*" He rested his head in his hand. "I should've known my stupidity would eventually return to haunt me. Listen. I can be that fool, you know? I had to try to build up my silly ego. I saw how happy Rip was with Adrian, and my life with Gordie was turning to shit because I'd made the same mistake with him that I did with Rip. I was flailing, lashing out, trying to hurt the world. Deep down I knew Rip would say no, throw me out, punch me in the face…pick one."

"I'd have done all three," I answered.

"I know. And he would've had every right to. And once I came to know Adrian better, I apologized for what I did. That's why I'm hurt he brought it up to you. I thought we'd moved past it. He's got his happiness. Why is he trying to destroy mine?"

"He's concerned you might be playing me."

"Playing you? For what reason?" He huffed. "I don't need to tie myself into knots to get a man into my bed."

I winced, both at his bluntness and the truthfulness of his statement. "Maybe for that very reason. It was no secret we didn't like each other very much when we first met. Maybe you saw me as a challenge."

"*Mais oui.*" The edge of laughter in his voice had me biting back my own smile. "You were and still are my greatest challenge. But not because of what you think, *mon cher.*"

My heart rate picked up. "Really? You know what I'm thinking?"

"I know what people want you to think. That it's all about sex for me."

"With good reason."

His eyes glittered. "Dammit. Can people not fucking change?" he swore. "I'm a human being who's made mistakes. I've apologized and regretted them all. And guess what? I'll probably make more mistakes in the future. Am I the only one who's supposed to be infallible? Does that mean I'm never to have any peace? That I'm not to be trusted ever again?"

"I understand, but it's hard for people to—"

"I don't give a damn what other people think," he shouted and smacked his thigh. "They're always going to color it with their own opinions or see what they want to see. I care about you. Your thoughts. Only yours. Because you're the one who matters to me. Not some random person who doesn't know shit about who I am, aside from what they're reading or hearing on the news. That's only an image on the screen or in the papers."

Hearing his passionate explanation broke down the walls I'd built around my heart. I didn't want to lose Denis at the expense of something that had happened years earlier, before I'd even known who he was. My stomach took a dive. "I'm sorry. I should've waited to talk to you before forming an opinion. I was wrong not to trust you, and I hope you can forgive me. I don't ever want to hurt you like that again."

"And now?" he asked quietly. "Do you trust me?"

"With everything I have."

The man I once was wouldn't have even listened to Denis's explanation. That Sterling would have dismissed him outright. I was so glad not to be that cold, locked-up man any longer, and I owed it all to Denis pushing me to accept that I deserved love. And that my love was worth giving.

"Then we're good, and I'm happy."

We sat quietly for a while after that. I could only see the outline of his profile in the gloom, but somehow the darkness was fitting, neither of us willing to reveal our faces or discuss hard truths. Maybe it was time to let the light shine in.

"I need you to know, I understand image. It's what shaped my life and created a person who's learned not to trust. My own mother, while saving my physical life, did nothing for my emotional well-being. She chose to reject me and motherhood to become a superstar based on the fake persona of a young, virginal girl. But along the way somewhere, somehow, she could've stood up to them. For me. Her son. She could've gained sympathy for what she'd endured and acknowledged me. But she didn't." Horrified,

I heard my voice wobble and catch. I drew in a deep breath to continue, but Denis left his seat to wrap his arms around my shaking shoulders.

"*Shh*, it's okay, *mon cœur, mon amour. Tout ira bien.*"

"No, but I've learned to be strong and live with it."

"Shutting people out isn't living. It's going through the motions, and that's depressing and dangerous. You see, I think we're more alike than different." His lips whispered over my hair. "My parents let me down in the worst way possible, making me a bitter, cold person. I used sex like others used alcohol or drugs. All those bodies numbed the pain of being alone, but only for a moment. And if I thought it could be something more, I had such little faith in myself after hearing my father's ugly words in my head, that I sabotaged it, preferring to walk away than risk being left again."

I pressed my lips to his warm skin. "Maybe we didn't like each other on sight because we recognized we were kindred souls. And it was too scary to admit, so we sniped at each other and fought the attraction."

Had it only been a few months since this all had begun? Yes, it was fast, but I'd waited forty years to find someone who challenged me, and when I fought back, didn't give up but came after me, wanting more.

"Well, you're the smart one, *n'est-ce pas*? I'm just the hockey guy who slaps pucks away from the net."

"Talk about never letting things go," I grumbled, and he kissed my cheek.

"I do it because I know it bugs you, and you're very cute when I annoy you." He tightened his hold on me, and I sensed there was more to that than our simple banter. "I talked to Gil today. My parents called him after I was injured, to find out what he knew. He told them to contact me, but of course they never did."

Dammit. "I'm sorry. We don't have to keep talking about what Adrian said. It doesn't matter."

Denis continued speaking as if he didn't hear me. "I'm so afraid when Gil leaves me, there'll be no one who knows me and will ever care about me again."

A chill ran through me, and I shifted in his arms. "I care. And I'd like to get to know you better."

I could barely make out the shadow of his smile. "This is me. The good, the bad, and the ugly."

"Underneath all our ugly is beauty waiting to be freed." I ran my lips over his wet cheek and kissed the tears resting on his lashes. "Let me free you. Because I think you're so beautiful. Outside and in."

Our kiss was soft and gentle, almost as if we were new lovers. Perhaps we were now that the masks were off and the shields thrown aside. One big hand cupped my cheek while my arm slid around his neck to steady us. I gave as well as took, sucking his tongue and pushing mine past his lips. He tasted like everything I'd been missing all my life. Love. Desire. A home.

"Please don't walk away from me," he whispered. "I knew something was wrong when you wouldn't talk to me all day."

"I'm learning. And I'll try my hardest to never shut you out again."

That potential cable news job offer crossed my mind, but I'd barely given it a second thought since the morning. I should check the email Charles sent, but I had little desire to move. Denis and I were having the most important discussion of our new relationship, and I was loath to stop it for something trivial.

"I couldn't bear if you left me, if in the future I'd be forced to see you kissing someone else...falling in love with someone who wasn't me." He covered my mouth with his, and I tangled my fingers in that glorious hair and gave in to the overpowering hunger to open myself up and give Denis everything he wanted.

"Don't you know by now I'm a stubborn bastard?" I said, and he nipped at my lower lip. I pulled off his sweatshirt to run my hands over his thickly muscled chest. "I don't give up when I want something."

"I thought that was only a news story." He took hold of my partly open shirt and ripped it down the middle, sending buttons popping in all directions.

Fuck, that was sexy.

"You are my top story. Beginning, middle, and end." I tugged him close and kissed him, leaving us gasping for air.

"I want you." Denis's husky rasp hit my ear, and I hissed. "Bedroom."

We ran and hit the bed so hard, both of us bounced. He landed on top of me and pinned my arms above my head. "Tell me how much you want me."

There was no ego in that statement, not with a fire blazing from his eyes so hot, I could've sworn it singed my skin. Sweat broke out from my pores.

"I'm not sure words exist to describe that feeling." I hooked my leg around his knee and yanked him so we were pressed skin-to-skin. "Even for someone who makes his living with them. So I'll have to show you."

I kissed him and slid my hands under the waistband of his sweats. He helped me pull them off, along with his briefs, and I gripped his thick, wet cock.

"Hurry," I whispered, and his devilish grin released such a rush of unprecedented emotions, I had to stop him from getting off the bed. I had to tell him. Right then. I grabbed his arm. "Denis."

He turned from reaching for the nightstand drawer and sat next to me. "*Quoi?*"

I sat up and held his face to mine. "I love you. Please never doubt it or me again."

A beautiful smile lit up his face. "*Je t'aime. Je t'aime.*" He kissed me until we laughed from the sheer joy of being together, and I wondered how I'd lived without this happiness for so long.

He took out the condom and the lube while I removed my pants and hung them on the valet next to my bed. Both of us now fully naked, we lay together kissing and touching. Hands sliding on hot bare skin, grasping and teasing, bringing long-dead nerves to life.

"Please," I begged, shameless for him as he played with me, two fingers pumping inside my passage. "Denis, I need you."

"I love to hear that. Say it again."

"I need you. I want you. Fuck me, come on," I demanded, and he chuckled.

"So eager. So perfect." He kissed me, hard at first, licking into my mouth, turning gentle until I was half-wild with lust.

He flipped me so I was on all fours, and I buried my head in my arms while he held my ass spread wide. Something wet and soft touched my hole, and I moaned as he played his tongue along my rim before nudging inside. A year ago, the sounds he made…the noises I made, would've made me blush. Now, for the first time, I was alive.

"Oh my God," I gasped. My entire world focused on the spot he mercilessly teased. I spiraled away to a place of pure sensation, my body screaming for release. He reached under me and stroked my shaft only for a moment before I fell apart. In my half-awake state, I felt him enter my aching body, and I clenched tight around him as his sank into me, inch by inch.

"Ahhh, so good. So good." Denis covered my body, his thick hair spilling over my shoulders as he moved slowly at first, then picking up speed, thrusting hard, touching that spot deep within my body that brought me to life again. I pushed to his pull, gave him my body for whatever he wanted.

He throbbed, hot and heavy, and came with a sigh, his face buried in my neck. "I play every game to win, but this is no game, and I'm not playing."

"Neither am I."

CHAPTER TWENTY-THREE
Denis

I had little desire to have a conversation with Rip about his husband, so for the following month, I stayed friendly but aloof. The times he approached me about getting together for a talk, or to have me over for dinner or drinks, I made excuses. I smiled and said all the nice things, made small talk about games, but stayed in my own happiness bubble, which had room for only two people: Sterling and myself. Rip was no fool, and on our away trip, after winning against the LA Seals, he cornered me in the locker-room bathroom.

"Can you give me a minute, please?"

Naked and dripping wet from the shower, I pulled a towel around my waist. "About what?"

He worked his jaw. "Come on, man. You know what."

I squeezed the water out of my hair and peered in the mirror. "Obviously not, since I'm asking." I sure as hell wasn't about to give him the upper hand and mention his back-stabbing husband's ugly insinuation.

"Adrian feels terrible."

"Ahhh, and it's all about *pauvre* Adrian. *Quel dommage.* His feelings are hurt?" I poked Rip in the chest. Other members of the team gave us the side-eye but wisely didn't interrupt and gave us a wide berth as they exited the shower area, leaving Rip and me alone. "And what he said to Sterling about me, someone he invited to your wedding, claiming we were friends and the past was the past, that was *nothing*? I should ignore it because...why? I said something stupid to you that most likely I would never have gone through with. For whatever reason, Adrian felt he had to warn Sterling about me?"

My thumping heart and pulse made me see spots, but I drew on my newfound strength in the relationship I was building with Sterling to use my words in a helpful manner and not be ugly and cutting.

"What do you want me to do?"

"Nothing. I am hurt. Very, very hurt that someone who acted like a friend would almost ruin a potential relationship. And I don't understand what he'd hoped to accomplish, but he failed. Sterling and I are together."

"You might not believe it, but I'm glad to hear that. Can we discuss this after you get dressed? I've been waiting for you for half an hour, and I'm sweating my balls off from the humidity in here."

I refrained from making a snarky comment about how I was surprised he'd forgotten I liked to take very hot, long showers and merely nodded. "Give me a few minutes to dry my hair and get dressed."

I didn't have time to call Sterling, who'd also admitted he and Adrian had been awkward with each other, but I did text him that Rip asked for a sit-down. Sterling quickly answered.

Don't lose your temper. Be nice.

My lips twitched. *I'm always nice.*

Rip waited for me outside the locker room, and I observed him with a frown—he was texting rapidly.

"Problem?" I strolled up to him, and he pocketed the phone.

"Nope. All good. Where should we go? The hotel restaurant?"

I waved my hand in front of us. "Lead the way."

When we walked into the restaurant, the hostess greeted us. The room was half-full even at this late hour. I saw several teammates, including Seb, who continued to drink his beer but gave me a side-eye.

"Table for two?"

"In the back, please," I asked before Rip could open his mouth.

"Of course." We followed her to a square table for two in the corner. "Zeke will be your server and will be right over to take your drink order."

We sat opposite each other, and Rip played with his wedding band, spinning it around and around on his finger. Finally, I had to break the silence.

"You look good," I said. "Happy."

Was that relief I saw flash in his eyes? Maybe he thought I'd come out swinging, but I decided to wait and allow him to make the first move.

"I am. Very. You look well too."

"I am. Very," I echoed.

"So, uh, you and Sterling are together?" At my nod, he smiled, his eyes crinkling at the corners. "I'm glad for you. I wanted you to find someone."

Funny thing was, I believed him. "Thank you."

"Although," he continued with a chuckle, "I am a little surprised it's him, simply because the two of you couldn't stand each other."

My smile was serene. "We've made *la paix*."

"Make love not war, huh?" Rip joked.

"Something like that." I didn't feel the need to go into a deep explanation of my relationship. Rip and I were friendly, but I wasn't about to share my feelings with him. Ex-lovers only went so far.

Zeke, our server, approached, and we ordered beers.

Again, I waited for Rip to speak.

"So, uh, I figured it's about time we hashed this out so we can return to normal."

"Hash it out?" I quirked a brow. "What do you mean?" No, I wasn't going to make it easy for him. It was his husband who'd stuck his pretty nose into my business.

The beers came, and Zeke hovered, pouring us ice water and getting us napkins and coasters. He was a young guy, in his twenties, and from how his gaze lingered on Rip and me, a bit starstruck.

"Can I, uh, get you gentlemen any food? Great game, by the way. I'm originally from the city and a big Blades fan."

"Thank you, that's great to hear," I replied. "I'll have the chicken sandwich, no mayonnaise please."

"Burger and fries for me. And thanks." Rip smiled, and Zeke left us.

"So you were saying..." I took a sip of my beer.

"Okay. Look. I didn't know Adrian planned on saying what he did. And frankly, I think he was wrong—it was none of his business. Whatever you and I went through, it's done with and we've moved on. I know he needs to speak to you and apologize himself, and I'm not here to pressure you to accept it, but I wanted the two of us to get back to normal at the rink and not have this hanging over our heads."

"Damn, Rip, take a breath." When he didn't respond, I clasped my hands together on top of the table. "I was offended. And blindsided that Adrian would do that to me. It felt like he was trying to sabotage my relationship with Sterling, which he almost did."

"Not to defend him, but I think Adrian was looking out for Sterling as a friend."

"By sabotaging a potential relationship and making it seem like I'm some sort of...I don't know, sexual deviant or predator? Which, by the way, having a threesome is so not."

His cheeks turned red. "Yeah, I'm aware. I guess he's a little sheltered. But please don't think I had anything to do with it. Honestly, I think it was pretty damn funny—not that I wasn't pissed at you at the time, but now?" He shrugged. "You were like a bad actor in a cheesy movie, dude."

I snickered. "And here I thought I was being seductive and persuasive."

"Maybe to someone who didn't know you as well as I did. And by that time I was in so deep with Adrian that whatever you said didn't matter."

Our food came, but neither of us made a move to eat. "I understand."

Rip studied my face, and a tiny smile played along his lips. "You know...I think you finally do. You're serious with Sterling." Not a question, so I didn't need to answer. I picked a fry off his plate and dipped it in ketchup. He huffed. "I always hated it when you did that."

I grinned. "I know."

Rip rolled his eyes and took several bites of his burger before resuming the conversation. "So, you and me. We're good? No more avoiding me?"

I didn't want to be at odds with Rip anymore. It made me an ugly, unhappy person who lashed out and was cruel and thoughtless. I didn't like myself, or anyone else, for that matter. The enemy was from within. Maybe the injury had exposed a vulnerability I wasn't aware of and shattered my cocky sense of invincibility. All I knew was that I no longer wanted to be that man.

I put down my sandwich. "*Ne t'inquiète pas.* It's all good between us."

"And Adrian?"

"Another story. He and I? *Non.*" I shook my head. "*Je suis pas prêt à lui pardoner.* He and I must speak face-to-face."

"I think that's a good idea. When we get home tomorrow?"

I knew he was eager to put this to bed, but I grimaced. "C'mon. It's a long flight. Let's do it on the weekend, when Sterling and Adrian don't have work the next day. Our next game isn't until Sunday night, so how about Saturday afternoon after practice?"

"I'm sure that'll be fine."

"*Ça va.* Are you finished?" He nodded, and I called over the waiter. "Put this on my bill. I'll charge it to the room."

"Yes, sir. Can I have your room number?" He bit his lip and gave me a sweet, lingering smile that left little to the imagination as to what he desired.

From the corner of my eye, I spied Rip watching our exchange with interest. In the past, I would've dropped an innuendo or even waited around for his shift to end and personally shown him the way to my room. But now I had Sterling and zero interest in having anyone in my bed other than him.

"It's 1045."

Rip pulled out his wallet. "Here's the tip in cash." He handed Zeke a hundred, and the kid's eyes almost popped out of his skull.

"Oh, my God. Wow. Thank you so much. Could I possibly get both your autographs?"

We scribbled our names on his order pad, and I added, *To Zeke, the best waiter in LA*, then posed for some pictures. By the time we finished, I was tired and grouchy because I knew with the time difference, I wouldn't be able to talk to Sterling until tomorrow.

"This sucks," I grumbled on our way up to our rooms.

"What?"

"The fact that we're three hours behind at home."

"Sterling?"

I nodded. "I haven't talked to him all day."

"I miss Adrian too."

The elevator opened on our floor. Rip was two doors away from me.

"G'night, Rip."

"You're in love with him, aren't you?"

I met his gaze. "Yeah. And this time I know the difference."

"I believe you do." He smiled. "See you in the morning. We've got an early flight, don't forget."

"*Oui, oui, mon capitaine.*" I saluted him and entered my room.

I undressed and got into bed, staring at the ceiling. My phone buzzed, and I saw it was Sterling. My heart raced. Was something wrong? It was three in the morning there. Why was he texting me?

"Idiot," I murmured. "You're acting like a schoolboy with a crush. Read it."

Just woke up because I discovered I don't like sleeping alone. Glad you won your game.

Sterling and I were never going to be the mushy hearts-and-flowers type, saying I love you at every turn, but I knew that was what he'd meant.

I hit the Call button. "*Bonsoir, mon cher. Je te manque?*"

"If you're asking me a question, I need it in English to understand what I'm committing to."

"Don't you trust me?" I purred.

"Not as far as I can throw you," he countered. "It might be something outrageous, like would I want to come home and find you naked and covered in chocolate."

I burst out laughing. "Is that your fantasy? Because if it is...*mmm*. I can totally make it happen." I hugged the pillow. "All I asked is if you missed me. You're the one who had sexy thoughts."

"Oh. Well, I mean, I did say it."

"No, my love. You said you don't like sleeping alone. That could be solved by getting a dog or cat."

"I don't have the time to dedicate to a pet. You take up enough of my attention."

He was too cute, and I rolled on my side, hating the empty expanse of the king-sized bed. "Then may I suggest a Denis-sized pillow. Extra, extra-large, of course." I smirked, and as usual, Sterling had a comeback ready.

"Obviously, to contain that massive ego."

"That's not all that's massive, *mon cœur*." I waited a moment. "I do miss you," I murmured.

"I miss you too," he whispered back. "Good night, Denis."

"Night."

I fell asleep with a smile on my face.

CHAPTER TWENTY-FOUR
Sterling

"I don't know why you agreed to this. Eventually the issue between Adrian and me will work itself out. And frankly, you don't have to talk with him at all. He's the husband of your teammate."

I ran an assessing eye across the large kitchen island. With three of the four of us living in Brooklyn, and Denis and Rip having practice earlier, it made sense to have the dinner at Denis's apartment. It was as much for my benefit as it was for his. Denis didn't need the reminder that he used to live with Rip at his place, plus it was where he'd made his ridiculous proposition that had gotten us into this mess.

Denis lay in a chair, one long leg flung over the arm. "Because enough is enough. And Rip is my friend. He says Adrian is walking around like a sad puppy and he can't take it anymore. It's affected our dynamic on the ice as well as off. Plus, I'm tired of hearing about it. We're going to discuss it like adults."

I took out the dressing for the salad and the tray of chicken and vegetable kebobs. I'd made sure the dinner would be at least a little healthy because I was certain Denis ate garbage anytime he was away.

"You've got more of an issue with him than I do." I stood staring at the platter. Much as I wanted Denis and Adrian to make up, I had other, more important things on my mind.

"And I fully intend to make sure it will all be solved by the time they leave tonight."

The buzzer sounded, and Denis hopped up to answer. A few minutes passed before the bell rang, and Rip stood with a visibly nervous Adrian by his side.

"Come in, *mes amis*." Denis stepped aside, allowing the two men to pass. "We are all friends here."

Rip squeezed Adrian's hand, and they both took off their jackets. The days were getting shorter and the weather chillier. I mourned the end of fall, when you could run outside without a jacket, scarf, and gloves and didn't have only the cold and dark winter to look forward to. Although now, with Denis to spend my nights with, it might be nice to stay at home and cuddle under the covers. I blinked. *What the actual fuck?* I didn't cuddle. That wasn't me, the hard-nosed reporter with a life dedicated to the news.

But realistically, who would've thought I'd be in love with a hockey legend whose ego was only surpassed by his talent?

"Hi, Sterling." Rip approached, and I put on my neutral friendly face. "Busy time for you with the political season heating up."

"Yes. But Adrian is doing a good job with the reporting."

My praise did little to alleviate the strain on Adrian's face.

Denis joined us and pointed at Adrian. "All right. Let's do this because I don't feel like sitting around all night waiting for one of us to bring the subject up. Adrian, I was very upset and hurt that you went to Sterling and told him about something that had been put to bed, *fait accompli.* If it didn't bother Rip or me, why did you feel the need to stir up the pot?"

My lips twitched. "It's just *stir the pot.*"

He arched a brow. "Whatever."

Adrian swallowed hard. "Well...I'm sorry, but I wasn't aware you two were serious, and though you'd been nice, Denis, I wasn't sure you'd changed."

"And again: I don't see how that's any of your business," Denis said, and behind the mild-mannered facade, I knew he was seething. "Sterling and I are adults. Older than you. Whatever our personal lives are, it isn't your business. If you have a problem with threesomes or any other sexual partnerships, that's your issue. But your insinuation to Sterling was that I planned to sexually trap him into something devious and dangerous."

"Come on, Denis. That's a little out there, isn't it?" Rip complained.

"I don't think so," I jumped in. "I didn't ask for Adrian's opinion. He's constantly tried to set me up with people, but I never asked him to do that. Adrian, I appreciate you thinking of me and your concern that Denis might not be who he seemed. But I don't need your or anyone else's dating help. You put your foot in it, and now you have to figure out how to win not only my trust, but Denis's as well."

Adrian met my eyes. "I'm sorry. I was wrong, and if you and Denis are together and happy, that's all that matters." He shifted focus to Denis, who stood with his powerful arms folded. "Denis. I apologize. I was totally out of line to dig up something that was put to bed. I won't deny it bothered me, and it's prevented me from trusting you, but the way I handled it was hurtful. I can understand why you believed I was sabotaging your relationship. I thought I was looking out for a friend, but in doing so, I only created more problems."

Denis remained silent, and I did as well. Both of us had perfected masks of neutrality to hide all the hurt we'd lived with, while Adrian, who wore his heart on his sleeve, grew visibly emotional.

"It was a very foolish thing for me to do, and I hope you can forgive my overstepping. From now on, I'll keep my nose out of everyone's personal business and concentrate on my husband and my own life." He ducked his head. "I'm really, really sorry. I don't know why I thought it was a good idea, but I can't undo it. I can only move forward."

Denis was the one most wronged, so I waited for his response. He pushed his hair off his face and blew out a breath. Knowing him intimately as I did now, I sensed his frustration.

"I don't like conflict. Rip and I play together, and it's been fucking with my head. But I do realize most of this is my fault. I was a fool to bring that ridiculous proposal to Rip in the first place. And why? Because I was jealous of your happiness at a time when my life was falling apart yet again. But even then, I knew full well Rip would toss me out on my ass."

It was fascinating to see Denis through this lens of love, now, and not scorn. He'd changed so much since those first days together. And so had I.

"We all do things we regret, sometimes even when it comes to love," I said softly and squeezed Denis's hand. He returned the pressure.

Denis closed his eyes for a second. "Shall we wipe the slate clean? I was thoughtless, and so were you, Adrian. Now we start fresh. *D'accord?*" He glanced at me and winked. "That means, okay?"

I pretend-glared. "No shit."

Adrian leaned over and asked Rip, "Does that mean he's not mad at me anymore?"

Rip chuckled. "I think so."

I nudged Denis. "That was nice."

"I'm a nice guy."

I picked up the tray of food. "I have to heat these through, but there's a salad while we wait."

Denis took out bowls. "I should've warned you both ahead of time. Sterling doesn't serve snacks like chips or all the little appys I love." He pouted. "He's a food warden."

"Somehow I doubt that." Rip took the tongs and put a generous serving of greens and vegetables in his bowl as well as Adrian's. "He looks great, and I'm sure he wants you to be in the best shape possible. It's nice to have someone who cares about you, isn't it? Especially when your family isn't nearby." He drizzled oil and vinegar on his and Adrian's salad.

A pang hit my heart seeing Denis pale and quickly turn away. Rip didn't know Denis's painful family history or how his casual words would hurt. I sought to change the subject.

"So who has been your toughest opponent this year so far? I've tried to watch the games, but I'm still such a novice. I can't pick up who is in what position. I only know the goalie." I smiled at Rip. "And the center because I know your number."

"Well, the goalie is the most important, as you know." Denis slipped his arms around my waist and kissed the top of my head. Adrian and Rip ate their salads, trying not to gawk at us but failing miserably. "What? You've never seen a man kiss his boyfriend?" He settled his mouth over mine, and I held on to his shoulders to steady myself. He pulled me close. "I know what you're trying to do," he murmured in my ear. "Don't worry about me. I'm fine."

But I couldn't help myself. I worried about his fragile state of mind all the time. Denis liked to project a tough-guy image, but I knew how devastated his family's rejection had left him.

"You're better than fine." I rubbed my cheek to his for a second, and he surprised me by catching my fingers with his.

"You too, you know."

I dipped my head in acknowledgment. "I've got to check the food."

The afternoon might've started out rocky, but it all ended up well between us. Adrian even hugged Denis before he and Rip left. When the door shut after them, Denis leaned against it with a sigh of relief.

"I am *so* glad that's finished. Come here." He held out his arms, and I leaned into his chest. "Now are you ready to tell me what's on your mind?"

Startled, I tipped up my face to meet his eyes. "What're you talking about?"

"You are a fabulous lover but a terrible liar. I've seen you staring off into space for the past few weeks. Now that this nonsense with Adrian is put to bed, we can concentrate on what's bothering you."

I made a face. "It's…I don't know what."

"Considering you make your living attempting to be articulate and that made no sense, you've got me concerned."

"*Attempting* to be articulate?" I pretended outrage. "How about some wine, and we can sit?"

"I won't say no."

I poured two glasses and joined him on the couch. I sipped and set it on the side table. "I had a call from a headhunter about a job as an anchor on a cable news network. I should've told you, but between your schedule and this thing with Adrian, I forgot."

A big smile broke across Denis's face. "But that's wonderful. It is, isn't it?" His brow furrowed when I didn't answer.

"I don't know. I told him I was interested, but I haven't received a call back. The job may not even be available anymore."

"So call the headhunter. Do it now."

I laughed. "It's past seven thirty on a Saturday night."

"So what? I bet he'll answer whatever questions you have. If I call my agent or lawyer, they always answer me—if not immediately, pretty damn quick."

Should I point out that he was a famous sports star with a multimillion-dollar contract and sponsorships, while I was a local news anchor with a small following but nowhere near that kind of influence? I tried to be diplomatic.

"You might have slightly more pull than I do."

He set his glass on the table. "Not where it counts." He ran his foot on mine. "For instance, I am putty in your hands."

"You are anything but. Putty is soft and malleable. You are hard as a rock. Everywhere." At his smirk, I settled into the crook of his shoulder.

"So what do you plan to do about it?" he asked.

My phone buzzed with an alert. I had my notifications set for the top stories of the day. "Give me one minute, and I'll show you."

"You're checking news stories instead of making love to me. We have a lot to work on, *mon amour*."

I was frozen. Unable to stop reading what was on my screen.

"Sterling? *Sterling*."

When I didn't respond, Denis plucked the phone from my nerveless fingers and read.

"*Merde*," he swore. "What now?"

As I had all my life, I gathered my strength and wits. "Nothing. Why should it matter? It is what it is."

He held me by the shoulders. "Don't lie to me. I'm not a stranger."

"Why would I lie? My mother, who was never a mother, might be dying." I picked up my phone again and read: "'Dahlia Dumont has been admitted to the hospital for a serious, undisclosed illness.' My world isn't going to be any different. I'm not going to miss the nonexistent birthday phone call or Christmas present." I shrugged. "You expect me to cry and be upset?"

I tried to break eye contact, but Denis cupped my cheek. "I don't know what I expect, aside from you feeling safe enough with me to be honest."

To my horror, my lips trembled and tears burned. "There was a time…I thought maybe she'd want to reach out. She'd retired from movies and was running her beauty empire. No one would care if it came out she had a son. But she never did. I'm sure the moment she wrote that check to me, she forgot I existed."

Soft and gentle, Denis kissed me. "I could never forget you. Now, come with me."

"Denis, I'm fine. Really."

He stroked my face. "Don't argue with me, or I'll have to carry you."

"Like you could," I scoffed.

He rose, grabbed me by the waist, and hauled me over his shoulder. "Never dare me."

"Denis, what the hell." I did my best to break free, but he paid no attention.

"You're only turning me on, you realize, with all that

wiggling." We reached the bedroom, and I slid off him. He held me close. "Let me love you."

I stood like a child as he undressed first me, then himself, and led me to the shower. He washed my hair and dried me off.

"You want your whole regime, *mon cher*?"

"No, thank you." I couldn't trust my voice above a whisper, and he helped me into sweats and a T-shirt. We got into bed, and he wrapped his big arms around me. No one had ever cared for me like that.

"I've been so wrong," I said, and Denis gazed at me, waiting for an explanation. "Being rejected by my mother...I thought I'd be alone forever. I never thought I had a home. Now I realize it's you."

With a smile lighting his face, Denis kissed me gently. "I've been waiting where I've always been. In your heart. I'm here. For whatever you need from me, whenever it might be."

Eventually, I heard his even breathing and knew he was asleep. Unlike me. I stayed awake almost until daybreak, thinking of everything that might've been and now would never come to pass.

CHAPTER TWENTY-FIVE
Denis

It had been a lousy week. We'd hit a three-game losing streak, and Coach was hoarse from screaming at the refs out on the ice and reaming us in the locker room. Thank God it was Friday and the bye week was upon us, because I was pretty fucking sick of everything and everybody at the moment. Myself included. I needed the reset that time away would bring to return to play, fresh and ready to get back on track.

I'd persuaded Sterling to take the time off as well, and we'd decided to go away to someplace warm, hoping that leaving behind the gloom of winter and the constant stream of news would lift both our spirits. Since hearing about his mother, he'd retreated somewhat, and I'd had to push him to spend our nights together. The excuse he gave was that our vacation required him to clear the work off his desk and he wouldn't be home until late, but I knew Sterling. He was locking himself away and hiding. I solved that problem by showing up at his apartment each night and waiting for him. After hearing a news story about his mother's health issues, I waited for him outside the news station with a car. His grateful smile didn't hide the shadows darkening his eyes.

We arrived home and I ordered us dinner, but he didn't have much of an appetite.

"Come. Let me take you to bed." I undressed him, we lay together, and I did everything I could to take away his pain.

"Denis."

We'd made love, and I'd yet to catch my breath.

"*Mmm?*"

"I know what you're trying to do, and I love you."

I rolled onto my side and skimmed my fingers over his cheek. "I don't like seeing you sad, with faraway eyes."

"I shouldn't be. After all, she and I are strangers, only connected by blood. So why do I feel like I might be losing something I never had?"

I had no answer for him. All I could do was hold him tight. "*Je t'aime.*"

The night before our bye week started, I'd allowed four goals for the first time that season. It was an ugly loss, and I took it personally. Then in the locker room afterward, I got a text from Sterling, saying he had an emergency meeting after the ten p.m. newscast and wouldn't be home until late.

I'll see you in the morning.

That left me alone, and when I was by myself and in a bad headspace, I tended to do foolish, self-destructive things. I went to a bar I used to frequent and drank a very large straight vodka.

"Hey, you're Denis Bouvier," some dude said, sitting on the stool next to me. "I'm an Icers fan." He wore one of their caps.

"That's nice." I beckoned the bartender. "Hit me up again, Tommy." There were two TVs on the wall—one had a West Coast basketball game on, and the other a replay of our hockey loss. My mood grew blacker.

"Sure, Denis. Been a while since I seen ya." He clinked the neck of the vodka bottle to my glass and filled it almost to the rim. Tommy always did have a heavy pour.

"Been busy."

"Busy losing a buncha games lately, huh?" the guy next to me said with a snicker, and I turned my head slightly, glaring at the dickhead.

"Fuck off."

"The Icers are gonna kick the Blades' asses in the play-offs this year. You're all a buncha old men."

"Hey, don't go bothering people in here." Tommy smacked a receipt in front of the guy. "That's your bill. Pay it and get outta here."

"Whatever. Place sucks anyway." He tossed a few bills and walked out.

"Whatta dick, huh?" Tommy took the money and stuck it in the register. "Don't let him get to ya." He kept up a steady stream of conversation as I drank. "So, where you been hidin'?"

"Nowhere. Just practice and the games."

"Well…" He leaned on the bar, his biceps bulging. "I know

it's the bye week, so if you wanna hook up, I'm free after midnight."

In the past, if I'd been out clubbing and no one caught my eye, or if I just felt like drinking and getting laid, I'd take Tommy home and we'd fuck. It was nothing more than pure sex, but it served its purpose. I met his gray-blue gaze, and even through my alcoholic haze, I sensed his lust. No one would ever know.

But his eyes were the wrong shade of blue, and I didn't want some stranger in my bed. I wanted my uptight, snarky boyfriend who spent half an hour every morning with his skin creams and potions. I didn't even mind the health food and all the vitamins and supplements and those fucking awful wheatgrass shots. God, I fucking loved him and missed his damn face.

"I can't. I gotta go." I took out a wad of twenties and gave it to Tommy. "Thanks."

A bit unsteady on my feet, I used the cold air and the three-block walk home to try and sober up, but it didn't work that well. My head still spun when I lay on my couch, and though he'd said not to, I called Sterling.

"*Bonsoir, mon bébé. Comment ça va?*"

Drunk Denis was in the house. Once I started speaking only French, I was in trouble.

"Denis? What's wrong?"

"*Tu me manque.* Miss kissing you. Can't you skip that stupid meeting?" If any of the guys saw me begging and pleading to see a man, they'd laugh in my face. I didn't care. I didn't want to be alone tonight.

"I wish I could, Denis, but the meeting is mandatory. I can't miss it. And it's going to go long. Did something happen?"

I couldn't tell him it was because I'd given up four goals and lost a game. He'd think I was silly and wouldn't understand.

"No, not really. I just want you. Wanna be with you."

"I want to be with you too. And starting Sunday, we're going to spend six whole days together."

"Not enough. *Je te veux. J'ai besoin de toi.*"

"Have you been drinking? Where are you?"

"*Home, home, all alone with my telephone,*" I sang and laughed out loud.

"I think you should go to sleep, and I'll come by in the morning and bring you breakfast and make you feel better."

"But—"

"I have to go. The station owner is here. Good night, Denis. *Je t'aime.*"

I smiled at his awful French accent. The phone went dead, and I stared at it. *No one wants me…not Sterling, not my parents…*

I rubbed my eyes and shuffled over to the refrigerator. A bottle of the wine Sterling liked was half-full, and I took it out, uncorked it, and not bothering with a glass, drank until my head buzzed.

I returned to the couch and picked up my phone. I was making a huge mistake, but I couldn't stop. It was as if I were separate from my body, watching from above as I made one bad, wrong choice after another. I found the number that was once as familiar as my heartbeat and touched the Call icon. After five or six rings, my father answered.

"*Allô?*"

"*C'est moi…Denis.*"

I heard the sharp intake of breath. "Denis…*ça va?*"

"*Oui, je vais bien.*" I braced myself and asked the question foremost on my mind—why did they call Gil? "*Gil m'a dit que tu l'as appelé après ma blessure il y a quelques mois. Pourquoi?*"

"*Je lui ai dit de ne rien dire. Ce vieil imbécile.*"

How could my father think that Gil would keep this from me, even if told to do so? And calling him an old fool…that was typical, unfortunately, and not something I could ignore. "Ne *dit pas ça. Il n'est pas un imbécile. Réponds-moi. Pourquoi l'as-tu appelé?*"

The conversation didn't last more than five minutes, but it was long enough for me to hear that twenty years had passed but nothing had changed.

My parents were angry that Gil and Mary had taken me away, but they had no regrets for relinquishing parental rights to their gay son. Me playing hockey was more important to them than understanding and accepting me. Now, like then, my father believed I was disgusting, a pervert. He had no interest in my life. The only reason he'd called Gil was because my mother had heard of my injury. But again, they'd called Gil. Not me, their son.

All the ugly truths had spilled out. I buried my face in my hands. I should never have gone out drinking. I wouldn't have called him and could've stayed in my bubble of ignorance. There were times I could even feel nostalgia for the way we were. Pictures in my mind of playing with my father on the ice. Him and *Pépère* showing me how to use the goalie stick and properly guard a net. My first game as a child and seeing them cheering for me in the stands when I'd block the shots. A life that no longer existed for me.

I did my second stupid thing of the night. I finished the bottle of wine and called for a car to Sterling's apartment. By some luck, I didn't get sick and managed to walk straight to the building. The doorman knew me, and Sterling had given instructions to let me up. I had my own key and opened the door. By that time, it was past midnight, and Sterling was sitting in the dark with the damn news on, of course. He jumped up when I opened the door.

"Denis?" He turned on the lamps.

I swayed and grimaced, flinging a hand to cover my face. "Too...bright. Turn it off."

He strode over to me, brows knitted. "I thought you were going to sleep." He reached up and brushed the tangled hair out of my eyes. "Wow. You're really drunk."

I belched and gave him a smile. "Very good obslervation. And it's your flalt...fault." My stomach heaved. "I'm gonna...throw up."

"Not in my living room, you're not. These floors cost me a fortune." Alarmed, he pulled me into the hall bathroom. I stumbled after him and sank to my knees.

"You always say the schweetest thrings...I love you." I stuck my head in the toilet and promptly got sick. I lay on the floor of his bathroom, my hot cheek pressed to the cold tiles. My stomach made some disturbing sounds, and Sterling huffed.

"I'll make you some tea." He left me, and I was grateful he did as I was pretty disgusted with my behavior. After a while, I managed to rise from my prone position and ran the taps, rinsing my mouth out first, then splashing water on my face. I glanced in the mirror and almost scared myself. My eyes were hollow black pits, my skin almost gray.

"Some stud you are."

I swished mouthwash and spat, found extra-strength pain reliever, and took three with water from the sink. That was about all I could do at the moment. My head still pounding, I left the bathroom and found Sterling sitting at the kitchen island, two steaming mugs of tea in front of him.

"Drink this."

Head bowed, I took my seat and waited for my hands to stop trembling before picking it up and taking a sip. "Tastes like shit. I hate tea."

"You're welcome. What're you doing here? I told you I was coming to you in the morning."

"I couldn't wait. I needed to see you."

He pulled up a stool to sit next to me and took my hands.

"Tell me what happened. I've never seen you like this. The Blades lost tonight's game, I saw."

"Yes. Because of me. I lost it. I've never given up as many goals in a game as I did tonight."

"No, that's not true. It's not your personal loss." He rubbed my back and leaned in to kiss my brow. "Don't blame yourself. You're part of a team. A loss isn't only on you."

"I can and I will. But that's not even the worst." I squeezed my eyes shut. "I went to a bar after the game to drown my sorrows. I was angry and lonely. I had a few drinks, and the bartender I used to hook up with wanted to have sex. But I couldn't because it wasn't you. I didn't–don't want anyone else but you."

"Denis..." Sterling began, his voice gentler, but again, I didn't let him speak.

"I came home, and that's when I called you asking to come over, but you said no. So, in my infinite wisdom, I took the bottle of wine from the refrigerator, drank some more, and thought, *What other dumb thing can I do to fuck up my night?* Oh, right. Let me talk to my parents."

"Shit." Sterling blanched and put his arms around me. "I'm sorry. Was it bad?"

"Worse." Sterling's warmth soaked through me, chasing away some of the coldness of my father's nastiness. "He said I was disgusting, a sin."

"Denis, no," Sterling whispered, pressing his face to my hair. "Sweetheart. I'm sorry."

I melted a bit at his endearment, knowing it was so pure and true. "It's not your fault. At least now I'll never have to wonder what they think or if they'd changed." My laugh was watery. "I tried to talk to him, but he wouldn't listen. How could he say that? He doesn't know anything about me. Or you. Because you saved me from being that man I once was who would've slept with anyone to stave off the loneliness."

He kissed my face, my eyes, and rested his cheek to mine. "Meanwhile, I sat here feeling sorry for myself because of my mother, ignorant to the fact that shutting you out was hurting you too."

"When I ended the call, I couldn't stay home." Finally, I had the strength to lift my head and gaze into his face. Those blue eyes I'd yearned to see shone with sympathy. "I wanted your disgusting wheatgrass shots and those silly face creams and serums you put on. I want to see you in that red-light mask you think I don't know you have hidden under the sheets in the back of the linen closet. By the way, it makes you look like a space alien. *Je te veux.* You. Only you."

"It must be love, then, if you're talking wheatgrass and red-light masks," he teased and held my face in the palms of his hands. "And I know I don't say it often, but I do love you. So very, very much. Even tonight when you're a mess." He kissed me. "Maybe even more because you're the most real right now. No posturing for your teammates or the cameras. Just me and you."

"That's all I want. One day everything else will end, and the only thing left will be the two of us. *Toi et moi.*" I kissed him.

"The two of us sounds like a pretty good thing," Sterling said, his arm around my waist. My strength. "Come. Let's put you to bed."

I leaned on him, and he led me to the bedroom, where he took off my clothes. I lay down, the sheets and pillow wonderfully soft and cool against my overheated skin. Sterling undressed and lay beside me, the curves of our bodies naturally fitting together. With all that happened, I'd thought I'd fall asleep without any trouble, but I remained wide awake, my mind racing, and from his breathing and body movements, I knew Sterling was up as well. The meds had kicked in, and I was feeling better. I kissed his neck.

"We've been so busy lately, we've barely spoken. Anything new with the cable job? What's happening with it?"

"I still haven't heard. I'd tell you if I did." He tensed, and under my lips, his pulse raced. "I-I might have to cancel our trip."

"Why? Something with work?"

"No. It's not that."

Something wasn't right. I sat up and turned on the bedside lamp. "Then what is it? Please, talk to me."

"I got an email today from a lawyer. From LA. My mother died last night. I was going to tell you tomorrow morning."

"Ahh, I'm so sorry, *mon amour*." I touched his hand, but my brow furrowed in thought. "That makes no sense. *Je ne comprends pas.* Explain, please? Why would a lawyer email you?"

CHAPTER TWENTY-SIX
Sterling

The room sat hushed, as if holding its breath, waiting for me to speak. What the hell could I say? I couldn't fathom the news myself.

"I was hoping this could wait."

"Wait? You don't want to tell me?"

There was obviously no sleep to be had in this bed, so I flung back the covers. "It's my–"

"If you say it's your problem and not mine, I will spank your ass until you like it," Denis growled, and I didn't know whether to be repelled or excited.

Openmouthed, I stared at him for a moment, then hung my head in shame. "I'm sorry. It's just that I'm used to doing everything on my own, without having to think about the impact on anyone else. No one's ever mattered like you do."

Denis left his side of the bed to sit by me. "This has nothing to do with me. It's all about you, *mon cœur*. Because you are all that matters."

The email had left me shaken, even without any real information. And now that Denis was here, I was grateful for his calm, steady presence.

"I'm not sure what's happening. All week I was busy preparing for our trip and setting up a time to interview for the cable job."

"You're going to take it?"

I allowed a smile. "I have to interview for it, you know. It's not like I'm such a big deal that they'll hand it to me."

"All right." He nodded, those dark eyes intent. "Continue."

"This afternoon I received an email from a law firm saying they represented Dahlia Dumont and she had passed. I was a named beneficiary. Before they would release the will to me, they needed me to verify my identity, which required my driver's license and birth certificate. I assumed it was a scam, so I called the State Bar and confirmed that this was, in fact, a true law firm and these attorneys were who they claimed."

"Aren't you the smart one? Good for you."

"I would hope you'd do the same." I smirked. "Anyway. After all this was done, which took up a great portion of my time, I received another email scheduling me for a video call tomorrow. That's when I'll discover what's in the will."

Denis's brows drew together. "So why do we have to cancel our plans? We don't leave until Sunday."

"I don't know. I guess I'm assuming something will come up that will need me to act immediately. But that's silly. It's probably a bunch of nothing."

He put his arms around me. "Either way, your mother has died and I'm sorry. It's closing a book on a sad chapter that will now never be finished."

"That's…a very insightful way of thinking about it."

His eyes twinkled, and that devilish grin tipped up his lips. "I told you once. I can be deep."

What would I do without him by my side? And how the hell had this happened? Denis held me tighter, and none of it mattered. He was here—my always and forever. Who was I to question the vagaries of life? I was finally ready to stand there with arms open wide to accept Denis's love.

My heart swelled, and I leaned my head on his shoulder. "I'm sorry you had such a terrible night, but I'm glad you're here. I missed you."

"It's ended well, though. But you shut me out this week, and I don't understand why."

"I'm forty years old, and for as long as I can remember, I've always handled everything alone." I bowed my head. "I'm not good at asking for help, and I'm not the best boyfriend because I don't know how to give you what you need. I know I've said it already, but I was wrong to shut you out when things get rough. But I didn't want you to know."

"Why? How can I help you if I don't understand?"

"That's just it. No one's ever been there to help me. I'm still learning that not everyone will walk away."

He kissed me, and I clung to him, never wanting to let him go.

"I walk toward you, *mon amour*. It's you and me, together."

Denis took my hand, rubbing his thumb to my palm, and a remarkable feeling of well-being settled through me. The sadness I carried with me in my bones for so long had dulled to a poignant memory, replaced by the almost unrecognizable emotion of happiness.

"I'm so used to carrying my burdens on my own, I didn't want to lay them on your shoulders. Not when your team's been struggling. You'll return from the bye week stronger and better than ever because I'll be there to cheer you on, every step of the way. You've been supporting me with my mother. Now it's time for me to be there for you. I know how important hockey is to you."

His troubled gaze met mine. "Hockey is my job. Yes, I love it, but you will always come first. And my shoulders are broad enough for the two of us. When Gil's wife, Mary, was sick, he told me he would've done anything to keep her from suffering. I'd often hear him praying, *'Give me her pain.'* That's when I learned what loving someone is. Sharing the bad as well as the good." He squeezed my hand. "Give me some of your pain."

How to explain something I didn't fully understand myself? "I've never told anyone this, but I always thought one day she'd reach out and want to be my mother. At least acknowledge me, if not to the world, then at least let me know she cared just a little bit." Denis held me close, and I shook my head, sniffling. "Here I am, a forty-year-old man crying for the mommy he never had."

"We will cry together, *mon cher.* And afterward, we'll move on and see what else the world throws our way."

I didn't realize how alone I'd been until the thought of all this happening to me without Denis to lean on sent shivers down my spine.

"I love you. Very, very much. I'm so glad you're here. We should go to bed because you've also had a rough night, and you need to recuperate."

We climbed in again, and this time when I closed my eyes, I slept.

I awoke before Denis and slipped out of bed to dress. I left the apartment to pick up some things, and at my return, he was standing in the kitchen, drinking a glass of water. His head was thrown back, blond hair streaming past his shoulders, and I watched the Adam's apple in his powerful throat bob as he swallowed.

Damn, I am a lucky man.

He set the glass on the counter. "*Bonjour.* Where were you? I woke up, and you were missing."

Walking toward him, I held up the grocery bag. "I had to pick up a few things I thought you'd need to recover from last night. Your body's depleted and needs reenergizing."

A smile kicked up his lips. "That's what I have you for, *mon cher.* Let's go to bed."

"Nice try, but first you have to drink this." I took out two small cups, and his smile faded, replaced by a horrified expression. He backed away with his hands up.

"*Non, non et non. Mon dieu, c'est dégueulasse.*"

I wouldn't relent and held out his cup. "Do it. It'll make you feel better."

"It'll make me sick. Do you know what this looks like? When spring came and the weather warmed up, all the melted sludge around the edge of the lake where the soil met the water." He opened the cover, peered inside, and shuddered. "Don't make me."

"Do it, and then I'll give you something else to put in your mouth you'll enjoy."

His brows flew up. "You're not playing fair, using the promise of sex to get what you want."

"I play to win too, you know." I lifted my cup of wheatgrass. "Bottoms up."

We drank, and while Denis moaned and groaned, he finished it all. "I'm waiting." He tugged at my pants, but I placed my hand over his.

"No. This one's for you." I sank to my knees and yanked his briefs off, freeing his rapidly stiffening cock. I needed to taste him. "Put your hands on the counter and spread."

He chuckled. "Are you arresting me?" But he did as told, and when I ran my fingers along the cleft of his ass, he widened his stance. I pressed my mouth to his rim and pushed my *tongue inside.* "Ahh, *mon dieu,*" he cried out, along with other words I couldn't understand. I sucked and licked, loving how violently he quivered. His hips rocked, and I knew he was close, so I sat on my heels.

"Turn around," I whispered, and he flipped forward, his engorged cock huge and wet. I dug my fingers into his waist and took him as deep as possible, until he hit the back of my throat. Almost gagging, I adjusted, and soon began to suck and lick his shaft.

"Sterling, please. *Mon amour,* oh God, fuck," he yelled and erupted. Thick streams of come overflowed my mouth to drip down my chin. I swallowed, and he joined me on the floor, catching me at the nape and pressing his lips to mine. "So much better than that fucking wheatgrass," he murmured and nibbled at my mouth. "I showed you mine. You show me yours."

He petted and played with my cock until I lay across his lap, gasping. He sucked my dick, the long, silky strands of his hair tickling my thighs. Sparks and pinwheels of light spun behind my tightly closed eyes as his wicked tongue and fingers played the most sensitive parts of me.

"Please, Denis, oh my God." My climax was long and almost painful in its intensity, but Denis held me as I cried out, then gathered me in his arms and held me like a baby.

"*Je t'aime. Je t'aime.*"

"*Moi aussi,*" I replied, and his eyes sparkled.

"Not too bad." He kissed the tip of my nose. "Now let's shower and get some real food. Not that green hell-water you like."

Hours later, we were lounging on the sofa, and Denis was watching a replay of the game the Blades lost. The phone rang, and my heart pounded.

"It's the lawyer."

Denis clicked off the TV, and I answered.

"Sterling Forest."

"This is Louis Jordan, Mr. Forest. I'm handling your mother's estate. Can we do this by video? I always find it more helpful to speak face-to-face."

"Let me get my laptop." Denis scrambled off the sofa, got it from the table, and handed it to me. "All right."

"Good. I'll call you right back."

While I waited, Denis massaged my neck. "Do you want me to leave?"

I clutched the laptop in my sweating hands. "God, no. Please stay right here."

The notification popped up, and I accepted the call. Louis Jordan appeared on the screen. He was probably in his late '60s, tanned, with a thick head of sparkling silver hair, and sharp brown eyes behind silver-rimmed glasses. His white shirt was impeccable, and his blue and white tie bore the discreet stamp of a luxury designer.

"Mr. Forest? Hello. Nice to meet you face-to-face, finally."

"Finally? I don't recall ever hearing your name. Have we had correspondence at some point?"

Jordan shook his head. "No, but I've been your mother's personal attorney for over thirty years." He met my gaze with a steady eye. "I'm aware of who you are and how you were raised."

A bit nauseated, I brushed the hair off my sweating brow. "I had no idea. Then you must be aware I've neither spoken to nor seen her since I moved out for college at eighteen. That's twenty-two years ago."

"Yes, I know."

The conversation was making me both irritated and sick to my stomach. "With that information, I'm sure you can understand why I'm a little confused. Can you please tell me what this is about? You said I'm a beneficiary. Is it something you can send me in the mail? Do you need my address?"

Jordan clasped his hands. "Mr. Forest, I understand your concerns. But as you're probably aware, your mother has amassed an incredible fortune. Her acting allowed her to purchase real estate and create her beauty company."

I was growing impatient. "Yes. She owns real estate in Beverly Hills, Malibu, the Hamptons, London, and Paris. I know all about it."

"It's all yours now. Aside from some personal bequests to long-standing employees, you are her sole beneficiary."

I froze, and I heard Denis whisper, "What the fuck?"

"I'm sorry. Did you say she left the real estate to me?" I waited for clarification.

"No, not only the real estate. Everything. Title and ownership of her properties are now passed to you. As for her beauty company, it's split into separate entities. One part—Dahlia Beauty—she owned in full. The other—Love Lessons—she was a fifty percent owner and board member. That is now you. Obviously, it's a complicated arrangement, and I urge you to have your lawyers review the documents carefully."

I blinked. Was I breathing? Alive? This couldn't be happening. "I-I don't think…I'm not sure I understand what this all means."

Jordan removed his glasses. "In the simplest terms, it means you're now an extremely wealthy man. Your mother's company has a market valuation of over one billion dollars. Her real estate is estimated to be in excess of one hundred million dollars. There are various investments which will be passed on to you—stocks, bonds, treasury notes and CDs."

"But…but…why?" Did I sound like a hurt child? The years of rejection and loneliness returned with a vengeance. "She ignored me. Her whole life was manufactured to keep me at a distance."

"And I urged her every chance I had to do something about it. She always replied the same: that she'd long ago known the decision she chose to prioritize her career over being a mother to you would be a wall between the two of you that could never be breached. Even after she fell ill and it became apparent she was terminal, I begged her to call you. Again she refused, saying that she didn't want a reconciliation based on impending death. I disagreed, but I was the hired help. I had to carry out her wishes."

"I still…I don't know what to say or do, even. This is not anything I ever imagined." My head spun, and I held out my hand, which Denis immediately grabbed.

"We can do this by mail, but my suggestion is for you to come out here. With an estate of this magnitude, it would be better to do it all in person."

"I…I'll have to get a lawyer. I haven't spoken to Greer Parsons—who helped me back then—once my mother gave me my payout and property."

"I know Greer. Sharp guy." His smile came and went like quicksilver. "I'm sure he'll take the case."

I looked to Denis. "Might as well, don't you think?"

"*Absolument.*"

"All right. I'll get in touch with him and let you know. Obviously, I'm still in shock."

"I know. And Sterling? I'm very sorry. I wish things could've been different. There isn't going to be a funeral. She was cremated, and her ashes are kept in an undisclosed location."

Odd, but on this remarkable day, nothing surprised me. Not anymore. "Thank you. I'll be in touch."

I closed my laptop and sat staring at its dull silver cover. "None of this makes sense. Why would she leave it all to me? We were strangers." Denis took my cold hands between his and rubbed them, but it did nothing to warm my numb emotions.

"It's only my opinion..." he began hesitantly.

"Which I'd like as my brain has suddenly stopped functioning." I was as weak as a newborn kitten and still hadn't fully processed this news.

"Perhaps all along she knew how terribly she treated you, and while she didn't seem to have the desire—or, more likely, the courage—to face you, this was her only way to try and rectify it. In her mind, giving you her entire fortune wiped the slate clean and she could die easier, knowing she took care of you."

"Her entire fortune." I held my head in my hands. "My God, Denis. That's more money than I can even imagine. I'm not equipped to deal with all this. It's a nightmare. I can't—"

"*Shhh.* Calm down." He took me in his arms and held me until I stopped shaking. "First thing we're going to do is call that lawyer you mentioned. We can fly out to California and meet with them. This is going to require an entire team of financial experts."

"California? B-but we were going to Barbados."

He cupped my cheek. "You need to do this. And where you go, I go."

CHAPTER TWENTY-SEVEN
Denis

I'd never pictured myself as a person someone would want to lean on, but ever since Sterling had received the news of his mother's death and his inheritance, I'd taken charge, changing plane and hotel reservations while also making sure he was mentally okay.

"Have something to eat." I pushed toward him the salad I'd picked up from his favorite health restaurant. I'd left him for forty-five minutes, telling him I had to get some last-minute things for our trip. In reality, I'd first stopped for a burger and fries at our local diner.

He picked at the lettuce. "I can't fathom so much money. What the hell am I going to do with it all? And the properties...I'm not leaving the news to run her businesses."

"Again, that's why we're going. You own it, which means you can sell it too. But I doubt you're going to want to get rid of everything. When you spoke with the attorney, didn't he tell you not to worry? Let's wait and see what happens when we get to California. We have the first flight out Monday morning. We get there nice and early so we can catch a nap and be ready for our meeting at two p.m."

Devastated eyes met mine. "I'm so sorry."

"For what, *mon cher*?" I stroked his hand. "You're a human being, and this isn't something anyone can ever be prepared for."

"I ruined your vacation, and I know you needed the time to relax and regroup. Instead, you're babysitting me and—"

I laid my fingers across Sterling's lips. "*Shhh.* Being with you is what matters. As long as we're together, it doesn't matter where we are. Barbados, California, here, my place. I don't care. Now eat your rabbit food."

His wan smile hurt my heart.

Sterling chewed the leaves with little appetite. A few minutes later, he shoved the bowl across the island, leaving half the salad. "I'm done. I can't eat." His eyes narrowed. "Where's yours?"

"My what?" I feigned ignorance. "Oh, you mean salad? I wasn't hungry."

"You are the world's worst liar." For a moment, a twinkle lit his eyes. "I know you had burgers. You tasted like ketchup and meat."

"Come to bed, and I'll take care of your meat." I slung my arm around his neck. "It's gonna be okay. I promise. We'll figure it out. After all, it's only money."

Sterling's brows rose high as he sputtered. "*Only money?* It's hundreds of millions of dollars."

"I know. I got myself a sugar daddy." Cackling, I gave him a big kiss on his cheek. "Can I borrow a few million dollars?"

With a laugh, Sterling smacked my ass. "You are such an idiot."

I pulled him close. "But I made you laugh, *mon cher*, so you can call me any name you want."

He laid his head on my chest. "Mine. I'll call you mine."

Sunday morning, I woke up early to an empty bed. Sterling had been awake all night, and I got out of bed to find him. It was a gray day, and I looked forward to the sun and warmth of California. A smile rose to my face when I saw him curled up on the sofa, and I was careful not to wake him as I covered him with a throw.

His laptop was open, and I touched the mousepad to see he was reading up on Dahlia Dumont's businesses.

"*Mon pauvre chéri...*" I murmured and left him to take a shower. I had an idea to take his mind off his problems, and I hoped he'd be okay with it. I'd been meaning to suggest it for weeks, but something always came up.

I was dressed and entered the living room again, and this time Sterling was awake. Tired and pale, he forced a smile. "Sorry if I kept you up all night. I couldn't sleep."

"I know. Let's have some breakfast, and then I have a favor to ask of you."

I turned on the kettle and poured myself a cup of coffee. I steeped his tea, brought it to him, and settled beside him on the couch.

"What is it?" He blew on it and took a sip. "Of course, anything you need."

"I'd like it if you would come with me and meet Gil. I don't often get the chance during the season to visit in person, and usually I do so on the bye week. I was planning on running up today anyway, and...I'd like you to come with me and meet him."

Sterling set the cup aside and reached for my hand. "I'd love to. Thank you for including me."

I kissed his fingers. "I want the two most important men in my life to know each other. After we eat, I'll call for a car."

Even more importantly, I hoped that at least for a few hours, it would give Sterling something else to think about.

We arrived before lunch and found Gil in the garden room, surrounded by his friends, talking hockey. I stayed by the door and grinned at Sterling, who had barely spoken all morning and during the car ride up.

"Watch. He holds court, telling them all about the stars he's coached and his predictions for the Cup."

It settled my fears of his decline to see him so animated and smiling. His voice rose strong.

"And I told Denis, never take your eye off that puck. It doesn't matter how many sticks are in your face. It's the puck that counts."

"And I've tried to listen, have I not, *Papa*?" I teased and strode into the room, Sterling several paces behind me. "Although it's been a bit harder lately."

The group of men—and, I noticed, several ladies—met my entrance with *oohs*, *ahhs*, and smiles. Several new faces gaped at me.

"Is that him? Denis Bouvier?"

"*Mais oui*," Gil answered them, then turned to me. "I'm so happy to see you. I was hoping you'd come."

My heart squeezed. I was the last of his students still actively playing, and I had no idea if anyone besides me came to visit him.

"And here I am. With a friend. Sterling Forest, this is the man who made me who I am. Gil Girard."

"Very nice to meet you, sir. Denis never stops talking about you."

He cocked his head and studied Sterling. "You're on the news."

"Yes. Channel 8."

"I watched the profile they did on you." He wagged a finger at me. "You, keeping secrets."

Laughing, I wheeled him over to a quiet corner where we could all sit together. Gil continued to question Sterling. He'd been waiting for me to bring someone to meet him for a while.

"And you and Denis. You're more than friends?" Sterling looked to me, and I winked.

"*Oui*. Very much so."

"Good, good. Denis needs a steady person who's not in the game. To be on the ice and at home again with the game?" He sliced his hand through the air. "No. This is much better." His sharp eyes met mine. "How long?"

I glanced at Sterling, who smiled for the first time that morning.

"You know…" he said, "I'm not sure. To be honest, we didn't even like each other in the beginning. Somehow, we just slipped into a relationship."

"And now he can't live without me," I added, to which Sterling returned an answering shot.

"Methinks it's the other way around. He chased me until I let him catch me."

Gil watched our back-and-forth with amusement. "*C'est comme ça.* This is what I love to see. The fun between a couple." His smile was filled with satisfaction. "Don't let that end. Mary, my wife, may God rest her soul, didn't like me much at first either."

"*Je ne te crois pas,*" I insisted. "Mary adored you."

"Not at first. She thought I was...how you say it...a jock. Too interested in sports and not her." His eyes twinkled. "I had to prove I was worthy. Because I knew"—he paused and searched my face, then Sterling's—"I knew she was the one. And nothing and nobody would get in my way of making her mine. When you meet that special someone, it changes you."

"In what way?" Sterling asked. "You didn't give up hockey."

"Never," Gil declared. "Your true love would never deny you something of such great importance. But this is where you must decide. What is your priority? In my opinion, you must always make your love number one. The ones who remain alone? They chose the game and glory."

The way Gil put it seemed so simple, yet it was something I'd struggled with my whole life. "You're right. I know people like that. I was that person," I admitted. "Since I came out and have been playing in the league, my main goal was winning games and having fun. I thought I wanted a relationship, but even once I had someone, it wasn't enough. I wanted more. I wasn't satisfied."

I felt like I needed to explain to Gil directly.

"Several days ago, I called my parents." Gil's brows rose high, but he nodded and let me speak. "I honestly don't know why, but I thought the fact that they called you meant they had some feeling left for me."

"And because deep down, you still care, you called them. I understand," Gil said. "You have so much love in your heart, Denis."

Sterling's hand crept into mine and held on tight.

My lips twisted in an ugly semblance of a grin. "Maybe I do, but my father doesn't. He hasn't changed—nothing's different from then to now. And it finally hit me that it didn't matter anymore. Whatever hope I had that one day things might be different, vanished. And I thought it would be terrifying knowing I was truly alone, but it was freeing instead."

"How so?" Gil asked, though I believed he already knew. But having me say it out loud made it more real. More honest.

"Because it forced me to realize I have to make my own happiness. I'm responsible for my life, no one else. I've made many mistakes and hurt people. People I've learned to care for. And I'm grateful they forgave me. But those mistakes made me stronger and able to recognize the real thing. I'm not alone. Not anymore. In the end, my biggest mistake is what saved me."

Joy shone from Gil's eyes. "And Sterling is the real thing."

"Yes. I understand what it means to put someone's happiness before your own. Because knowing they're feeling loved gives you pleasure. I don't wonder anymore about what I might be missing." I cast a loving look at Sterling, whose pain reflected in his eyes. "I have everything I need right here. You two are the most important people in my life." I kissed Gil's cheek. "I love you both, very, very much."

"And Sterling, you've been quiet. I sense something is troubling you."

I squeezed his hand. "*Mon cher*, you can trust him. Gil is the great keeper of secrets."

He bowed his head, uttering a wrenching sigh that tore through me. I hated how this was ripping him to pieces. "I've also had trust issues. Where Denis had a family who gave up on him, my mother never acknowledged me, choosing fame, and ultimately money, rather than tarnish her sweet, girl-next-door image."

Gil's brows drew together. "I am lost."

I leaned into Sterling. "May I tell him?"

Sterling nodded, and after I recited Sterling's family history, Gil couldn't stop shaking his head, his pain and disgust evident.

"*Mon dieu…incroyable.* Dahlia Dumont? I remember her. Beautiful woman. My wife loved her movies." With a slight smile, Gil's scrutiny of Sterling intensified. "Now that you've mentioned it, I can see the resemblance."

"She passed away two days ago. It hasn't been made public, but I'm sure the news will trickle in very soon. And once that happens and the sharks start sniffing around, my name coming out as her child won't be far behind. There's no way I can hide from all this publicity I hate so much."

"Get in front of it."

Gil's statement surprised both of us, and after Sterling and I exchanged bemused glances, he hitched his chair closer. "Meaning what?"

"You wouldn't be the first scandal, but because of your status as a news anchor, you have the ability to shape the narrative. Use your platform and say your piece, instead of scrambling to explain yourself."

"But we're leaving tomorrow morning for California."

I saw Gil's point and shifted gears to convince Sterling it was the right move. "Do it tonight. Ask if you can make a statement on air, but don't tell them about what. Look,

I've had experience with the gossip world and reporters who just want something ugly to print about you for clickbait. Tell the world first, on your terms, and you deflate their sails. Take away their story as they want to tell it with your truth."

"Do you really think it'll work?" he appealed to Gil, and I loved how Sterling turned instinctively to the father figure in my life.

Gil covered Sterling's hand with his. "*Absolument.*"

Sterling chewed his lip for a moment, gave a sharp nod. "All right. I'll call the news director and tell him I need to go on tonight's broadcast to make an announcement."

"*Bien.*"

A tall woman in a chic navy pantsuit approached us, her gray hair in an elegant twist. A colorful silk scarf was tied at her neck, with a beautiful pearl brooch pinned to the lapel. She used a cane, but her posture was straight, her brown eyes bright. Faint lines were the only marks on her face, and her minimal makeup was artfully applied.

"Excuse me, Gil. We were going to go to the two o'clock movie together?"

"Ahh, *mais oui*. I am so sorry. Please, let me introduce you. Denis Bouvier and Sterling Forest, this is Sarah Packard. She is a new resident."

"*Enchanté*, Ms. Packard." I smiled.

"Very nice to meet you," Sterling added.

"Oh, two stars, imagine that," she exclaimed. "I watch you on the news every night, Mr. Forest, and of course Denis Bouvier is a household name for me. My late husband was a Blades fan through and through."

"Gil, we will leave you to your movie date. I'll let you know how it goes." I kissed each cheek. "*Au revoir.*"

"Please do. And I'll make sure to watch the news tonight. Sterling, *c'était un plaisir de te rencontrer. Au revoir.*"

We watched as he and Sarah left the garden room. "I'm glad he's found people here. I hope it makes him less lonely and isolated." Knowing he had a lady friend made me feel it was the right decision to insist he move close to me. I slipped my hand into the crook of Sterling's arm. "Let's go home, and you can plan what you're going to say."

We waited for the car in the vestibule of the front office, and in a rare display of public affection, Sterling put his arms around me and hugged me tight.

"Thank you for bringing me here. It put a lot of things into perspective."

"Such as?" I held him, enjoying this quiet interlude, understanding that once he made his announcement, nothing would be the same.

He gazed up at me. "That no matter what, as long as we stand by each other, we're going to be all right. I don't think I could do this if I didn't have you to lean on."

"Then it's a very good thing I'm not going to be anywhere else but by your side." The car pulled up in front. "Come. Time to go home."

CHAPTER TWENTY-EIGHT
Sterling

My greatest fear was getting sick on camera.

On the ride home from visiting Gil, I placed a call to the weekend news director, Douglas Washington, who, though curious about what I planned to say, didn't press me for details. He agreed to give me three minutes before the end of the ten o'clock news.

With that off my chest, I managed to fall asleep, not waking until Denis kissed my cheek. "We're here."

A bit groggy, I followed him out of the car and into the building on autopilot. Inside my apartment, I sat on the couch, staring into space. A few minutes later, the buzzer sounded, rousing me from my stupor.

"Who's that?"

At the door, Denis waited. "I ordered some food so that when we came home it would be ready."

I managed a smile. "You're very sweet."

"I know." The bell sounded, and he took the package from the delivery person. "Sit and rest."

He brought the bag over, and I sighed. "I'm serious. I don't think I'd have been able to handle the last few days without you." It was the truth and even scarier to think about it. What would've happened if I didn't have Denis with me? Imagine finding out I'd inherited hundreds of millions of dollars while sitting here alone.

"Oh God," I whispered, and first a chuckle escaped me, which led to a spate of laughter and then full-on wheezing. I couldn't catch my breath. Tears rolled down my face and Denis grabbed me tight. Crying, I buried my face in his shoulder and shuddered, finally gathering my wits together. "I'm sorry."

"For what?" His large hand stroked my hair.

"Losing it. I don't know what happened. One minute I was thinking of what would've happened if I'd found all this out and been alone, and the next I was hysterical."

"You had a life-changing event. It's natural to be overwhelmed. Here. Drink this."

He handed me a small cup. "Wheatgrass? I thought you hated this stuff." I drank it, and his eyes crinkled with humor.

"I do. That's why I didn't get any for me."

"It's good for you," I insisted.

"You're good for me. Now I think you should go shower, take a nap, and we'll figure out what you're going to say tonight."

"Oh God," I moaned. "How can I even prepare for that? I'm cringing already. I'm a news story on my own."

"But Gil is right. If you do it first, you control the narrative."

"I know you're right, it's just not me to make my personal life public. I guess I've become so used to hiding who I am, it's going to be hard to switch gears."

"You can do it. You can do anything." He shooed me. "Now go do as I say."

"Yes, sir." I mock-saluted and walked halfway across the room. "Aren't you coming with me? I need someone to wash my back."

"I'm better with the front."

The nap with Denis helped, but setting foot in the studio, the nerves fluttered through my veins. I sagged into the chair at my desk, while Denis, who'd never seen my office, wandered around, picking up photos taken with various dignitaries I'd interviewed over the years and several awards I'd won.

"I'm going to be sick," I muttered.

"No, you're not." He grabbed my shoulders, forcing my gaze to his. "You're strong and confident and been through much harder things than this. Remember when you first discovered who you were and confronted your mother? You were only sixteen. Dig deep and remember how you felt."

I blinked. He was right. Compared to the moment that changed my life forever, this was merely a blip in the road.

"Thank you. You're right. I don't know why I'm being so silly."

He kissed my nose. "Because you're used to telling the story, not being the main character. Pretend you're talking to me. Remember, no one deserves to know any of this. It's your personal life. You are in control."

"You're pretty damn smart, you know?" Not that Denis needed an ego boost, but he deserved it.

"I know."

Someone knocked at the door.

"Come in," I called out.

Adrian stuck his head in the room. "Oh, Denis. Hi. I didn't know you'd be here."

"What're you doing here, Adrian?" I asked, not at all happy to see him. The last thing I wanted was to have to explain my story in greater detail to him, which I knew he'd expect. "Isn't Grayson Strong the weekend anchor?"

"Yeah, but he's stuck in Minneapolis. Freak snowstorm. They're giving me the anchor desk for tonight."

Great for Adrian. Not so much for me. I mustered a smile. "Good luck."

"They told me you're making an announcement at the end of the show. You're not leaving, are you? There's a rumor circulating that you're interviewing at one of the cable news stations."

"No, nothing like that. But I'm not prepared to talk about it ahead of time."

His brows shot up. "Oh, okay. Yeah, sure," he fumbled a bit. "I guess...I'll see you later, then."

"Yes." I waited for him to leave.

Denis chuckled when the door shut. "That was masterful. Keep that energy, and you'll be fine."

I drew in a deep breath. "I hope so."

At 10:27 p.m., I faced the camera.

"Thank you, Adrian. Good evening, everyone. I'm here tonight, not as your news anchor, but as someone who recently lost a parent. Now I'm sure you're wondering why I need to make a special announcement. In the coming days, you'll no doubt hear about the death of movie star Dahlia Dumont."

I gazed past the cameraman, focusing on Denis, who stood behind the cameras. I could almost feel his strength reaching out across the studio, wrapping around me. He nodded and gave me a thumbs-up and a reassuring smile.

"Dahlia Dumont was my mother. We had no relationship to speak of, and I haven't seen or spoken to her in over twenty years. Unauthorized stories about her life, and maybe mine, will be printed as her estate becomes public. I say unauthorized because I will not be giving any interviews or speaking about this again. Whatever relationship my mother and I had or didn't have belongs only to us. Let me repeat: I will not be speaking about Dahlia Dumont to any news source."

So far I hadn't fainted from nerves. A good thing. I picked up the glass of water and took a much-needed drink, then continued.

"You might also hear that I am the sole beneficiary of her estate. While that is true, I do not intend to leave my job as a news anchor to run her companies. My mother's businesses will stay intact, as is. My plan is to use her enormous wealth to benefit people through donations to medicine and science. To help seniors, children, and teenagers, the queer community, and those struggling with mental-health issues. I want to thank Channel 8 for allowing me this time to set the record straight. Thank you and good night."

I waited for the light to go off and the voice in my earpiece to speak. *"That's a wrap, Sterling."* I took out the wire, set it on the desk, and stood. Adrian hadn't stopped staring at me with astonishment since I'd begun speaking.

"Sterling, I—"

I put up a hand. "I meant it, Adrian. I'm not talking about it. Not with you, or anyone." The entire weekend news team stood gaping at me as if I were a sideshow in the circus or a strange new exhibit at the zoo.

Doug Washington waited for me. "Sterling, I'm sorry. I know you have vacation this week, but take as much time as you need."

"I appreciate it. I'm heading to California early tomorrow morning to take care of some business."

A troubled expression settled on his face. Washington had come from Channel 12, and I'd heard rumblings of him taking over for Rob DeVine, our news director, who had made no secret of his desire to retire. Washington had also brought in Grayson Strong, who'd captured big ratings on the weekend. "I do know you've made some inquiries into a national news spot. We'd hate to lose you."

I put a hand to my brow. "I can't think about that right now. Maybe when I return, we'll have a sit-down."

He grimaced. "Of course, I'm sorry. I should've kept my mouth shut. See you when you get home."

I left him to find Denis, who'd been corralled by Adrian. "Ready to go?" I asked him, and gave Adrian a perfunctory nod.

"Yeah. *Au revoir*, Adrian. Say hello to Rip." He hustled me away. "I do like the guy, but he's a pushy son of a bitch."

I couldn't help but smile. "Adrian has the instincts of a reporter. He knows there's a deeper story."

"You handled it perfectly. I'm sure your phone will be blowing up. There's nothing the media loves more than a juicy story." Prior to going on the air, I'd given my phone to Denis. He handed it to me, and I grimaced at the multiple texts and missed calls.

With my stomach in knots, I held Denis tighter, and always sensitive to my moods, he took control.

"Let's go home. We have an early flight, and you need to rest."

"Thank you for being here. And for everything. I'm sorry you have to deal with all this." I waved a hand. "It's not what you need in your life."

"You're all I need. Every game I take shots and prevent the puck from going into the net. It's what I do best. That's why my save percentage is top of the league." In the elevator, he held on to me. "On the ice I protect the goal. Here, I protect you. My ultimate save."

On Monday, after an uneventful flight, we stepped out into blinding sunshine and warmth. I hadn't been to Beverly Hills since I left for New York over four years ago, yet it was all still so familiar. I recalled myself as a lonely teen, roaming the streets.

"Have I ever told you how much I love being warm?" Denis raised his face to the sky. "Growing up, I was fucking cold all the time, starting in late August and lasting until almost June."

An insight into Denis I never knew. "And yet you picked hockey?"

"*Mon cher*, I did not pick hockey. Hockey chose me. And very well, I might add, don't you think?" He winked, and I groaned.

"Ego, thy name is Denis."

"*Oui*. But I think you like it." He nuzzled my neck. "And I love how you lose that control for me."

I couldn't deny it. And frankly his confidence, a turn-off for some, was part of what drew me to him. Was he a smug bastard? Yes, but he tempered it with his huge, generous heart.

"Let's go inside. Afterward, I have a surprise for you."

"Me? What is it?"

He patted my cheek as we entered the office building. "Silly. Why would I tell you?"

We received our passes from security and found the offices of Greer Parsons on the twenty-sixth floor. Sweeping views of the Hills spread out before us, so different from the high-rise skyscrapers of New York City, yet both awe-inspiring in their own way.

Greer came out himself to escort us to his office. I suppose if you inherited almost a billion dollars, you merited a personal greeting.

"This is Denis Bouvier. My partner." It was the first time I'd ever said it out loud, and I didn't miss Denis's smile.

"The hockey player?" Greer took my outstretched hand even as he eyed Denis with barely disclosed interest. "I grew up in Brooklyn, came out to LA when I was a teenager. The Blades were my dad's favorite team. Good luck this season."

"Thank you." He dipped his head, but by his reticence, Greer understood he wasn't there to chat.

"All right. Let's sit. I had my secretary order in some food in case you didn't have time to eat lunch."

A table had been set up with an interesting spread—platters of bagels, lox, and cream cheese, plus various salads. In addition, there was an elegant plate of sushi that looked as though it'd been made only moments earlier. A tiered dish of pastries sat by an espresso maker.

"Are you expecting half of Beverly Hills?"

"I always thought food makes everything easier." He sat behind his desk. "I looked through the papers, and this is going to require a team of people, not only attorneys.

We'll need financial experts, CPAs, people experienced with the SEC...you get the picture. It's not something I, or anyone, for that matter, could pull together in even a few days. Especially not over a weekend."

"I understand. What I'm here for is knowledge. As long as you can deal with what's coming, I'm good with you and your firm handling everything. I'm assuming Dahlia had a business manager? I didn't have a chance to speak about that when her lawyer contacted me. All I do know is, I have no desire to run a cosmetics business."

"Although he wouldn't mind the skin care," Denis interjected, and I appreciated his attempt at lightening the mood.

"If I wanted to sell, you could find a buyer, I presume?"

"Absolutely. It's a very, *very* valuable part of the estate—the largest share, in fact. So you'd probably see an injection of over five hundred million dollars."

I swallowed. "That is an awful lot of money."

"You might not want to sell after you think it all through." He clasped his hands on top of his desk. "Sterling. You are an extremely wealthy man now. I advise you to contact our financial advisor to think about investments for tax purposes. I can draw up papers to protect you and your assets." He flicked his steely gaze to Denis, who sat unperturbed. "A prenuptial agreement, for instance."

"We're not engaged. Don't rush me, *mon ami*," Denis drawled. He rose and went to make himself an espresso. "Could you get Sterling a green tea, please? He doesn't drink coffee."

Greer picked up his phone and made the request.

"I know I'm very rich. But so is Denis. I hardly need protection from him."

"*Mon amour*." Denis put a hand on my shoulder. "I have no problem signing anything. Like you said, I have money of my own. I'm not with you for your wealth."

"I know."

Greer said, "It's standard when someone has as much wealth as Sterling now has. Denis, I didn't mean to insinuate anything."

Denis sprawled in his chair. "Maybe you did, or maybe not. What you think doesn't matter to me. Sterling will make his own decisions, and I trust him implicitly, but I have no intention of taking any money from him." That sexy, intimate smile on his lips never failed to turn me on. "As long as I own his heart, I'm a happy and fulfilled man."

"You know the French," I joked to ease the tension. "Full of passion and romance. But I also trust Denis."

Greer nodded. "If you don't mind me saying, Sterling, you're a lucky man."

"I know."

Several hours later, having met with more corporate types than I'd ever known existed, I called for a car.

"Promise you won't ever make me do that again. All the money in the world isn't worth it," I moaned as we took off.

"*Mon pauvre chéri...*" He massaged my shoulders, his smile and the twinkle in his eyes making me happy. "Where are we going?"

"You'll see."

The car wound its way into Malibu and stopped in front of the house. I hadn't seen it in over four years, since I'd left LA, but I'd had someone take care of it.

"Come on, let's go." I exited the car, and he followed me.

"*Qu'est ce que c'est?*" Denis's brows pulled together as he craned his neck. "This is Malibu. Did you rent us a house on the beach, *mon amour? Très romantique.*" He slipped his arms around my waist and kissed my neck. "I want to make love to you to the sound of the ocean."

"Let's go inside." Key in hand, I walked up the front steps of the ultramodern home and opened the front door to the spectacular view of the endless Pacific Ocean. "What do you think?"

Denis's long stride took him across the large open living room to the slider doors that led onto a deck. The pool sparkled in the sunlight, and rays of sunshine streamed in, touching his hair, turning it to spun gold. "*Magnifique.*"

"It's ours."

He stood still. "What do you mean, ours?"

"Well, mine. Along with the money I got from my mother, I asked her for this house. I used to come here on weekends to get away."

"Did you ever bring anyone here?" he asked. "Other men?"

I flushed. "No. I was raised in secrecy, so I never let anyone into my personal life. No one knew where I lived. We'd meet in hotels. Sometimes I'd forget their names as soon as they left." I stared out at the ocean. "It was all a lifetime ago. Returning here takes me back to that time when I was basically going through the motions of life but not living. I never made friends—didn't know how."

"You can't dismiss who you were. It shaped who you are now. I have regrets as well."

I leaned on him. "Everyone does." His warmth soaked through me. "What are yours?"

It took him a while to answer, and when he did, the strain in his voice was evident. "It doesn't matter."

A sharp pain hit my heart, and I grimaced. "It's all too much for you, isn't it? The money, the notoriety I'm trying so hard to avoid..."

He grabbed me roughly and kissed me hard on the mouth. "No. Never. It has nothing to do with that."

"Then what?" Strands of hair escaped his upswept bun, and he brushed them off his face. I reached out and undid the tie, letting it flow to his shoulders. "Do you know how much I love your hair? You thought I was some uptight, hard-ass guy in a suit, but that was only because I had to be to keep away from you. One touch and it was over." I threaded my fingers through the heavy, silken waves. "What's wrong? Tell me and I'll fix it."

His eyes glittered. "The thought of you with other men. I can't stand it. I was no saint, and I was never the jealous type, but thinking about them being with you...touching you...making love to you...*Je t'aime de tout mon être*."

I rested my face against his chest. The comforting *thump* of his heart settled all the swirling pieces in my head. "None of them made a difference. Only you." The comforting smell of his skin, like the sun only warmer, brought me peace.

He kissed the top of my head. "Guess I am a fucking jealous bastard after all. I just love you very, very much."

"Don't be sorry. I spent my whole life never hearing that word from anyone until I met you. I didn't know what it meant, or how I should feel."

"And now?" A tender hand stroked my face.

"Now I think you saved me from a very lonely life."

EPILOGUE
Denis

Six months later

We had a chance to make team history at home. The Blades led three games to two against the Gold Miners in the Stanley Cup finals. If we could win this game, we'd have accomplished three Stanley Cups in a row. Not an unheard of feat, but by no means an easy one. Of course the other teams hated us for our domination, but we didn't care. They'd hate us anyway. We were brash, cocky, and made no bones about it. We played hard and gave everything in our hearts and souls to win. It was a New York thing, a Brooklyn thing, and why I loved playing for the Blades.

I adjusted my stance and waited, the ice vibrating under my skates. The whistle blew, and Rip took his position center ice to take the drop. Our fans roared, and behind my mask, I grinned. They seemed to want this win even more than we did.

I knew Sterling was there, in the lower bowl near center ice. Gil was next to him, and I was thrilled he'd brought his lady friend, Sarah. I'd chatted with them before the game.

"I'm glad you've decided to enjoy life again, Papa."

"You are looking happy as well, mon fils."

I cast my gaze to Sterling by his side. They'd become good friends, and Gil was teaching him French.

"I have my two best guys with me. What more could I want?"

"A third Cup?" Sterling pointed. "Go out there and get it."

Like an invisible line tethering Sterling to me, I could feel the power of those big blue eyes. And that was all I needed. Shot after shot came at me, but I smothered each one. I felt invincible and refused to be denied. And when the buzzer rang, we'd won. The fans shrieked and cheered. I tore off my gloves and mask, and after hugging it out with my teammates, skated to Sterling and Gil. I'd kept the last puck the Miners shot at me and held it up to Gil.

"Pour toi, Papa."

I kissed my fingers to Sterling, who smiled in return. As always, I didn't need grand gestures or declarations from him. I knew, and so did he. It was enough.

I returned to my team for the celebration and Cup presentation. Seb, who'd scored two goals and had an assist, was named Most Valuable Player and awarded the Conn Smythe Trophy, and holding up the Stanley Cup, skated first to his wife and girls. It was cute to see their little excited faces. When it was my turn with the trophy, I skated around the ice, returning of course, to Gil and Sterling.

"You have been my greatest accomplishment, Denis. Not only as a player but as a person. *Je suis fier de toi.* So very proud."

"I am as well," Sterling said. "You were magnificent." His smile warmed me through and through.

"*Merci, mon amour.*" I blew him a kiss, unaware we were on the Jumbotron, and the crowd clapped and whistled. Sterling turned red, but my grin grew wider. "I will see you later after the circus."

Seb, Coach, and I did the media circuit, and as usual, ever since the press learned that Sterling was Dahlia Dumont's son, the questions they directed to me shifted from my play to my relationship with him. I'd held out a faint hope that it would change with winning our third Cup in a row.

"Denis, how are you and Sterling Forest dealing with his newfound fame?"

"Denis, there's a rumor your boyfriend may be buying the team. Will you still play for the Blades?"

"Denis, there are rumors that Sterling Forest will have to move to LA to handle Dahlia Dumont's estate. Are you planning to go with him? Are you asking to be traded?"

That broke my casual, keeping-it-light-and-easy demeanor, and I slapped a hand on the rickety table. The microphones rattled, and Coach grabbed at the one in front of me to keep it from toppling to the floor.

"*J'en ai eu assez!* Do you hear yourselves? How ridiculous you all sound? Like a pack of wolves." The crowd turned silent. "We have just won our third damn Stanley Cup, and all you ask me about is my personal life. Not one question about the game. That is unfair to my team, our coaches, and me. We've worked our butts off to get to this point. Stop it. Please. It's demeaning. But let me say this." I drew in a breath and saw Sterling slip into the room. "I love being on the Blades. I don't ever want to play for another team or be anywhere but here. Playing for Brooklyn, with my teammates, is all I want." I couldn't help my lips curving. "But so you will stop asking me these incessant questions, before I slip away to the off-season, no. I am not asking to be traded. No one is moving to LA or anywhere else. Sterling is not buying the team—that's a rumor I hadn't heard, and it's a good one."

The entire room laughed with me.

Coach adjusted the mic and took over. "As Denis said, it's time to talk about the game. And I'll also add my two cents to say he's correct. He hasn't asked to be traded, and we're not looking to get rid of the best goalie in the league. Next question?"

They listened and finally directed their attention to Seb and Coach, and after another three or four minutes, it was done. The locker room was jubilant, and champagne was being sprayed everywhere. Press from all over were interviewing players, and when they saw me, I was rushed. Laughing, I put up my hands.

"Guys, guys, please. *Arrêtez!* Can I please shower? I need to get out of the uniform. Trust me, you'll thank me."

I left them there, stripped off my clothes, and jumped into the best and hottest shower of my life. Clean and dry, I put on my shirt and slacks. A young reporter with dark-brown eyes and a head full of curly blond hair approached me. He held a microphone with the logo of the Canadian news station from my hometown.

"*Excusez-moi, s'il vous plaît,* may I ask you some questions?"

I smiled, always happy to help someone from home. "Of course." Other reporters approached, shouting questions, but I wanted to give him a chance. He was very young but had a brazen confidence. Reminded me of...me, at that age.

"Do you have any plans to ever come to Canada and meet the fans there?"

I cocked my head. "I think that would be a wonderful idea. I can contact the league, and I'm sure we could work something out."

"Why haven't you ever returned to your hometown to meet all your young hockey fans?"

I blinked. "I-I've taught at many hockey camps throughout the years. I let my publicist pick which ones."

"When you were young, did you ever think you'd be this much of a star?"

That I could answer, and I flashed him a grin. "I wanted to be the best."

"You've said you owe everything to Coach Gil Girard. But isn't it true that your father, uncle, and grandfather started you on your road to playing professional hockey?"

My mouth dried, and my heart pounded. This kid...who the fuck was he with his piercing dark eyes and slight smile? Like he held the answer to a secret.

"I don't talk about my family." I glanced up to the other reporters. "Anyone else have questions?"

The interviews lasted about five more minutes, and I spied Sterling entering the locker room, shaking hands with Rip and congratulating Seb before making his way to me.

"Thank you, everyone. Time for me to go celebrate with my friends and family." The young Canadian reporter hadn't interviewed anyone else, and I shot him a curious look as I walked past. His fierce expression startled me. What was his deal?

I reached Sterling and kissed him, promptly forgetting about the reporter. Even after all our months together, his touch had the ability to drive away any other thoughts but how much I needed him. "Thank God. Where are Gil and Sarah?"

"They're with Rip's father. We sent them ahead with their aides to the restaurant to get to their table."

"Good."

The reporters had gone but for my young hanger-on, who lingered near my locker. Sterling noticed my attention. "Who's that?"

"He says he's a reporter."

"You doubt him?"

"No." I thought for a moment. "But I think he came with an agenda. He asked me questions about my family and why I never came to my hometown to meet kids."

Sterling's brows pulled together, and I waited. Ever since he left Channel 8 for his own news show on cable, he'd perfected the art of ferreting out information from the most reticent guests. "Let's go talk to him." Without waiting for my response, he walked up to the man. "Sterling Forest. And you are?"

"Davide." He hesitated. "Davide Bouvier."

Sterling's gaze flicked to me, and I licked my dry lips. It was possible. Davide had been a little boy when I left.

With a defiant tilt to his jaw, Davide met my eyes. "*Je suis ton cousin.*"

"I...see." I folded my arms. "And you asked me all those questions as what? A test?"

"I wanted to see if you were truly as arrogant as I'd heard." He smirked with no humor behind it. "And they were right."

"The fuck you come in here, pretending to be a reporter to ambush me."

Out of the corner of my eye, I watched my teammates gather beside me.

The little bastard laughed in my face. "I *am* a reporter for our local news station. And it's not an ambush. It's true.

You walked away from your family and never bothered to come home. Not when my mother—your *tante*—died, not when *grand-père* passed. No, you were too busy being a superstar."

I swayed, and Sterling put an arm around me. "Hey. That's enough."

"That's your boyfriend? The news reporter?" He seemed a bit starstruck by Sterling. More than meeting me.

"Yes. If you used any of the brains you were given, you'd realize I left because my family made it impossible for me to live there with their ignorant attitude about queer people. I'm sorry about *Tante* Isobel and *Pépère*, but you don't have a fucking clue what you're talking about."

White-faced, Davide wisely remained silent as my words tumbled out.

"I was bullied by my parents and threatened and intimidated because of who I was...who I am. And your parents knew and did nothing. They agreed with it. So don't stand there with that fucking cocky expression on your face like you caught me in a lie or you're embarrassing me." I smiled at Sterling, and when I felt a hand on my shoulder, I looked into Rip's solemn face. "I have my family. People who love and care for me. So unless you're willing to stand up for what's right and decent, you and your shitty, backward views can march your little ass out of here. I have a celebration to get to."

Davide stayed silent.

"Ready when you are, Denis," Seb said, and my brows lifted in surprise that of everyone, he'd spoken up first. I nodded and smiled at him, letting him know I appreciated his support.

"Let's go." I turned, and with Sterling's hand in mine, walked away.

—

The celebration had already begun by the time we entered Slapshots. I saw Gil, Sarah, and John Carver at a table in the corner with their aides, and they all had drinks and food.

"I'm gonna go over to make sure they're okay."

Sterling squeezed my hand. "I'll be waiting."

I kissed him, my lips lingering on his. "I'm counting on it."

To my amusement, I was summarily dismissed from the table when I arrived.

"Go celebrate with all your friends. This is a wonderful night." Gil raised his beer. "*Amuse-toi.*"

Sarah smiled shyly at me. "Thank you for inviting me. This is all so exciting."

"I'm thrilled you are here."

I pulled up a chair next to Gil. "I had a visitor in the locker room. My cousin." I replayed the conversation.

Gil's face was troubled. "Don't be too harsh on the boy. He had to live with the family you left behind. All he knows is what he's been told. Imagine the indoctrination. It's up to you to tell him the truth."

I hadn't thought of it that way. My defenses were always up whenever my family was mentioned.

"Maybe you're right."

A surprisingly strong hand gripped my wrist. "I know I am. *C'est ta famille.* Just try. Now go have fun."

I wasn't even sure how to get in touch with him, but I could find out through the station. "Enjoy yourselves, please, and we will see you later."

When I returned to Sterling, he was deep in conversation with Grayson Strong, who'd moved into his position as lead weeknight anchor. In his mid-thirties, the man certainly looked the part—strong, square jaw, neat, dark hair, and light-blue eyes. He projected warmth, charisma, and trustworthiness.

"Do you like doing more of the interview style of

reporting you're doing now with your own nightly show than simply reading the news?" Grayson asked in his smooth voice. "Before I came to Channel 8, I watched your profile segment and was looking forward to working with you." His smile was wry. "Then only a few months later, you were gone."

"You're doing a great job. I know it's hard at first, but Doug told me your ratings are climbing steadily. As for my new position? It's completely different, but I love it. I get to concentrate on the breaking national stories of the day, ask the hard questions, and now that I've been there for a while, they're going to allow me to travel for stories."

"No war zones, though." I draped my arm over Sterling's shoulders. "I draw the line at imminent danger to you."

Of course, Sterling disagreed and made a face. "Says the man who gets hockey pucks smashed into his face and body. I'll go when and where I'm needed."

"We'll discuss it when the time comes," I huffed.

Grayson laughed. "I didn't mean to set off an argument." Originally from Florida, Grayson had joined Channel 8 after Sterling and I had become a couple and wasn't aware of our less than illustrious beginning.

"Not to worry. That's how our relationship started. We hated each other." I winked at him.

"I wouldn't say hated," Sterling demurred, not because it wasn't true, but because he loved to disagree with me. He knew I enjoyed the push-and-pull.

"How about loathed?" I replied, with a tap to my jaw, pretending to think. "Detested? I mean, I thought he was an uptight, snobbish ass in a suit."

"And I thought you were an obnoxious thug on ice who only thought about sports."

"Thug on ice?" I grinned and waggled my brows. "Ooh, I kind of like that. Makes me sound tough."

Grayson watched our conversation with an open mouth. "Wow, well, this a complete turnaround, I guess, with the two of you together now."

I snickered. "I mean, he's still a hard-ass and uptight." I patted Sterling's cheek. "But it's a turn-on."

"And he still only thinks about sports." Sterling smirked.

"*Au contraire, mon cœur*," I purred and hugged him close to kiss the top of his head. I didn't miss the blush on his cheeks. "You're always number one on my mind."

The door opened, and my cousin Davide walked in. My good mood vanished, and I dropped my arm from Sterling, who'd begun to recount the hot-mic story to Grayson. With that innate sense he possessed to my mood swings, he immediately assessed the situation and took my hand.

No longer cocky, Davide approached me. "May I talk to you a moment?"

"You may. Right here. I have nothing to hide from anyone." Gil might think I should talk to my cousin, but I wasn't going to make it easy for him.

"I'm going to refill my glass." Grayson, perhaps sensing tension, excused himself and walked to the bar. Sterling moved closer to me. My rock.

"I-I apologize. I shouldn't have surprised you like I did on your big night."

"So you think it would've been better any other night?" His face flamed. "How old are you anyway?" I searched my memory. "You were just a baby when I left."

"I'm twenty-five. I was almost four when you left, but I was always sick, so I didn't go outside much. *Maman* was too afraid I'd catch germs."

It finally clicked. "I remember now. No one was allowed to visit. I don't even know if I ever saw you more than two or three times."

Davide's faint smile came and went like quicksilver. "Very rarely, but I watched you from the window, always playing in the backyard with *Papa* and *Oncle* Charles."

"I'm sorry I didn't recognize you, but if you're planning on attacking me, please walk yourself out the way you came in."

He ducked his head. "I-I'm not. But you got to leave at sixteen. Can you imagine what it was like for me? Alone, with *Papa* and *Maman* watching my every move, always preaching the Bible to me. And my illness made it even worse. I was trapped."

"Remind me because it has been so long. What was wrong?"

"My heart." Almost reflexively, he touched his chest. "I was born with a defect that required many surgeries."

Angry yet at the same time filled with regret that my exile had made us virtual strangers, I shook my head. "I am very sorry. But you're all right now?"

He shared a beautiful smile with me. "Yes, I am." His expression shifted, turning somber. "But when I asked where you'd gone, they said you were sent away because they were afraid you'd do the same to me that you did to Georges."

Bile rose to my throat at the implication, and pain worse than any injury I'd ever sustained sheared through me.

"I never...I need to sit down." Sterling steered me to a table, and shaking, I lowered myself to a chair. I rested my head in my hands before lifting my streaming eyes. "They are liars. We were both lied to. Are you still living up there? With them?"

"Not in the same house, but yes, in our hometown. I have a job with the local television station and got them to send me to your game. I guess they figured it would give them an inside scoop."

"I don't care what you have to do, but you need to get away from them. Maybe Channel 8 can get you a job."

"I'm not leaving," he said quietly. "I have a girlfriend, and we're going to get married next year. My life is there. I do believe you, and I'm going to go home and figure out what to do about *Papa* and *Oncle* Charles. But...it would be nice to talk to you and maybe return for a visit. Angelique has never been to the United States. Now that I know the truth, things can be different. At least I hope."

For the first time since I was a child, peace, not anger, filled my soul when I thought of my first home. And while I knew there'd never be a reconciliation with my parents, having my little cousin in my life might help ease the pain of loss.

"I'd like that. And I hope to meet her one day."

Davide was nervous facing Sterling. "Angelique raves about the Love Lessons cosmetics line. She wants to model and has been getting a few gigs." Like a good fiancé, he took out his phone and showed us a picture of the two of them.

Sterling chuckled. "I'm only an owner-slash-board-member of the company. I leave all the actual work to the people who've been doing this for years and have all the knowledge. But if you give me her address, I'll make sure to put her on the list to get our newest lines and PR boxes."

They were a beautiful couple, and I had an idea. "I've done some modeling. I'll make a few calls. Both of you could get work." He looked very similar to me in my twenties.

He blushed. "Thank you. That would be amazing. I know she'll freak." He checked his phone. "I'd better get back to the hotel. I have to talk to my news director, and I have a really early flight out."

We shared a smile, and I jumped up. "Wait a second." I brought over champagne and poured a glass for him and Sterling.

"Quiet, everyone." The bar turned silent. "I want to make a toast. To the Brooklyn Blades, the best damn hockey team in the world with the best damn players. I love each of you like brothers. We may fight and disagree, but deep down we have a bond that cannot and will not ever be broken."

"Damn right," Rip called out, eyes bright, his arm around Adrian. "No matter what, we'll always stick by each other."

I sought out Gil. "To my *Papa*. I owe my life to you and making my dreams come true." I hugged Sterling close. "And to my best friend, my lover, the other half of my heart…thank you for saving me."

"You French are so romantic," Sterling murmured, and laughter broke out from all corners of the restaurant.

"I'm Québécois. Not the same thing. For instance"—I dipped my head and touched my lips to his, and cheers and whistles rose from the crowd—"we are much better kissers." Sterling's face was bright red when I let him go. I tipped my head toward Davide and smiled broadly.

"We are a family, and that's why we're winners. To friends and family." I held the champagne bottle aloft. "The ones who save us."

Thank you for reading *The Ultimate Save*. I hope you enjoyed reading Denis and Sterling's story. I truly adored these two and had a hard time letting them go after I finished writing their story...which means you might see them pop up again in the future. With an ego as big as Denis', he'd not one to remain quiet for long.

I also hope you consider leaving a review, which is so important for indie authors. Thank you and know that I appreciate each and every reader.

FELICE STEVENS writes romance because what is better than people falling in love? Her favorite part of a romance novel is that first kiss...sigh. She loves creating stories of hopes and dreams and happily ever afters. Her stories are character-driven, rich with the sights, sounds, and flavors of New York City, and filled with men who are often deeply flawed but always real.

Felice writes gay romance because she believes that everyone deserves a happily ever after. Having traveled all over the world, she can safely say that the universal language that unites people is love.

Felice has written in a variety of sub-genres, including contemporary and paranormal, and she has a mystery series as well. You can find all her books listed on her website.

Felice is a two-time Lambda Literary Award nominee and a Lambda Award winner in Gay Romance for her book *The Ghost and Charlie Muir*.

BOOKBUB

https://www.bookbub.com/profile/felice-stevens

NEWSLETTER

https://tinyurl.com/y85e69ab

READER GROUP

https://www.facebook.com/groups/FelicesBreakfastClub/

FACEBOOK AUTHOR PAGE

https://www.facebook.com/felicestevensauthor/

INSTAGRAM

https://www.instagram.com/felicestevens

GOODREADS

https://www.goodreads.com/author/show/8432880.Felice_Stevens

WEBSITE

felicestevens.com

PAYHIP STORE

https://payhip.com/FeliceStevensAuthor

TIKTOK

https://www.tiktok.com/@felicestevens